Crossing Purgatory

Crossing Purgatory

Gary Schanbacher

PEGASUS BOOKS
NEW YORK LONDON

CROSSING PURGATORY

Pegasus Books LLC
80 Broad Street, 5th Floor
New York, NY 10004

First Pegasus Books cloth edition June 2013

Interior design by Maria Fernandez

Library of Congress Cataloging-in-Publication Data is available.

ISBN: 978-1-60598-443-8

10 9 8 7 6 5 4 3 2 1

Printed in the United States of America
Distributed by W. W. Norton & Company

For Sherri and Will, always

CONTINENTAL UNITED STATES 1858

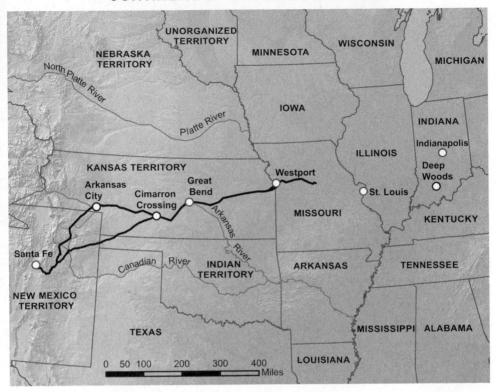

CONFLUENCE OF THE PURGATOIRE AND ARKANSAS RIVERS
NEAR BENT'S OLD FORT, COLORADO

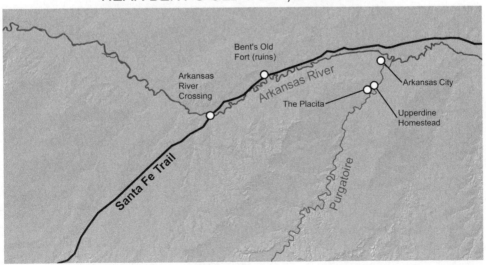

Crossing Purgatory

PART ONE

LEAVING DEEP WOODS, 1858

1

Thompson Grey quit his farm in Deep Woods, Indiana on the 20th of May in 1858. At first light after a sleepless night, he set out across his recently sown field, the tilled soil yielding beneath his weight. Dirt clung to his boots. Rich dirt, black and wet from rain. Holding him to his land. He felt its pull but resisted, pushed on. Once beyond the field and onto the road, he looked back the one time only. There, a trail of flattened corn shoots, slender and green and no larger than a baby's finger.

He arrived at the small township early morning and stood in front of Edwin Fletcher's door again to see if the constable might come out and confront him, but he would not. After a time, Thompson spat on the step and turned his back to Deep Woods, the drygoods store, blacksmith shed, livery, community storage barn, two churches, and twelve houses. At this hour, an ordinary day would bring the sights and sounds of awakening commerce: the report of hammer on anvil, the creak of a wagon, a scattering of people from the surrounding farms trickling into the mercantile. Not on this day. Shades were drawn, shop doors latched. The villagers had anticipated his passing. When he'd been gone half an hour, the shutter on Edwin Fletcher's front window inched open, and after another few minutes he stepped tentatively from his front stoop and squinted into the distance. He remained close by his entrance, as might a groundhog hug tight to its burrow until certain the fox had passed. And then, the bellows from the livery sent up a black column, the sound of two boys hollering broke the spell of silence, and the town of Deep Woods carried on with the business as usual.

Thompson Grey left the washboard road after six miles, cutting across country to the west. He had no destination in mind other than general direction. Westward, away from civilization. He carried a Kentucky rifle, a pouch of balls and caps, his powder, a water skin, and a rucksack containing a blanket, a small traveling Bible, cooking pot, and a tin cup. Around his waist a money belt cinched his wool jacket and protected two twenty-dollar gold eagles, three silver coins, and a few coppers. Tied to the belt were a gutting knife and a sack holding dried venison, a few stale biscuits, and a flint firestone. On his head, a felt slouch hat.

He walked through open farmland and the wooded hills of southern Indiana, walked with urgency, without rest, as if by exertion alone he might outpace his grief. He avoided marked roads where he could, having no wish for human contact and no need for trail mark or signpost. At dusk, he sat beside a black walnut tree, a windbreak, and ate a biscuit and a strip of venison, gnawing at the meat. He noticed the dirt lodged beneath his fingernails, embedded in his cuticles and in the creases of his knuckles. His dirt. From the last of the digging. Yesterday morning? Two days past? Three? Weariness bore down. His head slumped to his chest and, resting against the tree, he slept.

THE DREAM THAT HAD PLAGUED him these past days returned. Thompson stands at the brow of a hill overlooking a vast field of corn, endless row upon row stretching beyond the reach of vision, filling the entire valley. His valley. His corn. The stalks, broad-leafed and fully tasseled, grow tall during the day but at night they lie down with the animals, only to rise again with the sun. Thompson walks to his hill each day to survey his dominion and one morning discovers not corn but bones lying in the field. Dry bones, picked clean. Upon his arrival, they begin joining together, bone to bone, forming an army of skeletons that turn and march on him, a cacophony of rattling, the ground quaking beneath his feet. They beat drums, a thrumming pulse. He flees, but they pursue, calling to him in a language he does not understand but in a tone that clearly accuses, and in his heart Thompson knows they will never relent. Although for the moment he eludes them, he is certain the skeletons advance, he can hear the yowl of the wind through their ribs as they march.

HE WOKE UNSURE OF HIS whereabouts, dazed by fatigue and sorrow, the psalmist's lament in his ears. *There is no soundness in my flesh because of Thine anger; neither is there any rest in my bones because of my sin.* Daybreak brought a low, gunmetal sky, a chill breeze, and intermittent drizzle. Thompson again walked hard, pushed his endurance, the arcing of a blurred sun his timepiece. He ate the last of his jerked meat, kept moving. He came to a road leading west and he followed it, all that day and the next, occasionally chancing upon a cabin or small homestead. Once he passed close by a man and three children, a boy and two girls, working the field. The man looked up and mopped his face with a rag and followed Thompson's progress until apparently convinced he would not stop and then he turned back to his hoe. Near sunset, he sighted smoke in the distance, several individual columns rising from the horizon and dissipating in the breeze, and he left the

road for the cover of nearby woods to skirt the settlement. From a
hillside, hidden in the shadow of trees, he paused above the tidy row
of cabins. Several appeared newly constructed, a loose pile of scrap
timber, a pitch pot smoldering. Nearing dusk, the glow from cooking
fires blushed windows and seeped from beneath doors. People began
making their way from the fields, here a man with six children following in step like ducklings, there two men leading mules by their
harnesses. A pair of mongrels barked and nipped at one another and
worried a rawhide strip between them.

Day faded early in the woods and, in unfamiliar land, Thompson
sensed the ghost of memory stalking him, a chill presence descending
like a mist that drove him from the hill overlook on into the gloaming.
Past dark he rolled himself in his blanket and slept fitfully on the
ground at the edge of a meadow. Once during the night he woke
to the sound of a wolf far in the distance. A howl, a response? He
thought he was done with sleep for the night, but fatigue overcame his
churning mind and he drifted back into uneasy somnolence, floating,
dim noises, a light breeze through new spring leaves, the screeching
cry of a fox, or a baby, unable to distinguish dream world from real.

Thompson rose, stiff and weary, to a light rain. Tired, wet, but
marching as if he were fleeing the advancing enemy. His stomach protested, empty save for a stale biscuit from his sack and fresh water from
a clear running stream he'd waded. He sensed an unnamed adversary
coming from the east so he continued his westward course at military
pace long into the day. He passed one other township but encountered
no one on the road. By late afternoon he entered unknown territory,
country he'd not traveled before: limestone bluffs breaking the rolling
hills, the land opening a bit, the woods patchy. As the sun neared the
western horizon, he descended into the gully of a creek bed where a
small stand of hickory grew up dark against the paling sky. He drank
from the creek and refilled his water bag. The water tasted of leaves and

bog. After surveying the gully, he stood in the lengthening shadow of a tree and pulled the hammer of his rifle to half-cock and placed the butt between his feet with the muzzle at his shoulder. He poured the charge, fit the ball and compressed the paper wadding behind it with his ramrod. He shouldered the rifle and set the hammer to full cock. He waited. Motionless, alert. A quarter of an hour passed, and then the muffled sound of movement through the damp leaves, a squirrel darting along the ground and up the hickory where Thompson had spotted the nest. It paused on a branch and Thompson sighted his musket, but the squirrel sensed something, pending danger, the slight movement of the muzzle, and scurried to the far side of the tree where it scolded him with a repetitive, sharp chatter. Thompson picked a hickory nut from the ground and tossed it behind the tree and readied himself. The squirrel jumped from the sound back to Thompson's side of the tree, where the musket ball waited. Thompson's shot struck bark a fraction of an inch beneath the squirrel, killing by concussion without mutilating the meat.

Thompson pulled the skin from the squirrel and gutted the carcass. As dusk came on the rain eased, allowing him to build a small fire using a little powder and some branch shavings as tinder. He roasted the squirrel over the banked embers, and pulling meat from bone he ate greedily but without pleasure, ate because his fate was to live and life required nourishment.

THE FOLLOWING DAYS TOOK ON a sameness, rain continuing on and off, dimming clouds, early darkness, starless nights, the moon a gauzy hint, the going slowed by fatigue and by a road turned to mire, brown sludge puddling the low areas, food gone, game scarce. Thompson, bow-shouldered, mud-splattered, hair matted and tangled like a thicket of scrub brush, seemed more a feature of the landscape than a person moving through it. The constantly overcast skies deprived him of a clear view of the sun and the stars by which to guide, so he no longer was sure of his course, although he judged it westward still. He despaired time lost to foraging and rest, yet had not an inkling of his destination, a wanderer rather than a pilgrim. He felt compelled to move, but the why and where of it escaped him.

He must have appeared an ominous presence to the father and young girl he stumbled upon late one evening as he approached the cabin he'd seen from the rise. The girl held a slop bucket beside a small split rail pen holding four swine. The man stepped in front of the girl and loosely gripped the haft of a pitchfork. He was large and rawboned, wore a broad rimmed hat from which protruded shocks of hair the color of straw. He seemed to Thompson neither cordial nor threatening, but cautious perhaps. Thompson leaned his rifle against the fence post and stepped away from it.

"Hello. I don't wish to disturb your work. I thought only to fill my bag at the well. I've been on the road a spell." Thompson removed his water skin from around his neck and pointed it in the direction of the well. The little girl peeked from behind her father. Barefoot, she wore a calico dress checkered in blue and white. The man seemed to take Thompson's measure and then spoke.

"You're welcome to what water you can carry. Name's Madison. James Madison." He removed his hat and scratched his head. "No relation, but it's a topic of much merriment with folks around here."

"Thompson Grey. Obliged."

Thompson left his rifle at the post and walked to the well and filled his bag. Then, almost as an afterthought, "Where might 'around here' be? I come from Deep Woods and am headed west."

"Deep Woods?"

"Indiana."

"If west is your only destination you are on course," Madison answered. "A ways back you crossed over into Illinois."

"Again, I'm obliged to you." Thompson nodded to Madison, and Madison raised a hand to stop him.

"It's tight what with the winter stores getting low, but I'd be pleased to offer a little something to eat and a warm place by the fire."

Thompson considered his waterlogged chill and gnawing hunger. "I'm not fit for the table. But, some bread if you have it to spare, and a rest in the hay bin."

"As you wish," Madison answered and led the girl to the cabin. As the door opened, an older boy, almost a man, came from around back of the cabin wielding a flintlock musket and followed the two inside. As Thompson waited, he looked over what he could see of the farm and judged Madison to have achieved a measure of success. The log house was well constructed, the plank door tight in its frame, the stone chimney true, a window with glass panes. Cornfields stretched out behind the cabin in sufficient acreage that Thompson knew Madison must have several other children behind the door. The swine in the pen were heavy and of good color. Chickens pecked in the yard. Two milk cows grazed about their tether pins in a pasture off to Thompson's right, and a pair of mules shuffled in the lean-to next to the pig pen. A good life, Thompson thought. A good life. Not unlike his own, before.

THOMPSON HAD BEEN PROUD OF his quarter section in Indiana, the log cabin and the growing numbers of livestock, cultivated fields, and woodlands for lumbering. But his land paled in comparison to his father's estate, the two-story frame house with the front porch looking out over fields planted in tobacco and corn, sheep grazing on pastured hills, the forests beyond. And the outbuildings: kitchen attached to the main house by a covered walkway; the tenant shacks, base but tidily arranged in two rows and freshly whitewashed; the smokehouse; the tobacco barn and curing room.

Thompson believed himself born to farm and loved the comforting rhythm: plowing and sowing in spring, clearing land and culling trees during summer heat and winter pause, harvesting in fall, butchering after the first hard frost. He gave thanks for what he had in Indiana, what he had built for Rachel and the boys. But he dreamed of more and bitterly resented the curse of the second son. His father had told him he'd not see his future generations fall from comfort into poverty because of holdings divided and divided again. His brother Jacob would inherit the estate and Thompson despaired of ever being able to increase his own acreage. So, when the opportunity arose, he acted.

He'd been turning the soil early that spring when Cyrus Brawley rode over on his mule. Cyrus owned the farm adjacent to his own. "Giving it up," Cyrus told Thompson. They stood in Thompson's field. Cyrus bent and took a clot of dirt in his hand and crumbled it, sifting it through his fingers.

"They say soil in Illinois is black and rich." Cyrus looked to the woods bordering Thompson's five-acre plot. "And without these god-damned stumps to clear."

Thompson knew the Brawley farm. Yielded fair, would do better with his touch. Good sections of bottomland, acres of hardwood Brawley found excuse not to log.

"How much?" Thompson asked.

"A dollar and twenty an acre, I'll let it go. Looking to sell it all of a piece."

The property would double the size of his farm, if only he had the funds. He would request a loan from his father.

"MR. THOMPSON?"

Madison stood holding out a tin plate and a wool blanket, for how long Thompson had not a clue.

"Thank you." Thompson accepted the offerings.

"This should keep the chill off and the belly satisfied for a while," Madison said, and with a nod withdrew to the cabin. Thompson nested into the hay bin and shoveled food into his mouth with the wooden spoon Madison had provided. The plate held a generous slab of cornbread and thick gravy, milk and flour mixed with bits of fatback fried in a skillet. When he had sopped the last of the gravy with the cornbread and blotted the soggy crumbs with his finger, he wrapped himself in the blanket, burrowed more deeply into the hay, pulled his hat low, and slept uneasily with his dreams.

RACHEL AT HER VANITIES. THAT last evening, before he left to call on his father, Matthew in his crib and Daniel on his mat, she untied the string that bound her hair in its tight bun. Days, she kept it up, out of the way while at chores, but at night she let it down and brushed it each evening. A raven's sheen. An open, innocent face. Full breasts, firm despite three pregnancies in four years, the first ended prematurely to bleeding. She hummed a tune as she combed, and smiled over at him. He reached to stroke her hair, reached for the warmth of his wife.

SOMETHING WOKE HIM. A SOUND, familiar but out of setting for the wilderness. Music. The tune Rachel had been humming in his dream. He sat up and rubbed his eyes. He'd slept but little, judging by the hang of the moon in a night sky now swept free of clouds and filled with cold pricks of light. He stood wrapped in the blanket and listened. Still dreaming? There, from the cabin. Thompson retrieved the tin plate and eased to the window and peered inside. A woman, fair-complexioned and slim-figured, sat by the fire bracing a dulcimer on her lap, working chords with one hand while bowing with the other. Madison sat at a rough-hewn table with two older boys while two girls waltzed a toddler in a tight circle about the room. Madison and his wife sang quietly.

Thompson removed the blanket, folded it, placed it beside the door, and set the plate on the blanket. He backed from the porch and gathered his belongings and turned for the road and walked until the moon began to set, and then he ascended a slope into the woods and when he reached a leveling he stopped and built a small fire. As the fire glowed he lost his night vision and his world constricted, limited to the flickering reach of the flames. But he heard the animals, an owl high in a near tree, a deer picking through the deadfall, something foraging nearby, a raccoon perhaps. Thompson pulled his blanket around his shoulders, stared into the red glow of the coals, felt again solitude seeping into his bones with the cold night air, and, in the hours that sleep refused to come, tried unsuccessfully to wean from his memory his past life, a life forfeited by his transgressions, a life traded for this new, unfamiliar purgatory.

2

Sabbath day, June 7th, Thompson approached the city on the river. He'd been traveling though unfamiliar but generally recognizable country, every homestead reminding him of his own, every sow with her spring farrow, every cornfield. He felt unable to shake the dust from his feet. During sleep, marching armies, awake, haunting memories. Weariness his constant companion, a drugged consciousnesses, a vague awareness of the great river drawing near. A rising humidity, dense cultivation, and on the road, increasing commerce, wagons forcing him to step aside.

Thompson had heard of St. Louis, of course, and of the Mississippi River, but after traveling for so many days alone, avoiding the towns, sleeping in woods and ravines, he was ill prepared for the draw and sweep of it, the sharp delineation between east bank and west, the city rising from the bluff on the opposite shore, buildings like Sirens luring trail-weary Argonauts. The river, brown and wide and swirling. The city an impenetrable mass of brick and plank,

foreboding and indecipherable to a man of Thompson's experience and current disposition. As his ferry approached the landing,
they passed steamboat after steamboat moored along an endless
wharf. Although Sunday, an army of men were at work loading
and unloading boats, a clatter of iron wheels and horse hooves,
men shouting, cinder-belching steamboats fitted with hissing and
grinding machinery, sounds mixing and merging and rising in a
raucous din like the low rumble of a distant battle.

Once disembarked, he roamed the levee, uncertain of direction, stupefied by the confusion of activity, the bustle of people
and animals. He required supplies. He did not desire unnecessary
human contact, and he need not have worried. He observed little
neighborly interaction from anyone. Men jostled him, seeming
not to notice his presence on the street. No acknowledgements
except from those who wanted something: shills loitering outside
taverns bidding him enter; an aging whore with rouged cheeks
and a slightly humped back who cupped a breast in her hand and
asked if he might desire a place to rest his head for a spell; one old
hag with a goiter the size of a melon bulging from her neck who
pressed Thompson so insistently for a coin that he had actually to
push her aside to pass.

He came upon a mercantile and ducked inside. A dim and clut-
tered place, several men sat smoking pipes around a cold potbellied
stove in one corner. Dusty tins of hard biscuits sat mingled with sacks
of dried cod. The silent and dour proprietor eyed him suspiciously as
Thompson packed his rucksack with a small bag of cornmeal, a tin
of coffee, a square of salt pork which he wrapped in butcher paper.
His expression brightened when Thompson retrieved a silver coin
from the money belt and placed it on the counter. "Wasn't sure of
your intentions at first," the shopkeeper said. "You come in looking
fagged out, a little busted." He offered a few coppers in change.

"Looks don't tell the whole of it, I expect," Thompson answered. He returned the copper coins to his belt and walked back into the street.

Outside, Thompson left the wharf district and climbed into the city, walked through the heart of it, three- and four-story brick buildings throwing the street into early shadows, street after street, row after row of brick and stone, iron lattices over glass windows, gas lamplights along Main. A disorienting, unsettling maze; he did not comprehend the attraction of the place for so great a throng.

"COME SEE PHILADELPHIA," HIS BROTHER, Jacob, had urged that last night at the Reverend's table. He radiated enthusiasm when describing the crowds and the tall buildings. "Everything so convenient, one hardly has need of a mount." The city, his brother lectured, is the future. All that is progressive and forward-looking comes from the city.

"Perhaps," Thompson had countered. "But I can imagine no place better suited to my temperament than here."

His brother and he had converged at their childhood home because their father, the Reverend Matthew Grey, was not well. Chopping wood, the blade deflected off an oak burl and nearly severed his foot. The wound now festered, filling the parlor where Thompson first greeted him with a faint, disagreeably sweet odor. The Reverend was unable to rise from the settee, compelling Thompson to stoop down to embrace him, awkward for both, and decidedly cooling the reunion. Reverend Grey had pointed dismissively at the foot wrapped in a thick bandage seeping a yellowish discharge. "Administer what ointments you think best, I told the physicians, and let God's will be done."

God's will apparently was to take His time in determining His servant's fate, and with his father teetering between recovery and decline, Thompson petitioned him for an advance share of his inheritance. A land opportunity, he explained. The Brawley holdings adjacent to his own, the promise it held, the asking price better than fair. During moments of laudanum-induced magnanimity the Reverend readily consented to the advance, only to rescind later, when the effect of the drug lessened and his parsimonious nature reestablished hold both on his senses and his purse strings. The Reverend grew indignant, railing at Thompson's boldness during his time of peril. Thompson determined to stay on until he could resolve the matter. A few days stretched into a week, and beyond. Rachel would require help in the fields. Surely the neighbors would look in, lend a hand. It's what neighbors did. They knew of his mission. But time passed without resolution. A day short of two weeks, without having secured title to his inheritance, resentful of his father and of his brother who had no intention for the estate other than to sell it once he assumed ownership, ashamed over his own dereliction of family and field, Thompson returned to Deep Woods, returned to Rachel and the boys. Rachel and the boys. . . .

"Need directions?" Thompson stood in the middle of the road, Saint Louis, mid-intersection, immobilized by memory. He turned to the voice and recognized two men who had been smoking in the mercantile.

"I'll find my way."

"Look lost to me. Look lost to you, Neil?"

"Lost, and in a bad box," replied the second man, who was easing off to Thompson's left as he answered.

"Tell you what," from the first man, "you go on and show us what you got in that belt and we'll be off."

Thompson had been cradling his rifle in the crook of his arm, and now gripped it by the barrel and the neck of the buttstock and brought it out in front of his chest in a defensive position. The rifle was unloaded and the barrel visibly plugged for travel, plainly no threat to fire. As he half turned to keep the second man in his line of sight, the first advanced on him and grabbed the rifle mid-barrel to keep Thompson from swinging it on them. The man brought up a knife in his other hand and slashed Thompson twice on the forearm. Thompson held tight to the rifle and kicked up at the man, once, again, the second time connecting foot to groin. The man sucked in his breath, loosed his grip on Thompson's rifle, and doubled over. Thompson brought the butt down onto the man's instep, a crunching sound, and then swung on the second man, who had hesitated entering the fray an instant too long. The barrel of his musket caught the man a glancing blow in the forehead at the scalp line, dazing him and sending a rush of blood down into his eyes. Backing furiously away, he swiped at his face and seeing the back of his hand dripping with his own blood, turned for the alley beside two buildings on the near side of the street. The first man limped after him and together they disappeared into the narrow passage. Thompson did not pursue. He stood looking about, sucking for breath. The streets were still filled with passers-by. Other than two boys who had paused in their game of dice to watch the confrontation, no one gave Thompson so much as a glance. The boys turned back to their game.

The altercation shook Thompson from his torpor, awakened him to his surroundings. He retraced his steps to the mercantile and used a copper to buy a needle and some thread. With some grumbling the shopkeeper gave him an old flour sack which Thompson used to bind his forearm. He returned to the streets, walking quickly, and finally commercial landscape gave way to residential, and then to poorer frame houses of the workers and servants. He followed the Kingshighway to the city's western outskirts, where he took a room above a roadhouse. He carried a measure of whiskey in a tin cup and fresh water in a washbowl from the tavern to his room, drank half of the whiskey sitting on his bed, removed his tunic, and used the remainder of the whiskey and the water to clean the two gashes on his forearm. He took up the needle and thread and sutured the wounds as best he could, washed out the blood on his shirtsleeve, and sewed the ripped material with the same needle and thread. He judged the tunic more neatly stitched than the arm.

He washed himself, considered shaving, decided against it. He reclined on the stinking mattress and attempted to rest the night away but full sleep never came. The tavern dinned, floorboards creaked throughout the ramshackle structure, fights erupted and concluded downstairs, and thin walls offered no privacy at all. In the room to his right, he could not but eavesdrop on the adventures of a whore and her client, the escalatory slap of flesh against flesh so lusty and proximate that they might as well have been sharing his mattress. On his left, a man deep within the folds of drunken oblivion snored and snorted so loudly that the whore two rooms removed interrupted her partner's increasingly strident bed-rattling to pound on Thompson's wall and curse in protest.

Thompson lay there, his arm now throbbing, and wondered at this strange and hideous place, the city, where people seemed at once invisible and so inconsequential that almost no interaction between one person and another transcended the bounds of decency. To rob, to whore, to ignore common civility on the street? He realized he could never be a part of this place. He'd fled his farm, but the city would provide no sanctuary. So, then, where?

He turned on his side and attempted to doze. His arm hot to the touch, he shivered with fever.

COMING ONTO HIS FARM IN Deep Woods, he noticed immediately. The un-tethered horse grazing on dandelions along the irrigation ditch, the empty hog trough. A chimney free of smoke. Thompson jumped from the cart without reining the mule and threw open the door, calling. Dim indoor light, shadows only. A stench. Rancid meat from a cold pot hanging over dead coals. More, more than that.

"Rachel?"

Looking up from her bed, eyes shining, focused but unseeing. Face a mask of red sores, skin split and oozing. She did not answer, but turned back to Matthew, whimpering at her breast. Her finger weakly tickling his cheek, enticing cracked lips to suckle.

Thompson sat at the edge of the bed and put his hand to her forehead and could not believe the heat. At his touch her chin rose to him and her eyes grew wild. "Gabriel?" she asked, and then, inexplicitly, a line from a song, "Oh, my darling Nellie Gray, they have taken you away." Then she returned to Matthew, "Take," she said, offering her breast.

"Daniel?" Gently, the question. No reply, she coaxing the baby with incoherent muttering. Thompson looked about. The sleeping mat. He rose and approached. A stiff, bloated thing, the stench. An overstuffed sausage. He dropped to his knees, retched into the hearth, a great heaving expulsion. He could not bear to look at what days before had been his son. Could not bear to touch it. No choice. He dragged the mat on which his son lay from the house to a patch of ground beneath a persimmon tree and there he dug his son's pit, the mat his winding sheet. He packed tight the crumbled earth. Later, stones to shield him from beasts. He went back into the house with a bucket of water and sat with Rachel and Matthew, a cool cloth to one forehead and then the other, squeezing a drop or two onto tongues swollen and coated white with mucus. He sat with them into the night. Toward sunrise, Matthew's breathing grew shallow. Thinner, the breathing, and then nothing at all. The baby paled. Thompson had no prayer to offer up. Rachel woke just as he finished changing Matthew into his white baptismal gown. She sat straight up in bed and the look in her eyes told Thompson that this, she understood. That, for an instant, the veil of fever lifted. She opened her mouth but remained mute, as if there were no sounds for her grief.

Another grave dug, another son lowered into the ground. He kept his eyes shut as he scooped the dirt back into the hole. He returned to Rachel and sat at her side, holding her hand. She could not talk, a gurgling sound only, rapid breaths, and then she opened her eyes and stared at Thompson, stared through him. Eyes glazed. Unseeing in this world. He wondered if she saw into the next. He held a cup to her lips. "Try." He hummed a lullaby, or some tune that reminded him of something like a lullaby. He smoothed her damp and matted hair. Her beautiful hair.

He sat through the day. Light moved across the room. Against his will, he dozed. At some point during the afternoon he thought he heard voices outside, a horse sniggering. And then silence and then night came on again. He nodded in and out. He dreamed the precise words to console Rachel, the correct prayers to summon his boys from the grave. But when he awoke he could not remember them. Rachel's hand, cold, her stiff fingers intertwined with his.

THOMPSON AWOKE IN THE DARK of early morning, sweating, chest heaving. The memories would not leave him, would not permit rest. Awake and moving, he sometimes could distract himself, temporarily inhabit the present. But in sleep, the past returned, images crept back, burned anew, engraved themselves more deeply into memory, grew more vivid rather than faded with time. He sat up and swung his legs to the floor. The fever had broken. He tested his arm and found it stiff and tender. He tossed stale water from the basin out the window onto the street below and refilled it from the pitcher on the nightstand and changed his bandage. Before full light, he was up and on the road.

Thompson traveled for a week, following the course of the Missouri from its junction with the Mississippi, west by northwest across the state. In places the river bottom stretched for miles from either bank, fertile and, in places, cultivated. Sometimes the yellow bluffs

came up close to the banks and from them he sat looking out over
the expanse of river country, the hardwoods, the land's gentle rising
and rolling, the pale green of crops ripening in distant fields, and
felt an unspecified yearning for something lost. From the stillness of
the heights, he could look down on the world below and follow the
progress of paddle steamers churning upriver, and flatboats gliding
down with their loads of firewood or buffalo hides. Men going about
their business. Sometimes the bottomland became so swampy with
back eddies and side channels that he was forced to leave it altogether
for a stretch of miles. But always the river revealed itself in the cut of
the land, in contours carved from flowing water, coursing for millennia
after millennia, for years uncountable in human reckoning.

Ten days west of Saint Louis, the salt pork ran out. Thompson had
gone three days living on weak coffee and a thin mush of cornmeal
mixed with water and a pinch of sugar. But he refused to pass through
Jefferson City for supplies. His forearm yet throbbed, the wounds out-
lined in red and draining, a bothersome reminder of city hospitality.
West of the town, a day's journey, he located a promising oxbow on
the river, spongy banks carpeted in new grass gently sloping into scrub
flats cut with game trails. He camped off to the edge of the opening
and slept the night without a fire. He primed and loaded his rifle and
put it at half cock and slept sitting upright against a cottonwood. First
light, a rustling, and three does and two small spike bucks came out
of the brush to drink at the river. Thompson shot one of the bucks
cleanly through the lungs. It lurched with the shot and kicked for the
river but dropped before reaching it.

He dragged the buck by the forelegs up the riverbank and positioned
it on its back, head uphill so it could bleed out when he cut. He dressed
out the carcass and skinned it sufficiently to access the backstrap on
each side of the spine. He removed the meat and cut it into thin strips
on a flat stone he'd pulled from the river. After washing the blood

from his hands and arms, he built a fire and roasted the liver and the heart on skewers. While the fire was burning down, he built a drying rack by suspending willow switches over Y-shaped branches staked on either side of the fire pit. He banked the coals and put on some green wood to raise the smoke and draped the meat strips over the rack. While the meat dried, he ate a chunk of the liver and dozed and then turned the strips, ate part of the heart and slept again. Road-weary and sated for the first time in days, he slept without dreaming and woke midafternoon, grateful and rested. He sacked the jerky, and left the river bottom for firmer ground.

3

Gradually, the land stretched out, the woods thinning and the hills flattening into broad reaches of rolling meadowland. Heat built through the day, little rain fell, and locusts flew up from the road at his passing and buzzed into tall grass. Thompson noticed the change, his mind recording countryside not so much his own any longer. It made it easier somehow to forget, to associate his memories with another land, another time. For a day, sometimes, he could walk without falling into the trance of despair. For a night, sometimes, sleep came without visitation from the army of bones beating their muffled drums.

Although settlement thinned, traffic on the road increased. Thompson encountered growing numbers of emigrants striking for the western territories, small groups driving wagons drawn by oxen and mules. The traces, trails, and highways of the east converged at the bank of the Missouri on the border of Kansas Territory. He went by ferry into Westport the evening of July 2nd, passing through the city only because there existed no convenient detour. He did not stop, did not tarry, but hurried though a town that seemed constructed solely for commerce. Near the landing a tangle of ramshackle plank dwellings provided housing, he imagined, for the dockworkers, a cock-fighting pit and several taverns their entertainment. Above the landing, on either side of Westport Road, mercantile shops offered a dizzying array of goods to outfit the emigrants. Through glass display windows Thompson inventoried bolts of calico and flannel; kits of mackerel and dried codfish; coffee beans in hundredweight sacks; camp kettles of Russian iron; kegs of brandy; hardware, tools, rope and tackle. The household goods reminded him of his own home left behind, his family, his Rachel and Matthew and Daniel, and a wave of grief like a sudden nausea washed over him. He slumped against a hitching post until it passed, and then pushed on.

At town center, he stopped to fill his water skin at the community well. The water—clean-tasting, cool, and free of tang—refreshed him. He watched a merchant bargain with two aboriginals over a stack of pelts. The Indians were unlike any Thompson had encountered in the East. Taller, with long-muscled lines and skin more darkened by the sun. The strange ritual of trade, hands gesturing in pantomime, facial contortions, a few guttural syllables, were unintelligible to him, but obviously conveyed meaning for the participants. He left them haggling and on his way out of town passed a group of four Mexicans wearing wide cloth hats and colorful sashes. They played cards, laughing and talking in a melodic tongue, full of rolling consonants and soft vowels. Their skin was dark as some of the Reverend's field hands, and it occurred to Thompson that he was about to enter a territory populated by natives so attuned to their surroundings that they took on its shading.

Thompson followed the Westport Road past fenced corrals holding mules, oxen, horses, and a few sheep. The day was growing short but he wanted quit of the town before stopping. Toward evening he came across a large assemblage camped on open pasture that held good grass and a clear spring running through it. Livestock grazed, some picketed, some free-ranging. Smoke from scores of cook fires drifted above the pasture in a thin shelf of haze. The wagons appeared themselves almost living things with their long wooden tongues lowered to the ground and with canvas stretched over their arched ribs. Osnaburg-hided animals resting alongside the oxen and mules. The company appeared divided into two groups, a large congregation of sixty or so wagons and, to the near side of the meadow, a much smaller grouping of twelve to fifteen.

Thompson walked into the clearing, and to avoid concern, made himself seen to three men coming in from the animals. He raised a hand in greeting, although he did not stop to engage them. Instead, he retreated to the tree line, cleared a small patch of ground and built a fire. In his tin cup he cooked cornmeal mush. Just before sunset a man approached from the smaller gathering of wagons. He threw a long shadow as he walked across the grass. Thompson judged the man almost as tall as himself and heavier through the chest and shoulders. He wore buckskin pants, a dark shirt, black boots, and a hat with a large, flat brim. Thompson set his cup on the ground beside the fire and stood to meet him.

"Good evening," said the man, "name's Upperdine. Captain John Upperdine."

"Thompson Grey."

"Might I ask your intentions, stopping here?" Captain Upperdine said.

"Well, my immediate intentions are to finish my supper. I haven't much thought beyond that."

Upperdine smiled and removed his hat and scratched his head.

"I pilot a group of settlers. It is my job to think beyond your supper." Upperdine's tone conveyed neither anger nor threat, but he clearly expected a reply and he waited, hat in hand.

"I appreciate your responsibility," Thompson complied. "I am simply a traveler on the road."

"You are heading into the territory?"

"I am."

"Afoot?"

"Yes."

"Alone?"

"Yes."

"To farm?"

"Yes." Thompson said, without thinking. His answer startled him, caused a physical reaction, a cocking of the head, as if listening for a sound in the distance, unsure of what he had heard, and he amended his response.

"What I meant was that perhaps I will farm. I have not considered it fully."

"To trade, maybe?" Upperdine pressed.

"I have no wish to trade."

"Well," Upperdine said, "it's none of my concern." He pulled on his hat, adjusted the brim. "It's just that land is about all there is in the western territories. Cheap. Some of it passable fertile. If it's not land you're seeking, nor trade, I fear you are dead ripe for disappointment."

Thompson had no answer. He looked off across the meadow toward the smaller cluster of wagons. The fires began to glow in the twilight.

"I'll not interrupt your supper any longer." Upperdine started off and then turned. "Some advice?"

"Any advice is welcome."

"I've crossed these grasslands more than once. This time of year, daytime heat builds up, sweat like you was breaking a fever. Nights, the chill seeps in right to the bones because your clothes ain't dried out yet. I'd invest in a good wool shirt. Something that wicks. And maybe buckskin trousers."

"Appreciate your insight. Thank you."

Thompson ate his mush without tasting, added wood to the fire, watched the flames lick into the deepening night. He'd answered, yes. Yes, he'd farm. The realization stunned him. He had no heart for it, had no conscious intention of ever again putting plow to soil; but at the instant of his spontaneous response to Upperdine he'd voiced his destiny. He worked the land. That is what he was made for. He'd till and sow, reap and store, filling time between the present and that predestined moment in the future he would arrive at the gates of Hell. He'd farm, but not back East. He'd defiled that land and would not return.

Next morning, Thompson walked into town and spent a good portion of one double eagle on clothing and what food he could carry, splurging on a small bag of coffee. He would be pleased to be rid of the clothes on his back. He'd picked up fleas or lice or both from the roadhouse mattress, and the itching had grown progressively more irksome.

Returning to the woods, he bathed at the stream before it ran into the pasture. He stripped off his clothes and scrubbed his head and body with a scrap of lye soap he'd purchased in town. He inspected his arm wounds. His needlework had closed the gashes and allowed healing to begin, but was no work of art. The scars welted up, jagged and red. He discarded his old clothes after tearing a few rags from his shirt, left them in a heap beside the trail. He stepped into woolen underclothes and the buckskin trousers and began to pull on his new shirt, then stopped and hung it on a limb and returned to the stream. He wetted one of the rags and brought it to his face and soaked his whiskers. He used his skinning knife first to trim the beard close and then, after another soaking, to shave. Thick stubble remained and he made note to purchase a straight razor. But for the first time since Deep Woods, Indiana, since leaving his family, he exposed his face to the world, nicked and raw, for judgment.

He arrived back at the meadow rendezvous midafternoon just as a thundershower blew in from the northwest. He ducked back into the woods and sat under the overhang of an oak tree watching the rain slant in. Not heavy but windblown. It appeared that during the day a few additional wagons had arrived. After the quick shower, a golden light washed the meadow. The grass bejeweled. The oxen steaming.

Moving toward his camp, Thompson noticed a man working at one of the wagons. He had the back wheel off and was attempting to remount it on the axle. The man rolled the wheel into position while a boy and a Negro were struggling to raise the back end of the wagon using a large tree limb as a lever. The boy's feet were off the ground, hanging from the end of the limb, but the axle was not plumb to the hub. Thompson went to the boy and lent his weight to the lever and after some maneuvering, the back end rose sufficiently for the wheel to slide back over the hub.

"Obliged," from the man guiding the wheel. He appeared several years older than Thompson and slight, thin as a whip. A close-trimmed beard. Denim trousers that bunched at his waist, held up with suspenders. He wiped his hand on his blue work shirt and offered it to Thompson. "Obadiah Light. Sorry to inconvenience you."

"Thompson Grey. No trouble at all."

The Negro carried the limb off to the side and they all watched him as he began to chop it into firewood.

"Iron rim and brake lever wanted some work," Obadiah said. "Wagon's only as good as its wheels."

"That is so," Thompson said.

"I aimed to avoid having to unload the wagon. Left the back end overly heavy. Slothful, I suppose."

Thompson noticed the covered box of the wagon full of household goods: a spinning wheel, chests, two chairs, one inverted on the other, coiled rope, harness gear, sacks of grain, tools, a steel-tipped plow, grinding stone, and, near the back, a small parlor organ.

"I would not envy you that task," Thompson said.

"I'd be pleased to have you sup with us," Obadiah said.

Behind the wagon, a woman stood beside an iron pot suspended on a tripod over the low fire. A young girl, a toddler in blond curls, played in the grass with a cornhusk doll while the boy, the one who had been on the lever with Thompson, busied himself repacking tools in the box mounted above the front wheel. Thompson saw that the boy was older than he'd first judged, maybe just coming into shaving age, a faint presence above the lip. Slight of frame like his father, but undaunted, it seemed, about jumping to a man's work. The woman came over to the wagon, smiled at Obadiah, and folded down the rear gate into a table. She showed. How far along, Thompson wondered.

"My wife, Hanna. The boy, Joseph, and my girl, Martha."

Thompson nodded to the woman and the boy, and smiled at the little girl. Hanna set the kettle on the gate and retrieved a ladle and some tin bowls from a box on the far side of the wagon.

"Simple fare," she said, "some bread." She served a soup of desiccated vegetables flavored with field greens and a few wild onions.

"I've not had bread in a while," Thompson said. "Thank you." Bread from wheat, not corn.

"I can trouble to knead it proper when we're laying over. No time on the trail."

Obadiah pulled at the waist of his dungarees. "These were filled out when we left home. Had a little sickness. Some difficult times. But we're on our last leg now," he explained. "Barely two hundred mile to go." The Lights were from eastern Ohio, he said, on the road since early spring, bound for central Kansas Territory, near Great

Bend, beyond the far reaches of settlement. Hanna learned she was pregnant two months prior to their departure but kept the news from him. She knew his heart was set on homesteading and she did not wish to cause him to reconsider.

Listening to their story, Thompson sensed himself slipping back, and he fought to remain in the present. Still, images, like lightning strikes, flashed behind his eyes.

RACHEL HAD OBJECTED TO HIS being gone. "The fields need tending,"
"I'll be a few days only. I need to secure funds."
"We have more acreage now than we can put into crops."
"We'll grow into it. The boys."
"Coveting is a sin, the Bible says."
"Don't quote me the Book," Thompson said, angry.

THOMPSON SHOOK THE PAST FROM his mind and refocused on the Lights' company, Martha playing with her doll, feeding it scraps of bread.

They stood around the table, evening coming on, eating, talking idly of inconsequential matters. Weather, mileage, the soil. Presently the Negro came over from his work and Mrs. Light served him supper and he stood with them eating. The idea of sharing a meal with a Negro would never have registered with Thompson before, but he found himself curious rather than put off.

"This here's Ned, Mr. Thompson," Obadiah said. "Ned Frederick, named after the county in Virginia where he was set free." Ned inclined his head and said "How do?" and Thompson nodded back. Ned was a stocky man, ebony-skinned, with eyes that looked as though he'd had sorrow. As he ate, Thompson noticed that he was missing two fingertips of his left hand.

"Ned is a wonder with a saw and adze, a carpenter without peer in my book," Light went on. "He's traveling with us. I'm holding his papers for him until we reach territory where he can set hisself up without looking over his shoulder every waking minute."

"Is there such a place?" Thompson asked.

"We fixed on th' hope," Ned answered.

Obadiah set his tin on the wagon gate and stretched. "And you, Mr. Grey. Family?"

"No. I am alone." And, after a silence, "I best see to my fire before dark. I thank you for your hospitality." Thompson shook Obadiah's hand and nodded to Hanna and to the boy. And, as an afterthought, to Ned. He knelt in the grass and patted Martha on the head and then stood and returned to his camp. He folded some of the coffee beans in a flap of buckskin and pounded it with a flat stone. He shook out the grounds in his cup and boiled some coffee over the fire. A movement in the grass, a sound, and from the shadowy light Upperdine emerged.

"Mr. Thompson."

"Captain Upperdine, good evening." Thompson pointed to his coffee. "Have you a cup? I'd be pleased to offer coffee."

Upperdine untied the tin cup at his belt and held it out and Thompson poured half of his coffee into the cup. Upperdine raised the cup to his nose and inhaled the steam coming off the liquid.

"Simon Pure, the real thing. We normally get by on some god-awful adulteration, a few grounds mixed with dried peas, toasted grain, what have you."

Both men squatted on their boot heels close to the fire and drank the coffee without conversation. The rain had brought alive the mosquitoes, and the smoke from the cook fire helped knock them back. Crickets sounded in the tall grass. Upperdine broke the silence between them.

"I ride out tomorrow to see that the streams are not overly swollen by the rains. The following day we break camp."

"Will all the wagons form up?"

"It was decided yesterday evening that the two bands will remain separate."

"A disagreement?" Thompson asked.

"Most folks just want to be left alone to follow their plans. Buy land cheap. Put in a crop. Better their lot. But sometimes voices get raised and bad blood results."

"What company do you pilot?" Thompson asked.

"The smaller of the two."

Thompson had boiled more coffee, and he divided it between them. It was full dark and campfires dotted the field. Sparks flew up when one, then another was stirred up.

"Basically, Mr. Thompson, I am a freighter," Captain Upperdine said. "My commission is to deliver goods. Pelts and hides from west to east, housewares and equipment from east to west. Sometimes, emigrants to the opened territory. Makes little difference to me, except that truck is a sight less bothersome to handle than human freight."

"Less argument from a bolt of cloth," Thompson said, shaking the dregs of the coffee into the fire.

"Exactly." Upperdine stood and stretched. "I'd like you to consider joining our party when we depart."

Thompson thought to answer no, but instead asked, "Why me?"

"You said you were aiming west. My party is small. I could use another strong back. Another rifle, if need arises."

"I travel best alone," said Thompson.

"I understand. But this is perilous country you are about to enter. Men destitute of character roam this trail. Better traveled in company."

"I lack funds to pay my share."

"I've already settled with the company. I need hands. Mr. Light recommended you. A good neighbor, he vouched." Upperdine waited. Thompson thought about his offer, and his pause seemed to give Upperdine momentum to continue.

"I come out here a pup, signed up with Mr. Bent in the late '30s to teamster. Marched with General Kearny's Army of the West to Santa Fe in forty-six. Put down roots on the Purgatoire River in the western territory. Been up and down the Santa Fe trail more times than I can count. This is a harsh country. A challenge for a man alone. I don't know what you want from this land, but whatever your ambitions, I can provide alliance."

Thompson stood and kicked up the fire with the toe of his boot. "I promise you this, Captain Upperdine. I will sleep on it."

Upperdine left and Thompson sat facing the woods, staring into the maw of darkness.

A GOOD NEIGHBOR, OBADIAH SAID. Back in Deep Woods, when finally he resigned himself that the fever would not take him as he had prayed, he searched for blame and found a target. They should have looked after Rachel and his children, he'd asked as much of Edwin Fletcher the day prior to his departure. Look in on them? Of course, it's what neighbors do. Anger stirred him from his cabin. He willed himself upright, drank deeply from the water bucket, forced down a piece of stale bread. He strapped on his knife, took up his musket, and walked into the township of Deep Woods. He approached Fletcher's drygoods store. Fletcher also served as town constable, the first person Thompson thought to hold accountable for his family's neglect during his absence. Thompson stood unannounced before the store for several minutes until Fletcher appeared at the door and approached Thompson carefully, edging sideways, as if maneuvering around a rabid dog encountered unexpectedly in the road.

"Saw you was back," Fletcher spoke first. "Can't tell you how sorry—"

Thompson went for the knife on his belt. Fletcher extended both arms, hands palm out.

"Wait. There was nothing to be done." At Thompson's pause, he began to back away, pleading. "George sent his oldest out to your place, to help muck out the pens. Boy got there, looked in, the fever already on them. We put the boy up there in the shed off to his own self," Edwin pointed to the small rough-slatted hut beside the blacksmith shop. "Until we know it ain't got hold of him too. You know how fast it come on, how it spreads."

Thompson's intent had been to gut this man, to plunge his blade into the soft flesh below Fletcher's belly and slash upwards, opening him like a pig hanging from the bleeding rack. But he was not used to gutting a man, of course, and in the time between the willing and the doing, Fletcher fled into the mercantile. It would not have mattered had the constable remained standing before Thompson. The pause of indecision broke his spell, and the delicate balance within him between fury and grief shifted, and he was filled with a muscle-numbing sorrow. He could not lift the knife from its sheath; he could not move his legs. When next he came to his senses, the shadows had lengthened.

Thompson walked back to his empty farmhouse. The following morning, he took up what few belongings he determined essential, and he abandoned his land. He left the mule loosely tethered next to the feed trough in the lean-to that also sheltered his plow and equipment. He left the horse and the cow grazing in the near pasture. He left the chickens scratching in the dirt, left unfed the Duroc Reds: the boar and six sows. He left all the household effects, the iron cooking pot, the family Bible resting open on an oak reading stand, two patchwork quilts. He left the crops to fail, the tidy garden to wither, the new well he'd recently dug to fill with debris. He left the silent cabin to the miasma yet haunting its tight confines like a specter.

THE FIRE HAD DIED DOWN to embers. Thompson could not sleep. Memories too near the surface. Indecision about Upperdine's offer.

His mind drifting from past to present and back again. After a time, a full moon rose and washed the meadow in soft lambency. On impulse, Thompson retrieved the traveling Bible from his rucksack to test the moonlight. The passage he randomly opened to read clearly, "Two are better than one . . . woe to him that is alone when he falleth." A prophecy? Thompson decided to join the company. Two may in fact be better than one. For how long he had no idea, but for a time at least. He pulled his blanket close and fell almost immediately asleep. Sometime during the night he awoke to the sound of a cannon booming far in the distance. Independence Day in Westport? A groggy question, and he fell back into undisturbed rest.

Thompson woke later than was his custom, made coffee and stood watching the camp stir: three women returning from the stream hauling buckets; a man emerging from the woods with a fowling piece over his shoulder and carrying a turkey by the neck. In the pasture a clutch of men stood closely bunched. The stiffness of their postures, their gesturing, captured Thompson's attention. He set his cup on one of the firestones and walked to the men. As he approached, he recognized Obadiah. Ned and Joseph stood behind him. Confronting them were four men Thompson did not recognize. One of the strangers poked a finger in Obadiah's chest.

"Enough. I'm taking that there beast."

"It's not yours to take," said Obadiah. "The ox is mine."

"Get hold his nose rope, boys," the stranger said.

Obadiah stepped forward to claim the rope and another of the men pushed him aside, a beefy man, low to the ground and barrel-chested, himself resembling the ox he commandeered. Ned came up beside Obadiah and one of the men put his hand to the hilt of his knife and said, "Just give me the excuse, nigger."

Joseph sprang at the man who had pushed his father and the man cuffed him on the ear, knocking him to the ground. Joseph rose and lunged for the man again and the man knocked him down again. Joseph bled from the nose and his lip was split, and he stayed on his knees.

While the men were distracted, Thompson took the rope and led the oxen by the nose ring away from the ruckus.

"Hold on there," one of the strangers called. "Just what in the hell do you think you are doing?"

"Removing the cause for disagreement," Thompson said, and kept walking.

"The hell you will," said the ox-like man, and charged Thompson, head down like a battering ram. Thompson let drop the lead rope, sidestepped the man, and brought his knee up into the man's face as he passed. The man dropped, stunned, to all fours, and Thompson kicked him in the ribs, tilting him onto his side. Thompson suddenly felt rage, unfocused, not directed at this man specifically but at some unseen torment, and he kicked again, a cracking sound from the man's midsection. Another man advanced on him and Thompson's elbows flailed, finding nose, cartilage, an eye socket. Again he sensed an assault from behind him and attempted to swing, to kick, but he could do neither. Arms like staves encircled him, held him tight and immobile. He waited for the blows, but they did not come. Ned talked to him quietly. "Easy, sir. It's done. Easy."

Thompson relaxed, and Ned released him. Two strangers lay on the ground, groggy and bleeding. The two others showed little inclination to pursue the confrontation.

"I don't know who you are, but it is not finished. That ox is ours."

"Do you belong to a company?" Thompson asked.

The man jerked his chin in the direction of the larger congregation.

"And have you a wagon master?"

"Solomon Crank."

"This issue is best left for the wagonmasters to sort," Thompson said.

The two men on the ground were up now and the four started back to their side of the meadow. The one who had been talking said to Thompson, "You take up with their kind, no good will come of it."

"We shall see."

Thompson walked the ox to the vicinity of the Lights' wagon and set its picket.

"You will inform Captain Upperdine about the dispute when he returns?"

"I will," Obadiah said.

Thompson nodded and walked back to his fire to re-heat his coffee. He worried about Obadiah's lack of assertiveness with the men. He feared for a timid soul in this territory.

Upperdine returned to camp late afternoon. Thompson watched him ride in on his horse and saw Obadiah Light approach him before the Captain unsaddled and watched the Captain ride off in the direction of the larger camp. He thought about following but decided against it. Captain Upperdine appeared more than capable of managing for himself. Thompson instead took up his rifle and stalked the border between wood and meadow and returned in an hour with a cottontail. While it was grilling over the coals, Captain Upperdine walked up.

"Heard you had a little set-to this morning," Upperdine said.

"I regret losing my temper."

"Solomon Crank bemoaned your lack of restraint."

"I do not believe I initiated the skirmish," Thompson said.

Upperdine chuckled. "I've adjudicated the matter." He did not elaborate, and Thompson thought it advisable not to inquire further. "The stock is grazed and the streams are down. We depart early."

Thompson informed Upperdine of his decision to join them and Upperdine nodded in approval.

"I want to be on the trail ahead of the Crank party," Upperdine said. "Would hate to suck their dust, and we need to secure good grazing ahead of them. Grass been chawed out over the summer."

"Sounds reasonable."

"Our oxen are slower than their mules, but we are a smaller group by far and will be in motion long before they can organize their numbers."

"You do not use mules?" Thompson asked.

"Not for the trail. Oxen hold up better on the rough forage and they travel well over sandy soil."

Upperdine glanced at the grazing mules, spread out over the pasture. "We'll strike camp quietly. Pass the word wagon to wagon. Two in the morning, full moon, we should make do."

"I'll be about. Lend a hand where I'm needed."

"It would be appreciated."

"One question?"

"Of course," Upperdine said.

"One of the men today cautioned me about mixing in with 'those types'?"

"Abolitionists."

Thompson turned the rabbit on the skewer. The Reverend would approve. He must write his father about the events in Deep Woods.

"So, the larger company is pro-slave?" Thompson asked.

"Free-soil republicans," Upperdine said. "Want the territory free of slaves but free of the Negro as well."

"I see."

"Pro-slave ruffians are a sight rougher lot than you met today."

"That is not comforting news."

"I don't expect trouble. But I'll tell you this. Until I have this company a goodly distance from the Missouri line, I'll swear an oath to either side to see us safe on our journey."

Thompson tested the rabbit by poking and took up the skewer and offered a leg to Captain Upperdine. He declined. "Tomorrow, then," Upperdine said.

After dark, men went into the pasture and led the oxen to their wagons and yoked them while women and children loaded the cookware, tents and awnings, washbasins, churns, and other equipment that had been set out during layover. They slept lightly for a few hours in the open, and at two, Upperdine set the camp in motion. By first light the fifteen wagons had already covered several miles, and Upperdine continued to push them until late morning when they nooned beside a stream with good water. Far in the distance they could see dust raised by the large train, and Thompson was grateful they were making trail ahead of them.

Upperdine set the order of travel. Up at five, moving by six-thirty, nooning during the heat of high sun, resting the oxen, letting them graze unharnessed for a few hours, pushing on to a stopping point by early evening. They continued to catch sight of the larger wagon train by the dust signature, but each day it grew fainter until finally disappearing altogether. Their wagon train alone now on the prairie, a town on wheels, a town rolling inexorably westward with each passing day, it struck Thompson that he traveled with a community approximately the same population as the one he had abandoned. At ease with the idea or not, he'd rejoined the living.

4

They walked over rolling prairie and the unimposing flint hills of eastern Kansas Territory. It seemed impossible to imagine, those first days, that lack of good grazing could ever become a concern. Big Bluestem and Indian Grass grew as tall as a man's shoulder. When Thompson rested with Obadiah and his family, they had to keep watch on Hanna's little one lest she wander just a short distance and become lost entirely in the thick growth.

They walked beside their wagons at the slow, even pace of the oxen that pulled their every possession westward. The driver walked at the flanks of his team barking commands, "haw," "gee," his stock whip, or a prod, ready encouragement. The small children rode in the box. Older children at turns rode and walked with their parents or together in groups. The company: fifteen wagons, seventy-five Durham oxen, cattle, a few mules and horses, an assortment of dogs, fifteen families, sixty-seven people.

Even with so small a party, oftentimes the train spread out for a mile or more—a sore hoof, an axle in need of grease, an obstinate team—and Thompson found himself drifting from one family to another to help out, and he learned their stories. The emigrants were men who had made a go of it, for the most part, in the East but dreamed of more. They had to be well off enough to outfit the crossing and afford a year's stake in the new land before their first harvest. The Barksdale family, old Tom, fifty-four years, grizzled, a gray beard reaching down his shirtfront, widowed, led his five boys, stair-stepped in age. He planned to send for his young second wife and two infants in Springfield once the second crop came in. Hiram Calderwood was a wheelwright bound for Bent's new fort with his two oldest sons. Burrows Grissom traveled with his wife, Susan, and two oldest, but had left their three younger ones in Indiana with her sister. He first had come west in '48 for the California adventure and had lost his left arm at the elbow. He'd sliced his forearm while trying to separate a land turtle from its shell for stew. Infection. The West had gotten into his blood, but Susan refused to let him come alone again. Said she couldn't afford to lose any more of him than she already had.

Much of the walking was spent in silence, the creaking of wheels, the squeal of the brake lever on steeper downgrades, an occasional shouted command. They made good time, twelve, fourteen miles a day, dust always with them, coating their clothes, hair, beards. Although raw country, they still traveled within the bounds of civilization and they passed through land in places broken by fields of corn growing in ordered rows, an odd and incongruous sight in this unordered country. Log and wood shanties dotted the hills, fenced gardens growing root vegetables and bush beans.

Weather continued hot and dry, the trail dust-choked but firm as a barn floor. The miles passed. Water ran clear, and the bottomland still provided sufficient deadfall to feed cooking fires. Thompson proved an appreciated hunter for the company, killing a black-tailed deer one evening that provided small portions for each wagon. Another morning, three turkeys he'd called from a hackberry thicket just after sunup. He found comfort wandering alone in the wilds. Often without warning a dark memory would cloud his awareness for no reason other than he'd allowed his mind to wander back to Indiana before he'd thought to check it, and some unreasoned but necessary instinct would turn him away from the wagons and he would disappear into the grass or down a gully only to regain his senses hours later and miles away.

But on the days he remained clear-headed, he guided Captain Upperdine's wagon during the march, freeing the Captain to scout ahead on horseback or to check the position of other wagon trains along the trail. And, on those good days, he often supped with the Lights, drawn to the reassuring ideal of family. They'd sit together in the growing dusk and Thompson would race beetles against Joseph. They'd draw a circle in the dirt and spend considerable time selecting their specimen from the insects that were ubiquitous along the trail, feeding on the droppings of the thousands of animals that passed by.

"This one here is a brute," Thompson might say. "Bigger across than my thumbnail."

"But mine's sleek," Joseph might counter. "Built for speed."

They'd place the two insects together in the center of the circle and wager future riches on the first to break from the ring. Hanna expressed mild disapproval of their gambling, even on imaginary stakes, but did not forbid their game. Joseph quickly became a millionaire at Thompson's expense.

Other evenings, Thompson might spend time with little Martha, braiding necklaces from grass and wildflowers or whittling a stick figure for her. He'd linger around the camp watching Hanna put Martha to bed, and then perhaps he'd sit while Obadiah was at his pipe before retiring to his own fire, either to sleep or to lie awake into the night, staring into the endless black sky, imagining a life in

Indiana no longer within his reach, as distant and inaccessible as the stars overhead.

Whenever they could, the company set camp beside water where trees might provide shade and where there was good forage. Evenings, Thompson took to walking out into the tall grass, to whatever rise might present itself, to scout for game. If he suspected upland birds or waterfowl, he borrowed a fowling piece from Upperdine; if larger game, his own long rifle. On occasion, Obadiah's son, Joseph, accompanied him. Thompson found he enjoyed the boy's company because Joseph, like Thompson, had little use for extended conversation. Still, Thompson learned a little about him on their hunts. Sitting one evening on a hill looking out over an open meadow, Thompson asked:

"An expansive land, don't you think, Joseph?"

"A empty one, I'll give you that."

"You don't see opportunity out here?"

"No, sir; I see a whole lot of nothing."

They sat in silence. Thompson pointed to a shadow at the far end of the meadow. A black bear edged from shadow into light and back into shadow.

"Should we pursue?" Joseph asked. Thompson shook his head, no. Joseph seemed disappointed, looking first at the bear and then to Thompson, like a pup begging to retrieve.

"It is moving away from us and we are losing the day," Thompson explained. "Your mother would worry if we were long past dark chasing the beast."

Joseph laughed derisively, surprising Thompson. "Not likely," Joseph said.

They returned to camp and Joseph went to a cold supper while Obadiah greeted Thompson.

"Good of you to let the boy tag along with you."

"He seems unenthused about your journey," Thompson said.

"Difficult for him. He's of an age. Left his pards back home. May have been sweet on some girl, I don't know."

Thompson nodded. "It hurts to leave someone behind." He turned from the Lights' camp and walked alone into the outlying country as the day ended. The prairie sun had begun to burn the grass brown, but wildflowers were in bloom still, the goldenrod, the pink and purple four o'clock, and the brilliant blue flax. Many evenings when the press of other people tightened his chest, Thompson would sit alone out of view of the caravan and watch the blooms fold with the day and feel like the only human being on the face of the earth, utterly alone but at once filled with his surroundings, a bearable solitude.

THE COMPANY PUSHED ON, HOUR after hour, mile upon mile. Some days clouds brought shade, some days none. Most days brought wind, and, with it, dust. The settlers came to pray for the occasional shower that cooled the land and tamed the dust. But rain came at a cost. At first the drizzle was welcomed. Often, however, drizzle turned to rain, sometimes driving, and soon the road became slick on the grades and muddy on flat stretches. Progress slowed, boots caked with muck, wagon wheels mired. One discomfort exchanged for another. Day after day, a new challenge, a new test.

As they sank into the routine, travel grew tedious because of the mud, or because of the dust, tedium the one constant.

5

They came eventually into the valley of the Neosho River, an oasis of wooded draws and cultivated fields: corn and hay in the lowlands, cattle on the hillsides. They arrived in Council Grove midday and some wanted to pause, but Captain Upperdine pushed them through.

"River flow is unpredictable. We'll cross while the water allows."

They camped a few miles outside of town. Some of the men, Tom Barksdale's two oldest, the wheelwright Calderwood, and one other Thompson did not know well approached him after supper. The wheelwright spoke.

"Few of us of a mind to see what Council Grove is about, if you care to join us."

Passing through earlier in the day, Thompson had noticed the graceful set of the town, the wide main street, and the whitewashed shops advertising everything from sacks of oats to fine whiskey. He had use for neither, although he understood the men's curiosity.

"Obliged, but I have things to look to."

The following morning, Thompson noticed a group of men congregated around Captain Upperdine's cook fire, and he walked over. The men dispersed before Thompson arrived. Upperdine looked perplexed.

"Trouble?" Thompson asked.

"No more than expected. Calderwood has decided to forgo his plans for Bent's Fort and to establish his trade here."

"It's unfortunate to lose a wheelwright," Thompson said.

"Can't shackle him, I guess."

The company broke camp with one wagon fewer and pushed on to Diamond Springs, named after its clear, good water. The area was more sparsely inhabited than Council Grove, but a scattering of small farms dotted the landscape and the fields looked healthy. Upperdine laid over a day to graze the stock, and he bought a few sacks of feed at a fair price for insurance against barren stretches he knew the company would soon encounter.

Diamond Springs proved an alluring charm for three other families. At supper with the Lights, Obadiah sat with Thompson while a subdued Hanna put Martha to bed.

"The Grissoms will disembark here," Obadiah said. "Hanna is sore pressed to let go her friend Susan."

"Bonds form quickly on the trail, I imagine," Thompson said. "And there are few other women to visit with."

"We were tempted as well," Obadiah said.

"And why not?" Thompson asked. "This land recommends itself."

"I have my heart set on the open plains. Near Walnut Creek, perhaps, or just beyond. I hear there is an army outpost in the planning." Obadiah went to the front of his wagon and retrieved a leather pouch. "Friends in Ohio have kin in Odessa who sent them this."

Obadiah untied the drawstring and pulled out a handful of red-tinged seed and let them sift back into the bag. "A strain of wheat said to prosper in dry climates. Plant it in autumn. Sprouts early winter, goes dormant until spring. Benefits from the snows and early rains and ripens before drought sets in. I aim to try it."

Thompson absently listened to Obadiah go on about the potential for a wheat crop, while silently grateful to have them along for some miles yet. He enjoyed their company and, unsure of his plans, uncertain whether he'd ever come upon a place that would feel right for him, he found comfort in the Lights' unalloyed hopefulness. They dared plan a future, farming the great unplowed expanses.

The following morning, only eleven wagons departed. Two nights out from Diamond Springs, Thompson took last watch, from three until five. As dawn approached, a breeze came up from the northwest and stars began to disappear as a cloudbank rolled in. Daybreak brought rain. A steady, light shower fell early and let up, but the men all became soaked past the waist when they waded through wet grass leading the stock to harness. Rain had muddied the road as well, and travel slogged. Midmorning, high gray clouds gave way to a menacing black sheet that advanced on them from due west with a stiffening wind. They did not stop for noon. Upperdine pressed to make Cottonwood Crossing before rain, and indeed they forded just ahead of a blustery storm that churned the creek with runoff from the low banks. That evening, Upperdine confided to Thompson that he was happy to have passed Cottonwood Creek quickly lest its attraction lure yet others from the train.

"Did you notice the trees along the banks, those few log cabins on the hills?"

Thompson allowed that he had.

"That is the last community worth glancing at we'll see before Bent's Fort except for an outpost or two. And the last of the trees as well."

The weather took on a pattern. Clear mornings turning hazy, and by afternoon thunderstorms came on with a vengeance, clouds booming, lightning flashing across the darkened prairie, and rain in torrents. By the time they made Turkey Creek, its banks were over-flowed and six feet of brown, roiling water rushed the channel that normally held two. Thompson set camp with the Lights and they tried to dry off under the canvas of the wagon covers and eat a cold supper, cornbread and slices of dried apple. A lucky few had managed to keep bedrolls dry, but for most of the party, rain had found its way through slickers, between folds and splits in the wagon canvas, onto blankets and spare clothing and into boots. Night passed without fire, damp and shivering. Morning brought heavy drizzle and lifting skies, and they were able to light fires that put up dense smoke from sodden wood. They laid over all that day waiting for the creek to subside. Storms still raged to the northwest, and the creek ran fast and brown.

Midday, Thompson hiked to a rise and sat on his haunches and scanned the middle and far distances for game. In the gray light, the horizon blended into sky, so that he was unsure just where one ended and the other began. The grass, tall and returning to a light green from the rain, melted into the gray of the sky so that Thompson had the feeling he was staring into a flat, dimensionless sheet hanging from a line. Then, not a hundred yards away, a great beast stood from its wallow as if rising out of the prairie itself. The buffalo shook its head and its thick beard released a spray of mud and water. It started off at an angle toward the creek as another buffalo crested a small hill that Thompson had not even realized was there, and ambled after the first. Thompson kept low and maneuvered for a shot, but the animals moved with a surprising speed given their bulk and they entered the creek some hundred-fifty yards above him. The current mid-stream was fast and angry, and it pushed the buffalo downstream as they plowed forward so that they left the water on the far bank almost directly across from Thompson. They stood not forty yards from him, shaking the water from their mantles and pawing at the gravel of the creek bank. Thompson watched the two bulls. He could have taken them with his rifle but had no way of knowing when he might be able to retrieve the meat, so he passed up the shot and just watched them, all shag and sinew, until they climbed the creek bank and walked off into the high grass to the west. He wondered how they'd appeared from nowhere. An empty prairie one second and two behemoths filling his vision the next. Wondered how to develop eyesight in this strange land. A new perception required?

The grass still held the rain so that by the time he returned to the company early in the evening, Thompson again was soaked. He sparked his campfire to life, fed it dry grass he pulled from under the shelter of the wagon, then small twigs, then limbs. He removed his outer tunic and propped it on two sticks close to the fire to dry, and pulled on his one spare shirt. Afterward, he thought to inform Captain Upperdine about the buffalo, but he saw Obadiah talking with him. They looked in earnest discussion and rather than disturb them, he walked to the Lights' wagon and found Hanna at the back gate, tending to Martha. She'd wrapped her in a blanket against the dampness and had nestled her on a straw mattress. Hanna had placed a camphor poultice on the child's chest and was mopping her forehead with a wet cloth.

"A little sage tea," she said, to herself. She hadn't noticed Thompson approach.

"I'll watch her," he said. She started at his voice.

"I'll just brew up a little sage tea," she repeated, "and return shortly."

Martha appeared feverish to Thompson. Her hand was at her throat, massaging it. Her neck looked swollen. He stroked her head. He cooed, and then clucked like a chicken and Martha looked up at him and giggled. A little.

"Caught a chill from the rain, is all," Hanna said, coming up beside him, placing her hands to the small of her back, arching. A grimace.

Her pregnant belly swollen. Would she birth on the trail, Thompson wondered?

"She'll be fine," Thompson assured, and nodded to Obadiah who had returned from his visit with Upperdine.

A squall blew up at sunset. Winds carried a drenching rain, slanted and malevolent, as if seeking out every dry space, every comfortable nook. Campfires extinguished, paths mired, blankets soggy. They scrambled for cover under the canvas, under the wagons themselves. The rain sought them out and saturated them. Wet and chilled, they passed the night. Thompson crouched by his cold fire, the charred remains not even smoldering, stone cold. A flashing in the west, thunder. He nodded off sometime during the darkest watch.

Martha was dead by morning.

Thompson heard keening from the Lights' wagon at daybreak, and Captain Upperdine came to him shortly thereafter. "It's the diphtheria, I think," he told Thompson. "Comes on fast, can take the little ones hardly before you know it."

"Others?" Thompson asked, thickly. The word stuck in his throat. A glutinous, ugly sound. He feared the reply. The air heavy with mist, a veiled world. Where was he?

"None that I know of. The older boy, Joseph, shows no symptoms. A few others was around their camp yesterday. I will check on their condition, but I believe them to be spared. Thus far. But we should not tarry."

Thompson registered the salmon smudge on the eastern horizon. He focused on that thin line of color beneath a bruised sky. Concentrated on the far distance while hearing himself speak. "I'll see about a spade, maybe a place on the rise over there?" He vaguely pointed to the crest of a small hill.

"Not too close to the river," Upperdine advised. "And afterwards, make sure the men tamp it firm. River rocks, perhaps. Keep it from the prairie wolves."

That morning, Thompson and Ned went to high ground, to a level spot that had a nice view of the creek, and dug the hole. As he labored, Thompson found himself in Deep Woods, Indiana, digging beneath the persimmon tree, full summer now, the oval leaves providing shade from the high sun, the fruit just beginning to set. He looked down the hill toward his cabin, hoping to catch sight of Rachel hanging wash, but instead saw only the charred remains of his home, the chimney stones still in place, rising from the blackened heap. Of course, he thought, and he could imagine it perfectly. After he'd been gone a week, a committee from town, the pastor, the merchant Henderson, and Constable Fletcher went to the farm. They found the dried-off milk cow in the pasture but never did locate the horse they knew he owned. They sopped grain from the bin and fed the hogs, and untethered the mule from the lean-to, and between them determined a schedule to look after the livestock. After Thompson had been gone a month, they voted to keep the mule and the plow as community property, to divide the hand tools and the chickens, and to draw lots for the hogs. From outside, they covetously inventoried the farm house interior, the furniture and tableware, but none dared enter. Caution outweighed cupidity. Instead, they burned it. Burned it to white ash and black cinders in hopes the perdition that inhabited the rooms might leave them in peace.

"They burned it," he said aloud.

"Come again?" Ned asked.

Thompson, returned to Kansas Territory, shook his head. "Nothing," he said, and resumed digging.

Shortly, Ned set aside his shovel and went in search of a tree and felled a middling cottonwood, which he hauled back to camp with a borrowed mule. He cut a four-foot length, hewed out the core to form a coffin, and used his saw and adze to cut and shape rough planks for the lid. Some in the company debated the wisdom of keeping the girl and her disease above ground until the coffin could be finished, but Ned would not be dissuaded. "No, sir, this here girl to be seen off right. Need a coffin to cross over in." While he worked, Obadiah hacked limbs from the tree and with rawhide lashings pieced together a cross upon which he carved his girl's name.

Hanna would not be consoled. She sat by the fire, silent, staring into the embers until Thompson came with Obadiah to collect her for the service. She went with them silently, wrapped in a cloak Obadiah brought from the wagon. Even though the skies had cleared and the sun was throwing down heat, she shivered. After that first pre-dawn wailing, she had not spoken, neither at the grave nor after Captain Upperdine read a few verses from the Book nor as the men filled the hole that held her child. She did not speak but neither did she allow Obadiah to lead her from the grave. She would not be comforted and she would not be moved. She sat by the grave through the day.

6

Captain Upperdine decided to lay over an additional day even though the stream had receded to fording level. Early the following morning, storm clouds again building in the west, he could wait no longer. Hanna Light had stayed the night on the hill beside a fire Obadiah built for her and she showed no sign of giving up her post.

Thompson was helping Upperdine hitch the wagon when Obadiah approached from the hill.

"We must strike camp," Upperdine explained to Obadiah. "The weather threatens to strand us and we cannot afford another indefinite delay."

"I understand, of course," Obadiah said. "We'll catch up as soon as we can. Sometimes it's hard for a person to let go."

Upperdine gathered the wagons and directed the ford without incident and as the company reconvened on the western shore and assembled for departure, Thompson approached Upperdine.

"I'll be staying with the Lights until Hanna can see fit to be done with it," he said.

"I don't like being short another man," Upperdine said, "but I'd guessed your intentions."

"It's what a neighbor does."

"I'll not attempt to turn your mind."

"I'll push them hard as soon as they are ready to travel until we overtake the company."

Upperdine went into his saddle bag and retrieved a six-barreled Allen pistol. "I believe Obadiah carries only a fowling piece with him. Take this."

Thompson took the blocky pistol and a bag of caps and shot. The gun felt awkward in his hand, unbalanced. He held it at arm's length and appraised it with disapproval.

"It is an unsightly piece, and inaccurate at any distance," Upperdine said. "But it will do in close quarters, and may discourage someone from evil intentions."

The Captain stood his horse and took leave. The collection of wagons passed from view and the prairie grew still. Without dust rising above the trail to betray their proximity, once the creaking of the wheels and the clanging of the gear died away, the vast and empty expanse seemed to Thompson at once both utterly lonesome and intimidating. Although dark clouds rose in the west, the breeze did not pick up. Rain and wind held off and throughout the afternoon only the whirling of the grasshoppers and the occasional caw from a crow interrupted the silence. Obadiah and Hanna kept watch over the grave. Thompson and Ned minded the animals and Thompson cooked for them, a pot of beans and rice. They ate little and conversed less and evening fell solemnly on the camp. Joseph kept off to himself most of the day. Toward evening, Thompson carried food to Obadiah and Hanna but did not sit with them. He stood apart on the hill and looked out over the still plains until night closed in around him and he returned to the wagon. Ned busied himself with his tools, sharpening, oiling. The silhouettes of Obadiah and Hanna faded into the night and without speaking Thompson and Ned and Joseph rolled themselves into their blankets and rested with their private thoughts.

Next morning, Obadiah came down the hill to sit with Thompson and drink a cup of coffee.

"She cried last night," Obadiah said. "A weeping so deep I was brought low. Brought down as low as a believing man might be expected to fall."

"It's hard," said Thompson.

"I fear that some sin of the father has been visited upon the child."

"I've wondered the same before."

"She blames herself. And me, perhaps, for bringing us out here."

"Perhaps," Thompson said.

"I came to tell you, though, that she is ready to let go. I don't know if from weariness or resignation, or from the tears, but she allowed so to me."

Thompson stood and nudged a smoldering stick deeper into the embers of the fire with the toe of his boot.

"At daybreak, I saw some antelope down creek, watering. I'll see about getting us some fresh meat for the trail. Maybe ford the creek midday. Put this place out of sight before camping."

Thompson took up his rifle and set out across the creek, now shallow running and slow, so different from a few days earlier, and up a low bluff on the far side. From the crest, on his belly in the tall grass, he caught sight of the small antelope herd, fourteen he counted, grazing below. Perhaps a half-mile distant. He kept low in the grass and moved toward them in a duck-step. As he approached, an antelope raised its head from the grass and looked in Thompson's direction. Thompson waited motionless for several minutes until the animal returned to grazing, and then he inched forward. For an hour he crept in this manner. Finally he approached within rifle shot of the near animals. Back and knee joints stiff, he eased into a kneeling position, gun just even with the top of the grass, and sighted down his barrel and cocked the hammer. An antelope's flank twitched and its ears pricked but it did not bolt. Just as his finger cupped the trigger, the herd was spooked by a sharp popping sound, then another and a third, like firecrackers in the distance, and they bounded away.

Thompson lowered the hammer and watched the herd disappear into the grass. Then it registered. Gunfire. He took off at full sprint back toward camp. He almost fell splashing across the creek, and bloodied a hand on an exposed root while stumbling up the bank. He crested the rise leading down into camp and pulled up short at what he saw below him. A man's body lay prone on the ground beside the oxen. Another off to the side of the wagon. Three men were horseback. One held a rope that had been wrapped around the pommel of his saddle. At the end of the rope Joseph had been tied and had fallen and the man was dragging him in the dirt. As Thompson watched, the boy's head struck the wagon's rear wheel and the man continued to drag him. A fourth man had dismounted and stood hunched over Hanna Light, whom he'd bent face-down over the traveling trunk they had pulled from the wagon.

Some unrecognizable and horrible animal sound came from Thompson and he charged down the hill. One of the men on horseback raised his rifle as Thompson dropped into a buffalo wallow. Thompson saw a puff of smoke from the barrel and a shot buzzed past his ear, a sound like an angry insect. He propped his elbows against the lip of the wallow and aimed for the man reloading his rifle and fired before it even registered with him what it was he was aiming at. The hammer plinked against the nipple without discharging his load. He'd lost the percussion cap during his scramble. He pulled another cap from his pouch and jammed it onto the nipple and raised the rifle as the man in the distance fired again. Grit flew up into Thompson's eyes just as he pulled his trigger, and his own rifle resounded in answer to the stranger's muffled report. For a second, Thompson could not see. He set aside his rifle and rubbed at his eyes and through a teary film, he frantically struggled to reload. He glanced up expecting another round to come at him, but the man just sat motionless, staring in Thompson's direction as if trying to locate him hidden in the wallow. Then he let fall his weapon and rolled backward from his horse onto the ground.

The others in camp had stopped to watch the exchange of fire and now the one who had been assaulting Hanna mounted his horse and the remaining three set off at full gallop toward Thompson. They were wielding pistols, and their shots missed wildly, kicking up dust far from the mark. When they had advanced to within sixty yards of him, they seemed to a man to notice that Thompson's rifle had leveled on them and they lost resolve and all three wheeled their horses away from him and made for the creek. Thompson sighted his rifle on the back of the man who had been dragging the boy. A length of rope still flapped from the pommel where he had cut it free to take up the chase for Thompson. Thompson shot, and the man slumped forward and clutched his horse's neck but did not fall and the three riders splashed across the creek and up the far bank and down away from view.

Thompson reloaded and waited for a renewed assault, but after just a moment he climbed from the wallow and ran down into the camp. He approached the man he'd dropped from the horse cautiously, with his rifle at ready. The man was dead, eyes glazed and staring at the sun. Thompson had caught him just above the collarbone and the ball had blown away his throat. Blood flowed from the wound and pooled in the dust, and Thompson wondered at the amount a body held. He'd never shot a man before and although he viewed these riders as less than human, still he paused by the corpse, unable to look away. Just for a bit. Then he went to the wagon. Obadiah lay dead, shot through the forehead. The Allen pistol by his hand. Thompson bent and closed Obadiah's eyes. He passed by Ned lying alongside the wagon. He had been shot in both knees and was battered so badly about the face that he was unrecognizable except by the color of his skin. His adze was imbedded into the top of his skull as if someone had stood over him and used his head as a chopping block. He turned to Hanna. She had crawled to Joseph and held his head cradled in her lap. Blood trickled down her exposed thighs. He noted the faintest rise and fall of Joseph's chest. He watched for several seconds and the breathing held, shallow but steady. He ran to the water barrel but they had taken an ax to it, so he continued to the creek and filled a pail. He thought he heard a horse snigger and froze there for a minute, but heard nothing more so he returned to camp. He wet a cloth and cleaned Hanna's face and took Joseph from her and laid him in the bed of the wagon and placed the wet cloth across his forehead. To what purpose, he had no clue. He went to Hanna. She had wrapped her arms around her swollen belly and now moaned low and rocked forward and back, forward and back. She did not acknowledge Thompson's presence when he smoothed her dress over her legs or when he asked her where it hurt and what he could do. He wondered if the baby in her womb yet thrived. He knelt beside her and talked softly.

"I have to check those other men," he said. "Just to make sure they have left us for good. Then I'll see to things. Will you be all right here?"

She did not answer, did not even look at him but kept focused on the ground a foot in front of her.

"I'll only be a short time."

He took up his rifle and hurried across the stream and directly up the bank. He saw no purpose in stealth, could not afford the time. He would encounter whatever waited over the rise face on, quickly, to whatever end. He had in fact heard a horse when he had gone to the river. It was grazing not far from where the second man lay on the ground. The man was yet alive but unable to move, other than to lift his head at Thompson's approach. The man's right leg was bent at a sharp angle away from him. He did not appear to be bleeding, but his belly was distended and tight-looking as a drum. Something bleeding inside, Thompson thought. The man's pistol lay on the ground away from him, and he looked at it when he saw Thompson, but was unable even to move his arm. His eyes looked glazed and shone brightly.

"A drink," he demanded of Thompson.

"Go to hell, you son of a bitch," Thompson answered. He retrieved the pistol and tossed it far into the grass. Then he walked to the horse, took up its bridle and began leading it away.

"Don't leave me like this," the man said. "Finish it."

"It is finished. Look, the buzzards already circle."

"Goddamn them Free-Soilers," the man said. Pink foam bubbled from his nose and from his mouth when he spoke. His breath came in gurgles. "Goddamn you."

Thompson turned away and led the horse back toward the stream and murmured to himself, "Yes, I believe He has." He tried to hurry, but his limbs felt heavy as if wallowing through deep mud. He could not imagine what must be Hanna's burden and he struggled with what he could ever offer in way of succor.

Thompson went to work with the spade once again and took the better part of the midday digging. Afternoon, he stood over their graves. Ned. Obadiah. And beside them, the child, Martha. He tossed a handful of dirt into each hole and picked up his Bible and thumbed through the passages and felt nothing but hopelessness and despair.

Job: *"I cry unto thee, and thou dost not hear me"; "There is an evil which I have seen under the sun, and it is common among men"; "Lover and friend hast thou put far from me, and mine acquaintance into darkness."* He looked down into the hole that held Obadiah, and he tossed his Bible into the pit and began, shovel by shovel, returning first him and then Ned to dust.

The heat rose up off the prairie and he was drenched in sweat by the time he filled and tamped the graves. As he walked down the hill and drew near the corpse of the first fallen rider, he was startled by a green mist that hovered above the body. He drew near; the mist shimmered in the sun and made a buzzing sound. Blowflies. The flies had found the body and they swarmed by the thousands, a cloud of green. They alighted in the dead man's eyes and crawled into his nostrils and into his open mouth. The dung beetles and ants too had found him and one arm seemed to move with life as the insects tunneled their way into the sleeve of his jacket. Thompson shivered, felt a surging in his throat, suppressed it, and then left the man where he lay and went down to the creek and washed himself in the cold water. Then he returned to the wagon and found Hanna where he'd left her hours ago, unstirred. He asked if she was hungry but she did not answer, did not even look up at him. He dipped water from the pail and tilted her head and tipped the ladle to her lips. Most of the water ran down her chin and onto her dress. He dipped a cloth into the water and went to Joseph and put the cloth to his mouth. After a moment, Joseph's eyes fluttered and his lips puckered at the cloth, although he did not regain consciousness.

"Good," Thompson encouraged, and squeezed the cloth and Joseph suckled in earnest.

Thompson unhitched the oxen from the wagon that Obadiah had prepared for travel early that morning. He left them yoked to graze and he picketed the milk cow and the horse he'd taken from the raider.

He had a vague sense of himself at the chores, but no firm grounding in reality. What was happening? One moment he found himself at the hog trough in Deep Woods, Indiana, the next kneeling beside an unresponsive woman clutching her knees, rocking, gazing into space like an old woman lost in childhood. Night came on. He built a small fire and drank coffee and ate some of the rice and beans he'd cooked, when? He could not entice Hanna with either coffee or beans. He retrieved a blanket and draped it around her shoulders. She had not moved. He rested against the wagon wheel where he could keep an eye on Hanna and hear Joseph should he call out.

What course now? He could not bear the thought of returning them to Cottonwood Creek in this condition. Who would minister to them? He could reunite with Upperdine's party, but what then? He could not form complete thoughts, could not formulate a plan. His legs twitched, he ached to be up and moving. A part of him wanted nothing to do with this responsibility. He'd stayed behind with the Lights to lend a hand, to keep watch. And he'd failed. A part of him wanted to walk out of camp, off into the darkness, and to be done with it. He hated that part of himself.

Night deepened and he fought to stay awake. He feared sleep, but the day had exhausted him, and eventually his eyes closed against his will and his awareness dimmed. Somewhere out beyond, he heard the sound of prairie beasts, snarls and yips, a deep growl, and he hoped they had found the wounded stranger who had caused this pain.

7

In his dreams, the skeletons returned, the rattling of bones. From the horde rose up a monotone lamentation.

"Tell us. Tell us."

"Tell you what?" Thompson demanded.

"You know," the reply.

"Why do you persist?"

"You know," the reply.

"Why can't you leave me in peace?"

"You know," the reply. "Tell us."

"The children," Thompson said.

"Yes. The children. Go on."

"No."

"Go on, go on."

"The children. I knew. I knew. I knew."

THOMPSON'S EYES SPRANG OPEN. NOT even in his dreams had he confessed before. Not in dream, nor in prayerful confession, nor during waking hours. Yet the truth now opened his memory, laid bare his transgression. Raw, ugly like a rotting carcass.

He'd checked his boys that morning before starting off for his father's estate, first Matthew and then Daniel. Their foreheads burned. Cheeks flushed. Daniel had stirred, had reached for him, but Thompson settled him onto his mat without picking him up. Without an embrace. He'd debated at the threshold, stay or go, a moment only, and then departed. Rachel would look after them. He needed funds. He wanted the land.

What must it have been like for Rachel? To sicken, to witness fever overcome her children, too weak to nurse. Those moments, those slow fading days, did she know? The sinking, the aching and fever and then a moment, perhaps, of clarity? The thin veil between here and there, had she seen through it, passed back and forth until the question finally resolved itself? He recognized something of her travels in her eyes that last day, but the haunted whole of it he could only imagine.

Thompson stood. Dream world or real? Muzzy, he walked to the water pail and splashed his face. The muted light, a dim and mysterious world. A suggestion of form, a hint of substance, but indistinct. He fought to relegate his dark epiphany to the realm of drifting and unreliable imagination. This was real, this new day on the open plains. But truth stood firm, did not retreat. The world took shape, shadows solidified into wagon and firestone, but the truth remained before him, ox-like, stubborn, massive, and accusing.

Thompson took up the dipper and filled it, drank, and looked about. A clear dawn, high sky, and free of clouds. The animals docile in the pasture. The camp orderly. On the ground, her discarded blanket.

"Hanna," he called, his voice strident, causing the animals to raise their heads as if sniffing for danger. He scanned the riverbank, the pasture, the hill. There. On the hill. Digging. He called to her but she gave no indication of hearing. Running past the wagon, Thompson glanced in and found Joseph sleeping, and he ran on, pleading, "Hanna, no." He approached her and slowed, sucking for breath. She dug furiously. The girl's coffin was exhumed, the lid worried and splintered in one corner, but Hanna apparently had been unable to pry it open. A mound of dirt rose beside Obadiah's grave as well, his body not yet exposed. He took hold of her shoulders and pulled her from the hole and wrestled the shovel from her and threw it aside. She swung on him and connected with her open palm to the side of his face. Stunned him. With surprising strength she pummeled him, head, neck, pounding, kicking, silent, the huffing of her exertion the only sound resonating in the still morning. Thompson's knees buckled and he almost fell. He sensed that if he stumbled, she would take the shovel to him, and he almost surrendered, let it happen. Why not, really? So easy, just bow to it. But some instinct sparked him to action, would not permit him to go down into the pit with the others. He straightened and struck Hanna on the side of the head, and she fell.

8

The two of them rode in the bed of the wagon, Joseph awake on and off, groaning, and Hanna, mute, her hands and legs bound to the sideboards to keep her from climbing down and returning to the graves. Thompson had removed the parlor organ and a three-drawer oak chest to make room for them. He'd tethered the horse he'd taken from the raider to the back of the wagon but he'd left the milk cow lowing on the prairie because he could not afford its pace. Once on the west bank of the creek, Thompson turned and regarded their camp, the three hummocks of fresh earth on the hill, the parlor organ beside the cold fire ring, as if set out the evening prior for a recital, the abandoned cow rubbing its flank against the chest of drawers. The cryptic story of one emigrant family. Thompson prodded the oxen and hollered commands. He needed to put the camp behind him. He walked through the day and into night, eating and drinking on the move, stopping only to take water and food to Joseph and Hanna. Sanitation breaks for Hanna, Thompson the awkward sentinel.

Joseph began to recover an appetite, although Thompson had little to offer—stale biscuits, a few strips of jerked venison. The water in the pail running low. Hanna drank, ate little, and did not talk. Her expression remained fixed. Joseph and Hanna were inattentive toward one another and both toward Thompson.

Thompson did not graze the team. They bellowed in protest, kept plodding. The trail showed white under the partial moon and he pushed on. He would not stop, knew he could not sleep even as weariness overcame him. He walked. That first night his legs held out, felt strong with urgency. The second day, the sun tried to suck him dry, drain his resolve. But he came upon a stream and allowed the animals to drink and filled the water pail and then whipped the team onward. Compelled to rejoin Upperdine. Why, he did not know, but a goal, a goal he could focus on. He walked. The wagon creaked along.

The second night, the skeletons appeared and marched beside him. He was unaware when exactly they had arrived, but he did not care, they no longer frightened him. They'd heard his confession. He asked once if they bothered Joseph or Hanna, the rattling and clacking of bone against bone. The drums they carried, beating and beating, low, a vibration in the gut. Hanna did not respond and Joseph said only, "Nothing bothers me anymore." Sometimes, walking, he dozed. The clamoring of the bones kept him from drifting completely and falling and he welcomed their company. His tormentors, his inquisitors, became his companions on the road. The following day, he no longer noticed the heat. Dust raised up by the wind and by the thousands of shuffling feet covered his clothes and made him look as if he worked in a grinding mill. Fine grit in his nose and between his teeth. He did not care.

Night may have come again, and morning. He wondered if the oxen would fail, decide to kneel in the middle of the road and die, but he continued to prod them and they responded. He pressed on. Overtake the company. Upperdine would know what to do. The day passed, heat, glare, a softening, sunset, deep into deep. The oxen plodded, Thompson walked.

The skeletons began to lag behind. Hallo, boys, he encouraged them to keep up, but slowly they receded. Vague shapes in the distance, like trees in a snowstorm. Thompson needed them. They kept him awake; they held him up. He angered. Leaving the team, he backtracked a few yards to search for them. They were no longer in sight. It may have been nighttime, he did not know.

"Come back," he screamed. "You god-damned demons, come to me."

"Easy, boy." A voice. Confused, startled, he reached for his knife. Something restrained him.

"Easy, now. We'll take it from here."

9

Thompson awoke from so deep and un-dreaming a sleep that for a pause he imagined himself back in Deep Woods. He rested in transient drowsiness and ticked through the chores for the day: the mule needed shoeing, the new field cleared of stumps.

"Feeling human?" Upperdine asked, standing at the back of the wagon, peering into the cocoon of the canvas-shrouded wagon bed.

Thompson opened his eyes. He'd been resting on a straw-ticked mattress in the back of Upperdine's wagon. He sat up. "How long have I been out?"

"A day and a night and most of today." Upperdine handed Thompson a dipper of water, which he drained and handed back to Upperdine. Upperdine pulled a flask from a hook on the sideboard, uncorked it and poured a measure and Thompson drank the brandy as well, felt the burn of it in his throat, and almost immediately warmth in his gut. He couldn't say when last he'd eaten. Much he could not recall clearly. As the sleep left him, images came back in flashes, gunfire, and blood. Digging. Travel like sleepwalking.

"I don't remember overtaking the company," Thompson said.

"Actually, it was me what found you. Went scouting when you were over late. Saw the tracks where you'd wandered off trail. Wagon took a little beating, but we'll see to repairs."

"You've checked on the Lights?"

"Of course."

Thompson waited but nothing else forthcoming. "How do they fare?"

"The boy is healing. Knocked in the head, a busted rib, but he'll do."

"Hanna?"

"The girl has lost her senses, best I can tell. Seen it before."

"Will she recover?"

"Can't say. Some do."

Thompson attempted to climb from the wagon but wooziness overcame him and Upperdine helped him down and steadied him with a hand to his arm.

"Have you the news about Obadiah and the other, Ned?" Thompson asked. It came back to him now, the neat circle in Obadiah's forehead, painted red. Ned's hacked and mutilated body.

"Again?" Thompson asked. Upperdine had responded to his question but he had not heard, had been back on Turkey Creek.

"Bits and pieces from the boy. Enough. Didn't want to question too deeply."

"What men could do such things?" Thompson asked.

"Sons of bitches. That is who. Sons of bitches."

"I have one of their horses."

"I saw." Upperdine shook his head and waved his hand in dismissal. "A dragged-out beast. Won't make much either for the saddle or the plow."

"I don't want it. Someone might recognize it or its tack."

"A patrol out from Ft. Riley passed us yesterday," Upperdine said. "When they return, I'll send it back with them. Maybe something will come of it. Not likely."

"I failed them," Thompson said and his legs went wobbly again but he caught the wagon wheel and straightened.

"Plenty of opportunity to fail in this country." Upperdine handed Thompson another ladle of brandy. "A man does what he can. Take another drink and rest, and when you again wake, I'll see about food."

DURING THE FOLLOWING WEEK, DAYS passed in hazy anonymity. Thompson might remember rising, looking in on the Lights, and thereafter setting off into the barrens on a path roughly parallel to the trail only to find himself back in camp as evening drew near, recalling nothing of the interval between. One day he brought to camp a prong-horn draped across his shoulders but could not answer Upperdine's questions concerning the hunt. Some in the company began to shy from Thompson when he approached. Some complained to Upperdine about his queer behavior.

When aware, Thompson worried about the times he was not, the unaccounted hours and miles. Days when he could sense his mind beginning to blank, to drift into the insentient regions, he attempted to will it back into this world, focus on the tuft of grass, name it, the bird that flushed at his footfall, name it. Stay a while, he encouraged himself. On this piece of land, at this hour. Some days, he declined, could think of no compelling reason.

On good days, clearheaded, he often spent time walking beside the Lights' wagon. As Joseph regained strength, he assumed an adult role, sitting at Upperdine's council, tending the animals. But his recovery brought with it a sullenness that disturbed Thompson.

"Sounds like that hub could do with grease."

"Could be."

"I could stop over after we set camp."

"I can see to it myself." Joseph drove the oxen with cold severity.

Hanna kept to the wagon, rarely venturing out to walk in the open. She appeared competent in dress and hygiene, and she began eating again and cooking simple fare for herself and Joseph. But she remained mute and aloof. She did not visit with others during noon layovers or around the evening campfire. Except for Thompson, she did not acknowledge greetings or attempts at conversation. When approached, she fixed her gaze upon some distant object and remained silent until the well-meaning visitor gave up and moved on. When Thompson called, her eyes registered recognition and she watched him closely. When he went to the opposite side of the wagon, to check a wheel rim perhaps, she presently followed.

Hanna moved cautiously, as if anticipating danger. And she often sat with her arms folded across her stomach, hands probing here and there anxiously. The others feared her assault may have terminated her pregnancy, and she must have shared those same concerns. But it had not. Her belly grew.

THE COMPANY CONTINUED TO DWINDLE in number. Several emigrant families grew trail-weary and disillusioned with a country turning more sandy and less vegetated by the day. Upon meeting an eastbound freight train, they decided to backtrack with them to Council Grove. Three traders met a teamster near Middle Crossing who offered to guide them over the dry route to Santa Fe. The prospect of avoiding the mountain at Raton enticed them. Upperdine advised against the southerly route because of scarce water and Comanche presence, but their minds were set. Later, Upperdine confided to Thompson that the men also worried that Thompson might bear the curse of Jonah and they felt more easy away from him. Upperdine laughed when he related the story.

He said, "Only thing worse than their ignorance is their ill-judgment."

Thompson wondered.

Keeping the Arkansas River to the south, Captain Upperdine guided his remaining wagons into desolate country. A few isolated cottonwoods still sprung from the river valley, but the banks increasingly were overtaken by scrubby oak, hackberry, and willow brush. And then, no trees at all. Often, deep cuts and gullies forced the train from the riverbed onto arid tableland. The gentle rises and dips of the land and the swaying tall grasses of the prairie gave way to a flat, featureless plain, empty save for the ankle-high buffalo grass, brittle and brown. The isolated and denuded expanse was broken by sandy knobs populated by bunchgrass, sand sage, and yucca.

Thompson's mind began wandering less; he remained attuned to his surroundings. Passing through that barren and stripped territory gave him the sensation of walking the interior paths of his own mind, his soul, his body. No place to hide, all the scars, the deep cuts, the rolls and rifts lay bare. He felt the hum of its silence, the core energy working up through the cracked earth into the soles of his boots. The land seemed to Thompson almost like the beginning of creation. Unpeopled, the fundamental essence of being. Below, the earth; above, the sky. From these bare elements arose the potential for all being, Thompson thought. For life and for death, for good and for evil. If only it were possible to begin anew with this raw clay.

For days they traveled firm track under a white sun. Wind a constant: hot, dry, and always into their faces, the sand burrowing into hair and hide. Deep summer, heat borne down from the sun and reflected back from the trail which on the plains became not so much a marked road as a direction: westward. They saw little game afield, foraged no wild herbs or spices. Thompson found he could keep his strength by mixing cornmeal mush with bits of jerky, a chunk of salt pork. Coffee ran low. Upperdine insisted on conserving a portion for trade with the Indians, so they made do with weak, tea-colored adulterations, or they went without. Exclusively, buffalo chips replaced wood in the cooking fires. They collected dried dung by the barrelful, round discs the size of dinner plates, everywhere the leavings of the great herds, representing numbers unimaginable to Thompson. The chips burned like bark, a quick fire that sent up fine ash into the air. He wondered what Rachel might have thought about cooking stew while specks of cindered dung floated down into the pot. He thought about Rachel and walked out into the solitude.

Thompson took to the brooding silence of empty spaces. The plains whispered "come," and he found himself physically unable to sit idly, even after a long march. As he wandered out of camp silhouetted against the horizon in the flat light at end of day, he sometimes seemed almost an apparition, disappearing from sight as he climbed down into a dry creekbed, only to reemerge in a different place. The others would watch him and some wondered aloud if he might posses a dark power to come and go unseen, to float though the night sky. One evening he returned after nightfall and approached Upperdine's camp fire. Three men of the company sat with him, smoking and talking in quiet voices. One of them greeted him.

"Come, sit. It's not often you relax with us. Tobacco?" The man offered a pouch.

"Thank you, no." Thompson held out a rough oval stone the size of a child's fist that reflected from its cracks and fissures a robin's-egg blue in the firelight. "Found this along a dry bank."

Upperdine inspected the stone. "Turquoise." He held it up to the firelight. "Right pretty. Not from around here, I don't think. Some trader might have dropped it. The Mexicans and some Indians buff it up and make jewelry of it. Carvings."

Thompson put the stone in his pocket and stood at the fire idly discussing with the men the affairs of the day: heat, wind, miles traveled and miles to go. After a few minutes he grew restless and excused himself and walked to the Lights' wagon. He found Joseph spreading a bedroll out beside the dying fire. Hanna sat beside the fire looking into the coals, and Thompson wondered what she saw there. Sometimes, as his own campfire glowed and dimmed, visions appeared to him: the face of Rachel or one of the boys. Once, early on, he'd reached into the embers and burned his hand attempting to stroke a cheek.

"Hanna?"

She did not show sign of hearing him.

"I've brought you this. Something pretty." He held the stone out, and her eyes fixed on it, but she did not speak and her expression remained blank and unreadable.

"I'll just set it inside your wagon," he said. "You can look at it when you have a mind." But Hanna reached out her hand and Thompson gave it to her and traced the blue veining with her finger. "See?"

"Where'd you come by it?" Joseph asked, more of a demand than a question.

"In a gully north of here. A mile or so. Walk with me tomorrow and we can search some more."

"Chores need tending."

"I'd like to help."

Joseph looked down at his feet and then turned to his bedroll without answering.

THEY PROGRESSED WESTWARD. WITH EACH day, Upperdine grew more wary about the isolation and vulnerability of his charges. The heat and

the wind drained the livestock, demoralized the men, and parched
the grasslands. There had been no rain for two weeks, not a cloud in
three days. Scorched land, relentless sun. The trail turned sandy in
places, sucking at feet and hooves. Winds strengthened. West of the
Middle Crossing, they arrived nooning hour at a spring Upperdine
knew contained good water. Even though it lacked forage, their few
animals could manage. As Thompson helped close the wagons, he
noticed to the northwest a canvas tent shining brightly in the high
sun. After eating, he and Upperdine walked over. A man left his
plow and came to greet them. Jesse Rench, he introduced himself.
From the tent, a young girl emerged, holding the hand of a toddler
who followed, shyly. In the partially broken field, two older boys who
had been pulling the plow rested, harness straps hanging from their
shoulders, no animals in sight. A woman of sturdy proportions with
gray hair and a sun-baked face gouged the side of a low hillock with
a spade. Off to her side, a barefoot boy, just of an age for long pants,
sat stroking the head of a dead dog. Upperdine returned the greetings
and surveyed the surroundings.

"Snake-bit," explained Jesse Rench when he saw the men's attention
drawn to the boy and the dog.

"A test you've put yourself to," Upperdine said.

"Water's good," Rench answered. "Land for the claiming."

"But hard land," Upperdine countered. Thompson read his mind.
Days from market, Aboriginals about, a bleak and tenuous future.

THE COMPANY SPENT THE MIDDAY hours at the spring. Thompson
offered the Rench family what was left in his cooking pot, some beans
laced with salt pork, a few squares of cornbread. They accepted, took
the pot from Thompson and ate from it communally, scooping with
their fingers and sopping with the bread. After lunch, the Renches
returned to chores while the company rested under what shade they

could find or create by draping blankets from ox prods pounded into the earth. Thompson sat with Upperdine while Upperdine smoked. He watched the two Rench boys struggle to pull the plow.

"An ox or one of the mules would make short work of that small plot," he commented to Upperdine.

"If I tarried to assist every doomed immigrant we passed, I'd never complete a passage."

Toward two o'clock, Captain Upperdine broke camp; but they had progressed no more than a quarter-mile when the rear wagon hit a deep rut and broke an axle. Upperdine rode back to assess the damage, and then passed the word that they would lay over for the night.

"We have what we require to repair," he told Thompson, "but it will take some time." He turned his horse to join a group of men who were busy lightening the wagon and leveraging it onto blocks.

Thompson went to the Lights' wagon and shortly he and Joseph led one of the oxen to Rench's field and rigged it to the plow. Rench seemed uncomfortable working with the animal, so Thompson took the plow and continued in the field while the others hacked at the dugout and Joseph went over to the boy who had lost his dog and began talking with him. Thompson enjoyed walking behind the plow again, the rolled earth beneath his feet, the smell of newly turned soil and the draft animal close in front, the lathered flanks musty, its droppings mixed by the blade into the freshly exposed soil. Thompson spent an hour carving crooked furrows in the grudging soil with the makeshift rig and then, unwilling to overextend the ox, he unhitched and led it to graze. He went over to the incapacitated wagon to check on repairs, to lend what assistance he might, but several men already were at work. There was little to be added to their efforts, so he walked back to the Rench homestead.

Their dugout, an opening roughly a dozen feet across, extended into the hillside the depth of two men laid hat to boot. The ceiling height would have forced a tall man to hunch, but would prove adequate for the Rench family. Jesse Rench had already walled up a crude stone fireplace at the far end and sunk a stovepipe chimney through the hilltop. They'd extended the front of the dugout four additional feet from the face of the hill with a wall made of sod strips piled one upon another, grass-side down. He'd framed out a single window, one and a half by two feet, and a few men who had wandered over from the camp helped to build up the wall around the frame of the window and the door and across the face of the carved-out hill. Thompson noticed that Joseph and the boy were no longer over by the dog, which had begun to bloat and to go ripe in the heat of the day.

"Had someone better see to that dog?" he asked Jesse Rench.

"I tolt that boy take care of his own. But he done went off with that new chum."

"Where to?"

Rench pointed to the rise upon which the dugout was carved. Thompson hiked up to the crest and spotted the boys a quarter-mile away standing beside a copse of bushy oak growing around what he suspected was a dried waterhole. He started for them and as he approached to within a hundred yards he saw Joseph take an object in hand and point to the ground. A puff of smoke, followed a fraction of a second later by the crack of the pistol. Again. By the time Thompson reached them, Joseph had emptied the six barrels of the Allen pocket pistol into a rattlesnake that lay writhing in the deadfall of the oak. The snake's head was gone but its body still twitched and contorted, the rattles on its tail sounding a warning. The Rench boy excitedly danced around the snake, kicking dried leaves and dirt over it. "You done him good," he said to Joseph. "You done him real good."

Thompson recognized the pistol. "I'd forgotten that piece," he said to Joseph. "Why not give it to me. Head back to camp. Your mother will worry about you if she heard the shots."

"She's not my mother," Joseph said. "And I don't rightly care if she worries or not."

"Not your mother?" Thompson asked, attempting to mask his surprise.

"Step-mother," Joseph said. "Step-mother, half-sister."

That helped explain so much, Thompson thought. His lack of deep mourning for Martha, his indifference toward Hanna and her suffering. Thompson had wondered at Hanna's age, she seemed more youthful both in appearance and demeanor to Obadiah.

"The only one blood-to-blood with me is gone," Joseph added.

"He was a good man," Thompson said, extending his hand for the pistol.

Joseph tucked the gun back into his trousers belt. "My father refused to shoot it," he said to Thompson. "Tried talking reason to them."

"Hard to go against your convictions, sometimes," Thompson said. "Your father was a man of firm beliefs."

"My father was a coward," Joseph said.

Thompson placed a hand on Joseph's shoulder. "He did his best."

Joseph shook free of Thompson's hand. "How would you know? You weren't there. Not until too late." He turned toward the wagons with the boy tagging behind.

Stung, Thompson watched him go. So, there it was. The unwashed truth. Thompson had not been there with the Lights when they needed him. He'd not been with Rachel and Matthew and Daniel when they'd needed him. What atonement possible? How to respond to Joseph's indictment? The accusation in Rachel's anguished stare? Was it redemption Thompson sought, or punishment?

He walked back up the rise and stood looking over the Rench claim. What promise did the squatter see in these few acres? A spring that would provide water for his family, but not for crops; a small garden planted in turnips and potatoes that might or might not yield before winter set in; a few plowed acres that could not be sown until next season; a wretched, dark cave dug into the side of a hill. Obviously, Jesse possessed little aptitude for farming, his tools crude and the plot of land he'd chosen poor even for the buffalo grass. No livestock, little in the way of stores. Yet here they were, clinging to the sliver of possibility. What must have been his life before to uproot his family to this?

10

Once past the middle crossing of the Arkansas, traffic on the trail dwindled. Most of the large trade caravans turned from the mountain branch for the dry route cutoff to Santa Fe. Four wagons remained in Upperdine's guide other than his own: the Lights', a merchant, and two miners from Pennsylvania who had heard vague rumors of precious metals to be prospected in the Rocky Mountains.

The merchant, a family man from Ohio, left a prosperous trade for the opportunity at more. Thomas Pauperbaugh owned a two-story brick house in Oberlin, and rumor had it he was active in the Underground Railroad. Pauperbaugh was a hatter and a milliner, and John Upperdine had expressed to Thompson on more than one occasion his reservation about the applicability of such a trade in the wilderness, but Mr. Pauperbaugh explained that he meant at first to trade solely in men's headwear, not just for the gentleman but for the rougher sort as well.

The prospectors, Rice and Perkins, were coarse and hardy but inexperienced in travel. Their wagons seemed always to want repair, and on occasion they lagged behind not from laziness but rather from inexperience with their teams, even after weeks on the trail. They were Welshmen and conversed among themselves in their strange tongue, reverting to accented English with the others.

Midafternoon they came upon Chouteau's Island and Upperdine guided the wagons to sand hills overlooking the river. A larger company set out from Kentucky already had encamped nearby and gave Upperdine's small group a sense of security and companionship. They visited between camps, and Thompson couldn't help but recall memories of his father's estate in Kentucky, and by extension his own ambitions, but he kept his thoughts to himself. Toward sunset, he walked to the bluff and watched the Arkansas wash over the wasted barrens. The water ran brown and sluggish, wide and uninviting. Shallow but sandy, it looked a quagmire for lumbering stock.

Full dark, the companies disbursed to their respective camping areas. The night watch set, Thompson rested cross-legged by Upperdine's fire. His father's lush Kentucky, this stark plain, a journey between two worlds. What was before, what is now, just as sharp a contrast, he thought.

"Those men, that fell upon the Lights," Thompson said.

Upperdine understood. "Border ruffians, from Missouri."

"Why?"

"See the abolitionists as a threat. The large farms need labor. Slave labor."

"Still, a severe judgment to inflict on the innocent."

"Heard of Reverend Brown?"

"No."

"Abolitionist, strong in his views as well. Preaches that without the shedding of blood there is no remission of sin. Those are hard words. Hard actions on both sides."

"They are," Thompson said. "A harsh theology. But still you stood with these people."

"This country tends to make equals of us all. But my sympathy is with my oath. I agreed to pilot these people and I kept my word."

"That seems the honorable thing."

"I don't know about honor. That's something for grander men than me to claim. I just kept my word."

Night came on, and just as Thompson was about to retire to his bedroll, a sound came out of the darkness. Below, the silent river began to churn, a tumult of gurgling water and low-pitched animal mumblings.

"The river on the rise?" Thompson wondered aloud.

"No," Upperdine answered. "Buffalo crossing."

The commotion lasted into the night. Thompson walked to the crest of a sand hill, and peered into the murk but saw nothing except dark shadows the size of small wagons moving through frothing water that sparkled in the refracted moonlight. He returned to his bedroll and drifted off to the discordant melody of splashing hooves and sharp grunting, on and on.

The following morning, Thompson approached the bluff and looked out upon countless thousands of buffalo grazing on the far bank. The herd stretched from the water's edge across the bottom-land and up the low hills in the middle distance and over them out of sight. Animals rolled in the wallows, dust hovered above the herd like a talcum mist. Bulls pawed the earth and butted heads. A great caterwaul of lowing and snorting rose from the body and carried across the prairie. A chorus that mesmerized him: the sight and sound, the sheer numbers kept him rooted.

"Join us?" Upperdine approached from camp. "Hunting parties forming up."

They set forth a straightforward plan. A group of riders from the larger company set out earlier that morning, crossing the ford and turning immediately southeast, away from the herd. They currently were circling back from far side of the hill opposite the ford, intent upon breaking out a small group of animals and stampeding them back across the river to the northern bank where the others waited. Thompson took Joseph with him and together with Upperdine they established position on a steep bank adjacent to the ford. "Beasts won't be able to scale here, should be safe from trample," Upperdine explained. Presently they noted a general commotion spreading among the near animals, and within minutes the riders crested the far ridge, scores of buffalo ahead of them, making for the river.

"Take a cow or a yearling," Upperdine said. "Nearing the rut. A bull this time of year is strong-tasting and tough. Fighting and mating sheds all their fat."

Joseph removed the Allen pistol from his belt. "I need rounds," he said, holding the pistol toward Thompson. Thompson shook his head. "That will never do." He passed his rifle to Joseph and showed him how to load and to ready. "Tight against your shoulder socket, cheek to stock. Too loose, you dislocate an arm, break a jaw."

The first of the buffalo approached the near bank.

"Just sight down the barrel," Thompson instructed. "We're on high ground so aim a touch below where you want the ball to strike."

"Below the hump, mid-shoulder," Upperdine directed.

Thompson pointed out a young cow climbing from the shore onto the loose sand of the bank. "There."

Joseph took aim and fired, staggering back a half-step with the kick of the discharge. Thompson saw the thump of impact in the animal's midsection, a bit off the mark. It stumbled, and then walked on, but slowly. Thompson took the rifle and reloaded and handed it back to Joseph. "Once again, should do it."

Joseph took the rifle and raised it, but rather than dispatch the wounded animal, he swung to a large bull lumbering up the bank and fired on it. The ball struck the bull's foreleg, and it buckled but righted itself and turned back toward the river in a grotesque, three-legged hobble. Thompson grabbed the rifle from Joseph, again reloaded, and killed the young cow. His blood pumped in his temples, and then slowed. Joseph reached for the rifle but Thompson refused. "Meat enough," he said.

Now he noticed the others firing as well. Dozens of men, scores of buffalo. All about, the sharp cracking of gunfire, the explosive plumes from the muskets, the acrid scent of powder, men shooting indiscriminately as quickly as they could reload. Many wounded animals moved haltingly back across the river to rejoin the larger herd. From Upperdine's company, the prospectors and the merchant were not accomplished marksmen. The merchant fired his small-caliber belt revolver, a woefully inadequate weapon for killing buffalo, and he seemed intent on hitting as many of the creatures as he could, with little concern whether any of them actually fell. He shot at one and then turned his revolver on another. Downed animals were strewn across the ford, a low moaning, water running red, blood soaking into sand, more animals than an army could consume.

Thompson regarded Upperdine with bewilderment. Upperdine set the butt of his rifle onto the ground and gripped the barrel with two hands, rested against it. "I've seen it before, many times" he said. "Something about the animals brings out the blood lust in even the meekest of men."

Thompson and Upperdine took the tongue and the hump ribs from the yearling and divided it between themselves and the Lights while the others continued sporadically shooting at the cripples. Thompson noted Joseph walking amidst the carnage, bending low to a downed buffalo, looking into its eye, poking, moving on.

That evening Thompson and Upperdine roasted the tongue and ate while listening to the wolves at the carcasses out beyond the reach of the campfire. With only five wagons, they could not form a proper corral, so they had arranged them in a semi-circle and picketed the livestock up tight to the wagons and closed the circle with scrub brush from the riverbank. It would not do to have the wolves harassing the oxen and mules. And Upperdine feared the downed bison might attract a plains grizzly in due time.

"Seems a waste, leaving all that meat," Thompson said.

"Spoil long before we could finish it," Upperdine said, cutting a slice from the tongue. "No time to jerk." They sat by the fire and let it die down. Upperdine stood, stretched, and left for his wagon.

The next day, early, Upperdine led his party from the bluffs overlooking the ford of the Arkansas and rejoined the mountain route. The larger emigrant company was laying over for an additional day to graze the stock and to skin out a few of the buffalo for their hides, but Upperdine wished to push on. The season was growing late and they remained two weeks out from Bent's Fort.

"Robes is no good this time of year, anyhows," he'd explained when Joseph expressed disappointment at not taking a hide. "Need their full winter coats."

Fortified by meat and by rest, they made decent time over firm trail. But the oxen began to show the wear of travel. Having lost weight, they tired sooner than during earlier stages of their journey. Two days past Chouteau's Landing, they had to camp dry because the seasonal spring that Upperdine counted on for water had suffered from heat and drought and proved too alkaline for consumption.

The following morning as they were yoking the teams, Upperdine let drop his tow-line and walked to the rear of his wagon and rummaged through some sacks.

"Got any tobacco?" he asked Thompson.

"A little. You have a need?"

"I do." Upperdine found the sack he wanted and dug through the contents and brought out several strands of glass beads, a carved wooden horse, and a five-pound sack of coffee.

"For the Savages," he added.

"What Savages?" Thompson asked, scanning the flat expanse. And suddenly before him rode a dozen or so Indians, appearing, like the first buffalo he'd seen, to have sprung full-fleshed from the prairie itself. Not there and then, there. The Welshman, Rice, pulled his fowling piece from the wagon but Upperdine motioned him to remain calm.

"What shall we do?" asked Thompson.

"Nothing. We welcome them and hope they do not decide to harass us. Show your weapons. Do not shoulder them, but let our friends know we are well armed."

Thompson eased toward the Lights' wagon as the Captain walked to the mounted Indians and began conversing and signing. He took up his long rifle and rested the butt plate on the ground. Both the lead Indian and Upperdine appeared serious and at times sounded strident. Arms in pantomime, language a mix of English and incoherent guttural sounds, exaggerated facial expressions. The ponies shuffled in the dirt and dust rose from their hooves. The Indians were tall to a man, light-skinned and had what Thompson thought of as European noses, sharp and prominent. They looked sturdy and well-muscled with clean-shaven faces and skin more deeply copper than red. All appeared completely at ease on horseback. Only the spokesman dismounted to confer with Upperdine. They were armed with bows and lances, knives and hatchets at their belts. Two carried muskets. He noticed a few youngsters among the band, probably no older than Joseph. They concerned him most. No scars, hot blood. He watched them closely. He also found himself hoping that Joseph had not managed to procure additional rounds for the pistol he'd refused to yield up.

After a time, Upperdine turned from the Indians and walked to his men.

"Trouble?" Pauperbaugh asked.

"It's as I expected. They want tribute for the buffalo we've taken from them."

"Nonsense," Rice said. Upperdine ignored him.

"Thompson, I'll take that tobacco now, if it suits you."

"I will fetch it up."

"And Mr. Pauperbaugh, I'll trouble you for one bolt of that purple felt you are carrying."

"If I must."

"You must." Upperdine turned to the Welshmen. "I'm afraid you don't have much in your wagon that would appeal to them. But they trade up and down the trail, and a little currency would sit well with them."

"I'm thinking my buckshot would sit as well," said Rice.

"There are twelve of them, and all able to fire off four arrows to your one load. I do not believe they wish to harm us, or they would have done so. But do not doubt that they are capable of it." Upperdine spat in the dust. "Now, gather me a few coins."

Upperdine presented the Indians with his trinkets and the other ransom. The lead Indian placed the coins in a leather pouch hanging from his neck and fingered the calico but made no motion to gather up the goods. He stood silently, arms crossed at his chest.

"No more," Upperdine said, crossing his arms as well.

The mounted Indians began slowly to space out their ponies in a row, facing the wagons. Thompson took a deep breath to steady his nerves and calculated his first target should a skirmish ensue. His positioning, how best to protect Hanna and Joseph. For several moments, no one spoke and no one moved. A snort from one of the ponies, a twitching tail. Then, to his left, Hanna Light climbed from her wagon, walked over to Upperdine and the Indian fixed in impasse, and placed the turquoise egg on top of the calico bolt. The Indian picked up the rock and turned it in his hand, held it up to the sun. He watched Hanna return to her wagon, and, pointing toward her, spoke with Upperdine.

"No," Upperdine said, and re-crossed his arms, set his feet apart, a wall.

The Indian stood in place a short time longer and then put the turquoise rock into his purse with the coins and motioned to one of the young Indians to collect the tribute.

The mood between Upperdine and the Indians seemed to lighten almost instantly, with Upperdine uncrossing his arms and motioning with his hands, take, take. The lead Indian adorned himself with one of Upperdine's bead necklaces, mounted, and led his men into the plains. The company watched until the ponies disappeared below a gradually sloping depression and up the far side, and down again. Captain Upperdine retrieved the tow-line and led his ox to the yoke. "Let's not tarry," he ordered.

They pushed the animals hard. They did not noon and they walked into the evening, covering eighteen miles, according to Upperdine's calculation. When they stopped for the night, he ordered the men to pull the wagons close and directed that they sleep on the ground between the back wheels. As was becoming their habit, Thompson and Upperdine supped together. Thompson mulled the events of the day, the Indians, but more, of course, than that.

"So, she is aware?" Thompson said.

Upperdine understood his question. "I'd guess as much."

"She observed your negotiations. She understood the stakes, and she acted."

"Yes."

"What does that mean?" Thompson asked.

Upperdine picked a piece of grizzle from his teeth. "I do not pretend to know."

"Perhaps she is recovering her wits," Thompson said. Then, after a pause, "Perhaps she never lost them to begin with."

"Perhaps," Upperdine said.

"Yet still she will not speak." Thompson used a rib as a pointer. "I attempted to talk with her, and it seemed like that mania just came back down over her face, like a widow's veil."

"I ain't a physician," Upperdine said. "I got no answers."

Thompson shook his head, questions still buzzing, and changed subjects.

"What are they like, the savages?"

"That's like asking what's a white man like. All sorts, like we got Irishmen and Welshmen and Englishmen. All different sorts." They ate in silence, Upperdine chewing on his meat, and then he went on.

"Take your Cheyenne, kind of like royalty, tall and quiet and never shows you what he's thinking. Crows, they like a good time. Seen a brave one time lift up his squaw's skirt and just plant his corn, right out in the open. The Crows can steal a horse right out from under you and you don't even realize it's gone until your feet hit the ground."

"Thieves," Thompson said.

"But, they're not too much for killing our kind," Upperdine said. "Would rather keep us around to steal from. The Comanche, now that's another story. Bandy and mean and got no use for whites. Think we're disgusting creatures, all hairy and pale." Upperdine laughed at his characterization.

"Who were they we met today?"

"Arapahoe."

"They didn't give us too much trouble."

"Not today. But they call themselves the 'bison path people.' Them buffalo herds, that is their whole life out here, and I expect it makes them dead ripe nervous to see us laying waste to them." Upperdine walked off into the night and Thompson could hear the stream of his piss, and then he returned. "Tell you this. They know how to make a living off them animals, food, shelter, clothing, everything. I once seen some winter-starved squaws drag a drowned buffalo calf from a tangle of deadfall in the river bend. I couldn't figure what they was going to do with that beast, all swelled up and putrefied. They ate it. Raw."

Thompson tossed the rib bone into the fire. "How do you know what to expect when they come up on you like today?"

"Don't, and it don't much matter. It's a big land out here, and you ain't likely to see the savage often, and only then when they want you to. And they won't make theirselves known until they want something from you. Your life or a little sugar, hard to tell." The Captain tossed a few dried chips on the embers, and sparks danced from the flame.

"I once passed a evening with a nice enough Indian. Had a little whiskey, a pipe, I slept easy. That very same Indian and his boys come up on a Texan riding alone not two days later. They took his horse and drug the man back to their camp and slit open his stomach and let the dogs chew on his guts while the Texan watched. Just never know."

Thompson spat into the dirt.

"That is inhuman."

Upperdine stood.

"Careful to judge. I heard that the Texan's kin came up on the Comanche camp when the men were out raiding. Laid waste, killed everyone in it. Mostly squaws and young ones. A few old men. One old boy skinned out a squaw's female parts, hung them from his saddle horn." Thompson looked up at Upperdine, dumbfounded. Upperdine started to his bedroll and then turned back.

"I know you are tore up over what happened with the Lights. Those men. But you got to face up to it. This land is wild yet. A hard place. No civilizing influence, and men forget themselves." Upperdine left Thompson to his thoughts.

Thompson wrapped himself in his bedroll and watched as the fire went to cinder and darkness crept in around him, blinded him to the vast beyond, and centered him to his own consciousness. Sound only. His heartbeat. The soft breeze riffling the short grass, the gentle agitations that went unnoticed during the day. Coyotes sounded, and were silent. What's to become of the Lights? Joseph, his instability and flashes of aggression so unlike the boy he knew a short month ago. Hanna, sweet, innocent, now damaged, perhaps beyond repair. Could she survive until returned to sanity, and to the states? The Indian had wanted to trade for her, of that he was certain. A man's domain, this western territory. How to protect them, from others, from themselves?

Thompson peered into the darkness, and then, slowly, eyes adjusting to the night, he detected the outline of his foot, then the ghostly arc of the wagon canvas. He surveyed the dim world reappearing before him and thought, "This is my life. A shadow." The long night ahead. The yawning emptiness within. He reclined onto his back and stared up into the band of stars crossing the universe.

11

They passed through washed-out prairie, bleached flats, cactus and bunchgrass growing in tight fists. Sand hills and low plateaus intruded on the horizon like sea swells. Heat still burdened the land and pressed into their skulls. But Thompson knew they had been gaining elevation as they moved west, and with higher ground came an easing coolness at end of day. Imperceptibly, a few feet a mile, but mile after mile. During the day, clear skies, white heat; at dusk, the hint of chill creeping in like the melancholy memory of a lost love. In the lengthening nights, his blanket became a close companion. The high plains seemed to Thompson a desolate, wondrous cathedral. The sky a towering arched ceiling of blue, the horizon an unapproachable altar, a solemn, quiet, endless space. The vast openness, a place to ponder, to pray, although he'd all but forsaken belief.

The days passed with affirmative sameness, so when the landmark known as Big Timbers first came into view it seemed a mirage. Cottonwood trees lining both banks of the river jutted into the sky and appeared almost simultaneously with the imposition of great billowing clouds advancing from the west. What for days had been a monotonous, faded background transfigured into a landscape of radiant whites, sharp blues, subtle greens, and almost infinite shades of brown as sunlight played through the clouds and threw shadows across the plains and against the bluffs that rose from the river flats.

The five wagons crested a small rise and caught sight of Bent's trading post, a collection of stone and wooden buildings sitting below the bluffs on a stretch of high ground. Horses grazed on the broad floodplain, and a dozen tepees occupied that same bottomland: conical, symmetrical shapes against the stark angles of the buildings. Rock and timber, hide and pole, civilization in the territory. People milled, miniature in the distance.

"A sight," Thompson remarked to Captain Upperdine, who rode beside him next to the wagon.

"Nothing like the old fort," Upperdine commented. "Upriver a ways. Adobe brick, walls taller than two men. Plaza could quarter a hundred-fifty men. A icehouse sunk deep beside the storage bin."

"Plaza?" Thompson asked.

"A town square. Come in out of high country, a man could feel civilized again, for a bit. A bath, a woman if you wanted and had a coin or a pelt for trade. Conversation. Bent kept books, and periodicals."

"What's become of it?"

"Mountains got trapped out. Fur trade slowed. In forty-nine, Bent offered to sell it to the Army. Army declined. Figured Mr. Bent would abandon and they'd have it for free. Mr. Bent was a businessman, and that notion did not set well with him. Blew it to rubble. Moved here and took up on a smaller scale."

Blew it to rubble. The idea that someone would destroy something he'd built with his own hands struck Thompson as almost inconceivable. Then it occurred to him with such startling clarity that he stopped in place as the oxen plodded on. It's exactly what he had done with his own homestead, his family, his life. Blown it to rubble.

Coming into the perimeter of the trading post put Thompson ill at ease. Indians, of different ilk, distinct in skin coloring, dress, size. Mexican traders, brown like the earth. A scattering of free Negroes, scores of white men of various dress and deportment, all hard-lined and trail-worn. He noticed only three females as they came into the confines of the post, Indians, who were dressing hides in proximity of the tepees. Among the stone buildings, traders sat under lean-tos that sheltered wares and pelts. Several men squatted in the shade of a cottonwood, talking a bit too loudly, laughing, and passing a jug. Thompson's attention drew to a cock-fighting bout underway in the stone ring: men hollering, bills scattered, blood on the sand. One cock had an eye dangling from its socket, but fought on and the crowd yelled encouragement. The noise of greeting and barter and argument ebbing and flowing in the dust-stirred air. He felt on guard, the world closing in around him, his senses assaulted after too long in solitude. He tensed, and then relaxed a bit when Upperdine moved the company through the outpost without halting.

Upperdine decided to camp west of the trading post a half-mile, where a level bench for picketing the animals held tolerable grass. As they passed the tepees below the post, Upperdine reined his horse and asked Thompson to handle the encampment. Thompson watched Upperdine dismount and walk up to three Indians who greeted him in friendly animation.

While the others explored the trading post, Thompson remained in camp. He watched the comings and goings from a distance, heavy Murphy wagons pulled by six teams of oxen, wiry Indian ponies flying among the plodding mules on the grazing fields. He walked along the river to where bluffs threw both banks into shadow and the temperature cooled by at least ten degrees. He discovered geometric designs carved into the rock face by ancients, he supposed. On the plains, he walked a land of low hills and ridges rising from the expanse of dry flatlands, and he began to notice details he'd neglected while in constant movement on the trail: shallow depressions where jackrabbits might nest; the whirring sound of prairie chickens flushed from the sagebrush; turkey roosts in low timber along the river and in thickets clogging the side channels; how a scrub patch in the distance might lead him to a pothole or a seasonal pool holding water, or, perhaps a mallard. He had a notion to winter somewhere near, and he needed to become familiar with the land.

For two days, Upperdine stayed away with the Indians and Thompson ate with Hanna and Joseph. The others were rarely in camp. The two miners, Rice and Perkins, had met several prospectors at Bent's Fort who were preparing to set out for the foothills to the north and west. They talked excitedly of gold nuggets the size of pigeon eggs strewn along the stream banks just waiting for the plucking. Pauperbaugh, the hatter, had negotiated a license to market at the fort and was busy during the day disassembling his wagon for the ready planks with which to begin building a display table and trade booth. Thompson kept close watch on the Lights, and he slept nearby, and guardedly. Men from the post had heard that a white woman was traveling with the company and a steady stream of hungry-eyed, wolfish strangers crabbed about, hoping to catch sight of her.

The layover provided Thompson opportunity to meet an obligation he'd been putting off while on the trail. The afternoon of the first night at Bent's Fort, he spent a few of his coppers to purchase a pen, paper, and postage. He wrote a letter to his father, a straightforward, unemotional account of his life since that past spring. He repeated what he suspected his father had already been informed, that he had lost his family and abandoned his farm, and in the letter he renounced any inheritance due him. He would not be returning home. He offered his best wishes to the Reverend and to his brother, Jacob, and he signed off. He deposited the letter in the leather mail pouch that hung from a peg in the trade room.

He'd written the letter without sentiment but later in the evening as so often happened, his mood darkened with the ebbing day. His thoughts carried eastward: Jacob biding time in Philadelphia, waiting for the day the estate would come into his possession and provide for him a comfortable city life either through sale or tenancy. Thompson did not begrudge his brother that future, but he did mourn the forfeiture of his own due to covetous greed. Had he not lingered on his father's estate, he possibly could have saved his family, nursed them, or, failing, died with them in honor. Yet, filled with self-loathing as he was, when he wandered in memory over the ripe fields and green pastures of his boyhood home a yearning came over him almost like love-sickness.

The morning of their third day at the fort, Upperdine rode up to Thompson while he was sitting on his heels by the fire, drinking coffee. The Captain dismounted and accepted a cup from Thompson.

"I plan on striking for home first light tomorrow. Except for you and the Lights, the company has dispersed."

"I'd noticed as much." Thompson glanced toward the fort. Curiosity loosened his tongue. "Acquaintances there?"

"In the Indian camp. I paid respects to the elders, learned of news across their range, and attempted to secure pledges of peace through the winter. I believe I succeeded."

Thompson offered a hard biscuit, which Upperdine accepted.

"So, you get along with the Indians?"

"For the most part. The Cheyenne and the Arapahoe. The Comanche is a wild card." He retrieved two strips of jerked venison from a pouch at his belt, gave one to Thompson, and absently gnawed on the other. "When I first come out here, I was with Mr. Bent when he hid a couple Cheyenne from the Comanche. I ended up marrying into the tribe."

"You took an Indian wife?"

"I did. Weren't no churches out here, but yes, I took her. And she did right by me. Strong worker, obedient. She was a good woman."

"Was?"

"Lost her to the cholera one spring when she went to visit her people. That all was years ago. But the Cheyenne remember me."

"That is comforting news."

"It is, for now. But I do fret. They are nervous about the numbers of whites they see crossing the trail. They have heard that a man found gold north of here. They had a strong wish to kill him before he passed on the news, but failed."

Thompson stood and tossed the dregs of his coffee into the fire. "Rice and Perkins have heard the same rumors."

"No good will come of it for the Indians. They're concerned about the spider people overrunning their land."

"The spider people?"

"That would be us." Upperdine paused, removed his hat and scratched his scalp, eyed Thompson. "But misfortune for some could mean opportunity for others."

"Others?"

"I got plans. The Arapaho have been in council with the Cheyenne. Prospectors are already coming onto their lands. Not many, yet."

"Then it's true? There is gold to be had?"

"Don't matter to me one way or the other. If there isn't, a lot of people will have wasted their time. If there is, the Big Bugs in the states will get hold of it before the scratch miner has a chance to sneeze. But I been through the rush of forty-nine, and I seen enough to know that it's not emigrants who will prosper but those that provide for them. They come ill-prepared for life out here. Linen shirts, poor tools, few provisions."

"A trade post where they stake out claims?"

"I don't know. Just rumors so far. But if they come, opportunities will arise."

"Sounds like you got it figured out."

"I'll need help."

"I'm neither teamster nor trader."

"I have land on the Purgatoire. Hay that needs cutting, wood split for winter, stock to tend. Help with my fields while I am away. Winter over, and then decide your future."

Thompson thought over the offer for a few minutes before answering. A part of him wanted nothing more than to work the fields again; he was not by nature a wanderer. But another part felt responsibilities weighing on him.

"I cannot leave the Lights. I have no solution for their circumstances."

Upperdine stood and paced, frowning. "I told you, this is no place for a boy and a woman, let alone one so incapacitated with melancholy."

"I cannot abandon them."

"Eastbound wagon trains stop at Bent's Fort, for another few months, until the weather turns. They can join one and return home."

"The boy is also damaged in spirit, not ready to cut loose to his own devices. There's an anger inside that could cause him hard times." Thompson knew that with Hanna incapable of handling their affairs, they'd be taken advantage of. "If they decide to return, I'll have to accompany them."

Even as he said it, Thompson dreaded the thought. But what choice? He'd traveled with them for weeks, grown fond of the family, and Joseph needed watching, and guidance. Moody like all boys his age, but normal until his injury. Thompson remembered his own awkward age, how he and Rachel had played together as children, their families close neighbors and Anglicans, both, until one day almost simultaneously with hair appearing on his body, chest, armpit, crotch, he began to notice her in a different light altogether from that which illuminated their adolescence. He too had grown moody almost overnight, fidgeted in church, and in school, barely able to sit, wanting only to run, to test his legs, his breath, to feel the energy surge. When in Rachel's presence, some unknown and frightening urgency to seek her glance, to contact her, a brushing of arms. What outlet for his energy had Joseph? And Hanna? What of Hanna?

Upperdine spat. "Damn it all, bring them along." He spoke with vehemence. "We'll find quarters for them until she gives birth and hopefully recovers her mind."

"It's not my decision to make," Thompson answered evenly. "But I will attempt to learn their desires." How, he did not know, but before reticence dissuaded him, he walked the short distance to the Lights' camp. He found Hanna on a campstool, mending a shirt. Her belly was heavy now and served as a shelf for her sewing. Joseph was not around that he could see. He'd shown excited interest in the trading post, the exotic sights and activities, and spent much of each day there. Thompson approached Hanna, who glanced up from her work. He crouched so he could talk softly and levelly with her, explained patiently what he and Upperdine had discussed.

"I will see you through," Thompson said. "Wherever you decide to go. But I must know your wishes. To remain here a while? To return to your home back East, your people? Some other destination? What do you want?"

Hanna looked up from her needlework and for the first time since her ordeal regarded him straight on, unblinking, and her eyes spoke to him as clearly and as persuasively as any conversation possibly could. They shone with a controlled but pervasive sorrow and with resignation and with a determination that communicated clearly her intent.

She held his gaze, forever it seemed, and he could not look away. And slowly he intuited a distinct sense of this woman. Her tranquil expression, face softened by grief but unlined, revealed a younger Hanna than Thompson had taken her to be, perhaps only a few years older than himself. He'd never appraised her so closely before. She'd always been Obadiah's wife, or Martha's mother, or the widow, ravished in body and spirit. She must have been young when she came into Obadiah's household. She must have had to deal with Joseph's cold reception and jealous guardianship of his father's attention. Obadiah, older by a decade, must have served her both as counselor and husband. Thompson understood that there was no home to return to back East in Obadiah's absence, and that she both loathed this new land for its mournful bequest and determined to make something of her husband's dream. Other truths about Hanna he struggled to bring into focus, but they remained murky and unarticulated. Truths like a forgotten name, on the tip of the tongue, but irretrievable.

So, a decision reached, all without a word between them. He stood, felt momentarily lightheaded, and walked back to his camp.

12

They departed the following morning, the two wagons only. Without the others, they pushed the teams hard and covered ground quickly, eighteen miles the first day, stopping only because the oxen appeared worked out. The trip had covered more than five hundred miles, and the animals had lost one-third of their body weight. They had departed Westport stocky, with glossy hides and clear eyes, but now ribs protruded around their midsections like the staves of a barrel and they moved with a shuffle that kicked up dust with every step.

Two days out of Bent's Fort, they came to the confluence of the Arkansas and Purgatoire rivers. Captain Upperdine halted the wagons and rode down the embankment and urged his horse into the Arkansas upstream from the junction. His horse struggled mid-river but made the ford. Upperdine remained on the far bank for several minutes, riding upstream and back, testing the banks, and then he re-crossed and returned to the wagons.

"Fresh teams, I'd ford here and make for home," he said. "It's only a few miles down. But I won't risk my trade, not on this team. They're done for." Upperdine's wagon was laden with eastern goods highly prized in the western territories: factory-made clothing, machined tools, milled lumber, glass window panes, books and maps of newly surveyed territories, sulfur-tipped matches. Thompson recognized Upperdine's cautiousness as their travels neared completion.

"There's a good natural ford farther upstream," Upperdine said. "We'll double back."

Early the following day the wagons had passed the rubble of Bent's old fort, a mound of broken adobe and blackened rafters. Upperdine did not slow his team and he barely glanced at the wreckage. Thompson studied the ruins until they disappeared from sight around a curve in the trail. His homestead in Indiana a similar ruin. With the new fort downstream, no one would likely rebuild here, as no one would reclaim the burned cabin in Indiana. His fields in time would return to forest. No trace that a family had once built a life there; that laughter had echoed from the woods and dreams seeded the fields.

Just southwest of the fort the banks of the Arkansas leveled and Upperdine led the wagons across at a point where water would not threaten the storage beds and footing was sure for the oxen. Thompson crossed the river standing on the Lights' wagon tongue, encouraging the oxen with his prod. Joseph stood beside him, and Hanna sat in the back.

On the south bank, they camped one final night. The four sat into the night, each quiet in their own thoughts. Thompson experienced no rush of excitement or anticipation, only a vague melancholy. His travels were over, for the present, but what now? Could he remain in one place without memories overtaking him? How to fill the hours, how to avoid wandering back into the past as he had yesterday upon catching sight of Bent's ruins?

The next morning they turned east and doubled back on the south side of the river until they met with the Purgatoire. Captain Upperdine halted the wagon and his sweeping arm panned from the river along the floodplain to low rises in the west.

"I foresee a great city here," he said. "The river and the stream coming together near the main thoroughfare. There on higher ground I'll lay out a town site."

Thompson noticed a few abandoned shacks by the river, one of sod and one of rough-cut planking.

"This is your land?" Thompson asked.

"From the confluence upstream a good ways, until the river cuts into the canyon."

"Those huts?" Thompson asked.

"Folks come and go," Upperdine said. "Help me out for a season or two, don't stick."

Thompson thought of the cities he'd passed through and could not imagine one desecrating this terrible and wonderful country. "The bottom land looks promising for crops," was his only reply.

"Sooner rather than later," Upperdine continued, "the emigrants will flow into this country and I'll be waiting for them." He grinned at Thompson and slapped the team forward.

Following the smaller stream a few miles over easy country marked by wagon ruts, they rounded a broadly sweeping oxbow and passed through a field where several dozen sheep grazed. Within a quarter-hour, Thompson caught sight of a squarely constructed two-story log house nestled in the shelter of a cottonwood grove. September, the leaves turning a pale green, a few golden sprays foreshadowing the turning of the season. A curl of smoke rose from stone chimneys set at opposite ends of the house, and a covered porch ran the length. A well had been sunk not a dozen feet from the front entrance, and beside that a hollowed-out tree trunk served as a trough. To the east was a solid-looking barn with a foundation of river stone, and beside it a lean-to that stored farm implements. Farther off, a chicken coop and split-rail stock pens were visible.

Upperdine pulled ahead of the wagons and tied his horse to the post and went inside. By the time Thompson and Joseph had led the wagons to the far side of the barn, unhitched the teams, and put down fodder around their tether, Upperdine had returned outside and from the porch waved them over. As Thompson approached, a woman came from the house and stood at Upperdine's side. Thompson judged Upperdine to be in his late forties. The woman appeared younger, perhaps because of the smooth skin of her face, unwrinkled, the color of finely tanned suede. Plump, but sturdy, she wore a red calico skirt and a long shirt-like blouse cinched at the waist with a leather sash. She had expressive eyes as black and shining as her hair, which she wore in a tight bun. A slight, inquisitive smile, she regarded them with curiosity, a tilt to her head. But if she was surprised to see three strangers arrive with her husband, she did not show it, although she did glance briefly at the pouch of Hanna's belly.

"This is my wife, Genoveva. This here is Mr. Thompson Grey. Hanna Light, and her son, Joseph."

"Pleasure." Thompson gave a slight bow.

"Welcome," Genoveva responded. "Mi casa es su casa."

Thompson followed her lead when she waved them into the house. They entered into a large room with colorful woolen rugs covering smoothly finished plank floors. A well-crafted dining table and six high-backed chairs occupied the center of the room. One corner nearest the dining area was partially walled as a separate kitchen, and Thompson could see an iron cooking stove set on a flagstone hearth that extended the full width of the room. The opposite end of the cabin led to a bedroom with a second fireplace, and a sturdy ladder on the wall opposite the front door led to a storage loft. In one corner near the bedroom, two leather-upholstered chairs were arranged on either side of a small table holding an oil reading lamp. A bookcase sat against the wall behind the table. The house was well lit, with glass windows located on three of the four walls. Upperdine apparently noticed Thompson's silent inventory.

"Trading as many years as I have, a man has occasion to strike a bargain or two along the way," Upperdine offered.

"Well done," Thompson replied, "well done."

That afternoon, they butchered a young goat and roasted the kid over coals in a cooking pit while Genoveva prepared bread in an outdoor oven that looked to Thompson like a clay beehive. On the indoor stove she simmered beans with rice and crushed red peppers. Upon their arrival, Hanna had stayed close by Thompson, at his elbow. But once meal preparation began, she moved into the kitchen and helped Genoveva. Thompson noticed her handling the silver dinnerware and the china settings with reverence. For her part, Genoveva conversed amicably with Hanna but did not pause for response, and Thompson surmised that the Captain had briefly conveyed to his wife the state of their small company. Awaiting the meal, Joseph remained for the most part silent, but he did admire a fowling piece hanging by the front door, and Upperdine took time to point out the walnut burl stock, and the engraved American eagle on the silver frame plate.

Invited to the table by Genoveva, Thompson felt some awkwardness after so many weeks on the trail. He sat in a chair at table rather than cross-legged on the ground. He had at his disposal a linen napkin rather than the sleeve of his tunic, and crystal glassware rather than a dented tin cup. No soot from buffalo-dung fires coating the meat, no muddy water to filter through a charcoal bag before drinking. He hesitated at his plate while Genoveva recited grace in a melodious, rolling tongue, and then she took up knife and fork and the others followed. They ate the meat and sopped up the beans and rice with the freshly baked bread. Genoveva served them water flavored with lemon crystals and sugar. The water was cold from the well and free of alkaline and tasted fresh as a new day.

After eating, Genoveva brought coffee and sweet custard that reminded Thompson of butterscotch. They finished eating with an hour left of good light and Upperdine asked Thompson to walk with him by the river. In late summer, the stream ran weak, following only the main channel, leaving wide sections of the riverbed exposed. The water showed green as it flowed over moss-covered pebbles and it gurgled pleasantly and offered a soothing, meditative backdrop to their stroll, an excuse to walk in silence. They followed a worn footpath that skirted the thick brush on the lowlands and turned close to the stream when the trail climbed and the banks were high and free of under-growth. After a half-mile or so they rounded a bend and ascended a small swell and came upon another homestead under construction. From the ruins of Bent's Old Fort, Thompson recognized the same soft red brick of the buildings. An adobe wall partially enclosed a plaza, three sides complete, eight feet high, a foot and a half thick, and three feet of the remaining wall put up. He could see that the wall formed the back end of a series of small rooms that opened to the inner square. The adobe brick had been finished in a reddish mud plaster and the corners smoothed and rounded so that the walls of both the outer perimeter and the inner rooms swirled together in a curving, symmetrical architecture that gave Thompson the impression that it flowed up from the earth like an outcropping.

"A Mexican homestead?" he asked Upperdine.

"Well, technically an American, now. Although white folks don't necessarily see it that way. This is his *placita*."

"An acquaintance?"

"The husband of one of Genoveva's cousins. Her favorite. The husband, Benito Ibarra. A country man, not as refined as Genoveva.

But he knows the land. This land. Turn a patch of rock and prickly pear into the Garden of Eden. And can sense water. Located the wells on both our sites. In exchange for his help, I let him cut out some of the acreage for his own. He'll pay it off over time, with work and with share. In return, a home for his family. Company for Genoveva."

"Indentured to you?" Thompson asked.

"No, no. He's Genoveva's family," Upperdine said, defensively. "It's just that in his gratitude, he insists on lending a hand."

"Of course," Thompson said.

Thompson surveyed the compound. The area to be enclosed by the adobe square was bare, cleared of grass, brush, and trees, and a well had been sunk in its center. A series of wooden forms lined the partially completed fourth wall along with several stacks of adobe brick. A corral of cedar limbs and oak snags extended from the outer side of one completed wall, and another larger corral enclosed a garden of ripening vegetables, red and oblong like pudgy fingers.

"Peppers," Upperdine explained. "Genoveva tends his little patch."

"He is away?"

"With his family down south, outside Santa Fe. He spent the most of last year here, helping me with planting, harvesting in the fall. Started on his placita when he could find the time. Don't know when he rested. He wintered over, working on his quarters as the weather allowed. Helped put in the crop this past spring, then back down to Santa Fe. Due back presently, but this time he'll return with his family, his wife, daughter, and two boys, and stay for good."

"Seems a schedule to drag out a man."

"It does, but he refused to bring up his family until the rooms were at least livable. Hard enough country as it is."

Upperdine led Thompson into the partially walled compound and opened the door into one of the completed rooms. "Benito's quarters," he explained. From the doorway, Thompson could see that the compartment held a table, three chairs, a cupboard, and two narrow beds covered with buffalo robes. A fireplace in the same oval shape as Genoveva's outdoor oven occupied one corner and above the hearth hung an ornately carved wooden cross, inlaid with tin, and a string of dried chilies. Upperdine pointed to the corner. "That one fireplace provides all the warmth you could wish for, what with these thick walls." An archway joined Benito's quarters with another room. "For the boys," Upperdine said. They walked to an adjacent room that had a separate outside entrance and joined Benito's quarters by a shared wall. This apartment held no furnishings but was the same basic design as the first, roughly twelve by fifteen feet with an adobe fireplace in the corner. "For his daughter. I thought the Lights could room here temporarily. We'll see about more permanent arrangements once Benito arrives. One of the spare rooms, perhaps, once finished." On the second wall of the compound, two similar rooms had been roughed out, and smaller storage rooms begun along the third wall. Upperdine ran his hand over the smooth plaster of the adobe. "For his relations, if they follow. You might lend him a hand, here and there, as you see fit."

"Seems a fair trade for the Lights' quarters," Thompson said.

"You might could take one of the unfinished rooms," Upperdine said. "Still protection enough from the elements."

Thompson's silence must have struck Upperdine as indecision. "Or, I got a little shack on that bluff down by the river." He pointed toward a thicket of sumac, and Thompson made out the cabin, almost hidden in undergrowth. "Put it up first season here, before I built the house."

"Looks like a pleasant view from there," Thompson said.

"Some of Genoveva's kin lived in it on and off," Upperdine said. "Come up to watch over her when I went running trade. But they never did take to the land. No one's lived there for a few years now. Might have to clear out some varmints, but it's got a iron stove that still works, far as I know. And, I laid a plank floor. In off the trail, I didn't want nothing more to do with dirt under my feet."

"I expect it will do just fine," Thompson said. He could tell from a distance that the cabin would need work to make it habitable. But he was not comfortable housing within the same complex as Hanna and Joseph. He felt responsible for them but also trapped, entangled, and he found appealing the idea of being a short distance removed.

Thompson returned with Upperdine to the log house where Genoveva had waiting for them two glasses of pear brandy which they took out to the porch while evening came. Genoveva and Hanna moved about inside, and occasionally a silhouette passed one of the windows. Joseph, a darkening shadow down by the river, sat on a boulder and whittled with his pocketknife. A white heron glided silently past. The harsh, high cry of a curlew cut through the quieting day. Thompson relaxed, eased into the slowing rhythm of evening, watched the birds alighting to roost and the farm animals circling to bed, imagined the fields almost exhaling the day, and a sense of familiarity washed him like a warm zephyr. He finished his brandy and went to the wagon to collect his bedroll and camp gear.

In wan light he made his way to the Purgatoire and washed himself and scrubbed his clothes. There was the well available at the placita, but he'd tasted the water and, finding it pure, it seemed to him almost a sacrilege to waste such a treasure frivolously. So he bathed in the river, and afterwards, full dark, he returned to the placita, draped his clothes across the garden corral and, naked, returned to one of the unfinished rooms and dressed in his spare set of underclothes and wrapped himself in his bedroll. Indoors for the first time in weeks, insulated from the wild sounds and shielded from the stars, he lay straining for the familiar murmurings, the chorus of wind and wild, and for the familiar sights, the blossoming night sky, and suddenly he felt entombed. Presently, he heard a small wagon approaching and

Upperdine leading Hanna and Joseph to their quarters. He listened to them settle. With the Lights so proximate, his sense of confinement increased. He looked forward to moving to the shack on the rise. When the buckboard had creaked away and the night quieted again, he rose and went outside onto the plaza and, wrapped in his blanket beside the water trough, fell asleep almost immediately and did not stir once during the night.

The following morning, refreshed, Thompson went to the river, splashed his face, and shaved in the reflection of his tin plate. He had felt compelled to remain clean-shaven upon joining the emigrants outside of Westport. Upperdine had cautioned him that in the western territory some might take him for an Indian at a distance, but he persisted in this new habit, for whatever reason. A form of grieving, a refusal to hide his mourning behind a mask of whiskers, a confession; he did not understand the why of his decision, only the firmness of it.

After shaving, Thompson stood beside the river and looked downstream to where the summer flow trickled around the bend, upstream. There, where the channel cut close near the bank, he saw a purposefully placed collection of large stones, stones not native to the river but to the limestone bluffs and rimrock formations rising from the folded-up prairie south of the Arkansas. He walked to the rocks and recognized it as a man-made creation. Someone, Benito he guessed, had built a diversion dam so that the channel water pooled against a steep section of bank before returning to the main stream. On the bank a floodgate had been constructed of half-round planks that could be raised or lowered using a rope pulley system. The gate was lowered so that no water flowed into the partially finished irrigation ditch stretching out behind it. He could see that the trench was to run the length of a long narrow strip of field and that a secondary ditch marked by stakes was planned that would bisect the field into two

smaller sections for row crops. The main channel, four feet across and
four feet deep, had been dug two-thirds the length of the field, with
the remaining one-third staked out like the side ditch.

Thompson at once understood the importance of irrigation in this
rain-starved country. The sun-baked earth, hard as Benito's adobe
wall, grew only shortgrass a few hundred yards removed from the
river's flow; only bunch grass, sage, cactus and prickly pear as the
ground rose from the floodplain. He appreciated the simplicity of
the ditch layout and the grand design of what could become, with
water, productive cropland. Benito had not plotted too ambitious a
section, several acres only, and that suited the harsh conditions. A
row of young fruit trees within a year or two of bearing, he judged,
lined the ditch bank. This land, a yellow, flaky crust, fed by rain and
flood, so different from the soil back east. Yet promising still, with
nurturing. And vast tracts, the line of sight defined by two elements
only: earth and sky.

Thompson returned to the placita as Joseph arrived with the Lights'
trail wagon, retrieved from the Upperdine pasture where the team
had spent the previous night grazing. Watching Joseph lead the oxen,
Thompson judged that during the past few months the boy had been
subjected to burdens beyond his years, and that his mouth, fixed in
a tight-lipped frown, and his eyes, downcast and devoid of joy, of
wonder at this new land, bespoke a childhood prematurely ended.
Together, they worked unloading the wagon, moving the travel chest
and the spinning wheel into the room, and the few furniture items that
Thompson had not abandoned on the prairie: a bed frame minus the
head and foot boards; four ladderback chairs with cane seats; a table,
legs disassembled for travel. Hanna walked with a splayed, flat-footed
waddle, encumbered by a belly dropped low and heavy, and after a
few trips from the wagon into the quarters, Thompson dissuaded her
from heavy lifting, so she busied herself with arranging the furniture

and replacing their mattress ticking with fresh straw Mrs. Upperdine had provided.

With the wagon empty, Thompson inspected the stowage box and discovered a large bundle tightly wrapped in canvas to protect it against the elements. He removed the canvas to expose a seed bag, a hundredweight, and an image came to him of Obadiah opening this same bag on the trail and scooping a sample that he'd shown to Thompson. Wheat, he'd explained, hardy and drought-resistant. This seed had encouraged him to venture out into the great barrens, had lured him and his family beyond the boundaries of settlement. If not for this seed, might Obadiah have indulged Hanna's desire to remain with friends in the relative safety of Diamond Spring? Or, never left Ohio at all?

Suddenly enraged, Thompson hefted the sack onto his shoulder and carried it past the placita gate, struggled across Benito's field to the bank of the Purgatoire. Descending, he slipped under the weight and fell hard and slid on his backside, cursing. He recovered his footing, brushed dirt and debris from his pants, and dragged the bag to the riverside. He unstrung the opening and drew out a handful of seeds and threw them into the water and watched them float downstream. Another handful followed the first. Obadiah's dream, Obadiah's curse, floating in the weak current, grain swirling around exposed rocks and mixing with foam in the eddies. He began to turn the bag wholesale into the river, angry at life, at fate. Grain poured in an arc, but before half empty, he stopped himself, or rather, some feeling like a hand grasping his shoulder turned him from his intent. Was it his place to pass judgment on Obadiah's hope? He retied the bag and climbed the bank and looked out across the floodplain, the flat expanse laid out before him unbroken, challenging. The future? Could such harsh land produce bread? Rough forage, yes. A little grass and, perhaps corn. Wheat? He could not imagine it. But he'd not squander

Obadiah's bequest: the dream his only legacy. He returned what remained of the seed to storage at the placita.

MIDMORNING, THE WAGON EMPTIED AND the oxen set to pasture, Thompson crossed the field toward the sumac thicket that sheltered the log-and-plank cabin Upperdine had offered him the evening before. Approaching close, he saw that the roof sagged at the midline but remained intact and sound for the most part. The only window lay open to the weather, the oiled paper covering long since lost to parching sun and scattering wind. The rough-hewed plank door was set on cracked leather hinges but closed true and tight against the jamb, and it resisted his testing of the latch. He forced it open and inside, the dark, abandoned interior seemed well preserved. It smelled of piñon fire and the faint muskiness of tanned pelts. The iron stove was without rust, the floorboards tight, and daylight filtered through mud chinking only here and there. A bed frame of posts and leather straps still looked serviceable. The corners of the room held droppings; squirrels, rabbits, mice. In the far corner, he noticed tight fur balls and small piles of bones, and he heard a scratching from above. There on the center beam an owl perched, ear tufts like the bushy, arched eyebrows of a disapproving judge, implacable yellow eyes following him.

"So," Thompson said. "Another tenant." At the sound of Thompson's voice, the owl took flight, a great swooshing, and then a practiced folding of its wings to fit through the open window frame. Thompson went to the door and watched the owl sweep low over the willows and then rise and alight on a cottonwood branch not thirty yards distant, where it positioned itself to keep watch over its domain. "I meant myself," Thompson called to the owl. "Not you."

After sweeping clean the cabin floor with willow switches he'd bundled into the semblance of a broom, and arranging his few possessions, Thompson walked beside the creek collecting firewood and cutting stove length sections from deadfall with a hatchet he'd found hanging from a peg on the doorframe. He stacked the wood and turned toward the placita a quarter-mile distant. His cabin sat on a low bluff above the river and the placita was built on a flat bench just where the land began to rise again from floodplain, and between the two stretched the field cut by the irrigation ditches. The simple act of walking across a ground destined for the plow, and of cleaning out a permanent living space, began to instill in him a sense of place, of belonging, and at once he felt both the yearning to be of this land and a rising guilt at imagining for himself a future here, without Rachel, without the boys. He reached down and took up a handful of dirt, pale, dry as cornmeal, sifted it through his fingers, let the fine grit drift back to the earth. He'd seen Upperdine's corn, noted the grass on the south-facing slopes above the bottomland. Still, he marveled how anything might take root in this soil.

Afternoon, the sun still high, Thompson walked the path to John Upperdine's house and from the lean-to storage shed he shouldered a mattock and a spade. When he turned to go, Genoveva came from the house onto the porch.

"Would you care for a cup of water?"

"Thank you," he said, setting the tools on the ground and taking the ladle from her outstretched hand. "Is Captain Upperdine in?" he asked.

"He's ridden out to meet a freight wagon."

"But he's just in from the trail," Thompson said, and, realizing his indiscretion, blushed, turned his head.

Genoveva smiled. "It takes a while for him to grow accustomed to home."

Thompson took stock of the house, the outbuildings, the fields, and it occurred to him that this woman must have managed alone during long stretches of Upperdine's absence. He looked to the east, a day's journey, two days, visible in the distance until convergence of sky and earth. He turned to the west where the land climbed gradually in dips and rises. He marveled at Genoveva's endurance. And now, what of the new arrivals, uninvited? Does she welcome, or merely abide us, he wondered.

SUDDENLY AWARE OF HIS AWKWARD silence, his inner musing, he gestured to the tools. "I don't suppose he would object to me borrowing these?"

"Of course not."

"I noticed a small grove of fruit trees downriver," Thompson said. "Apple I recognized, the other I did not."

"Pear. A gift to my cousin's husband." She smiled. "Perhaps more a bribe. His family had orchards, and I've presented him a few saplings to tie him to this place."

"You will be pleased to have them settled here for good?" Thompson asked.

"Very much so," she answered. "She is dear. He is a great help to me, and I adore their family. I've not seen any except Benito in three years. The little ones so grown, I imagine."

"They do sprout," Thompson said.

"You have children?" Genoveva asked.

"No," Thompson said, and started to add something that caught in his throat, and he bent for the tools without further conversation.

He walked to Benito's field and stood beside the unfinished irrigation ditch and studied the property, imagined he could understand the Mexican's design, sense his purpose. The initial rooms on the placita were almost complete. Benito would finish the walls this season. Rooms would be added out from the inner wall as his extended family grew, and this would become home for his children, and his children's children, generation after generation.

Again, the dull ache of loss began to overtake him. A vacancy of hope. *My days are like a shadow that declineth; and I am withered like grass.* He let drop the tools and looked at his hands. Hands long rid of the black soil of his farm but stained yet with the blood of his family, and of the Lights'. Hands good only for digging graves. The blackness fell upon him. He took up the pickax and swung it above his head and into the hard earth to continue the irrigation ditch. He swung the ax again. And again, establishing a mindless rhythm until his breathing labored and sweat stung his eyes. He paused to mop his face with his shirtsleeve and then took up the spade to remove dirt he had loosened from the ditchworks with the pick.

"I can dig for you," Thompson said aloud as he fell back into the cadence of the rise and fall of the pick. "That I can do. I can dig."

PART TWO

THE VALLEY OF LOST SOULS, 1858

13

The cart came into view along the river path below the pasture that Thompson was mowing. He glanced up from his work just long enough to take notice. A man guided the burro while two children rode in the cart and two women on foot followed behind. Mexicans, by their appearance: Genoveva's cousin? The man raised a hand in passing. Thompson did not acknowledge. Face hidden by a wide-brimmed hat, the man walked with the cautious, deliberate gait of one older than Thompson assumed the architect of the placita to be, and his slight frame again belied Thompson's preconceptions. Not much taller than the burro he led, and insubstantial as a shadow, could this be the person responsible for the grand plan of the adobe compound and the irrigation system Thompson had so admired?

The cart and the pilgrims rounded the sweeping bend toward the Upperdine place and Thompson continued mowing. He moved smoothly, cutting the swaths, guiding the scythe with the two-handled snath, passing it close to the ground, curved blade glinting in the sun, grass deposited in neat rows as he walked. Downslope, cuttings from two days earlier had already dried, pale yellow lines running the length of the field. Baked out by a September sun just beginning to lose its summer force. Heat still rose up, but with reluctant intensity, the nights consistently had begun to cool, and afternoon breezes carried just the hint of an edge down from the mountains.

He felt at ease in his labor, a liberation to be lost in motion unforced and effortless and so closely a part of his nature. But, occasionally, that same movement triggered memory, and his mind would wander back to other reaping, other fields, and his rhythm would break, the scythe moving with an uneconomical jerkiness, and he'd find himself hacking at the ground. He'd stop, drop the tool, move his hands to the small of his back, stretch, knead flesh on muscle, attempt to return to the here-and-now, his breath, taking in this air in this place at this time, and after a while, he'd take up the scythe and continue on.

The sun overhead now, walking in his own shadow, Thompson did not notice Captain Upperdine's approach.

"Making progress," Upperdine called out. Thompson laid the scythe across the humped grass and walked to Upperdine.

"Some. Those were Genoveva's relations?"

Upperdine nodded. "He's already asking about you. Wanted to know who was mowing his grass."

"His?" Thompson asked.

"He over-seeded last fall. Thought the field might hold moisture and produce good hay for my stock."

"Well," Thompson said. He removed his hat and swiped his forehead with his sleeve. "He was correct. But, I guess if he was worried about his field, he should've planned on being here when it needed mowing."

Upperdine laughed, shook his head. "Genoveva asks that you noon with us."

Thompson glanced about. "I've grass to cut."

"It's important to Genoveva," Upperdine said.

Thompson replaced his hat and pulled the brim low. "I'll be along, then."

WHEN THOMPSON ARRIVED AT THE Upperdine house, he washed his face and neck at the trough and cleaned his boots at the scrape. Before entering, he removed his hat and ran his fingers through his hair. Inside, they were already at the table, chatting quietly in Spanish but apparently waiting on him before eating. He stood awkwardly by the door until Genoveva glanced up.

"Thompson, come," she waved him over. "This is Señor Benito Ibarra, his wife, my cousin, Señora Teresa Ibarra, their daughter, Señorita Paloma, and los muchachos, Benjamin and Alejandro." The boys flanked Genoveva and she caressed each in turn as she introduced them.

Thompson bowed slightly to Benito and Teresa. "Pleasure," he said. Benito rose and returned the acknowledgement. He stood no taller than Thompson's shoulder, his face etched and furrowed as an arroyo, of indeterminable age, dark hair streaked with silver, his expression courteous but guarded. Teresa smiled at Thompson, her face open and welcome. Paloma kept her eyes fixed on her plate. Her features, what he could see of them, looked finely carved, but the mask of her face was sharp and scowling. Although they had freshened and cleaned the dust from their clothing, the family looked haggard, run-down. Even the boys were sunken-eyed and hollow-cheeked.

"Here," Upperdine said, waving to a seat beside him, opposite Benito. Genoveva said grace and they all ate in silence and with enthusiasm for a few moments: a stew of chicken with carrots, squash, and onion, spicy eggs cooked with dried beef and chilies, bread, tortillas, and, on the sideboard, a crumb cake sprinkled with cinnamon. When the eating slowed to a more leisurely pace that accommodated conversation, Teresa and Genoveva began chatting quietly at the opposite end of the table. Upperdine fished a chicken leg from his stew. "This man here's been a whirlwind since we come in off the trail," he said to Benito.

Benito regarded Thompson with polite neutrality. "Yes, I've already seen him at work." It surprised Thompson that in his presence, the men switched to English.

"Wait until you see what he's accomplished with your irrigation ditch," Upperdine said. He gnawed at the chicken leg and then set it on his plate and pointed a greasy finger with emphasis.

Benito's expression tensed and with great deliberation he sipped at his coffee. Thompson began to understand why Upperdine was so insistent he noon with them. Eliminate surprises, set boundaries, test nascent relationships. He put himself on guard.

"My *acequia*?" Benito asked. "What do you know of my acequia?" He still held his coffee cup near his lips, sipped, set it down with care.

"Nothing of the mechanical works," Thompson said. "But you laid out the course, and I just continued from where you'd left off."

"How far?" Benito asked.

"To the windbreak at the far end of the field. And a start on the secondary ditch, edged out with a spade, maybe a third complete."

Benito stared at Thompson as if suddenly unable to comprehend his language. He turned to Captain Upperdine. "This is not possible."

"He don't sleep much, seems to me," Upperdine said. "Went over there just after dawn the other day to see about help with the cutting and he was in that ditch, going at it hammer and tongs, lathered up like he'd been digging for hours."

"When did you return home?" Benito asked.

"Few weeks back," Upperdine answered.

"But even night and day . . ." Benito began, and then seemed at a loss for words.

Thompson shifted in his chair, glanced toward the door. "I am restless at times," he said. "Ill-suited to inactivity. So, I work."

"I figure we can both use the help," Upperdine said.

"I have no money to pay," Benito said.

"Please," Thompson said. "I ask nothing. I'm just here to lend a hand for a time."

"You do not intend to stay?" Benito asked.

"I haven't given it much thought one way or the other," Thompson said.

Benito appeared to relax. The grip on his coffee cup noticeably eased.

"Forgive me for sounding sharp," Benito said. "It's been a tiring journey. It will be good to unpack, settle into the placita." He smiled wanly.

"The placita, now there's another story," Upperdine said, his voice rising. Teresa stopped talking with Genoveva and inclined her ear toward the men's end of the table. Paloma shot Upperdine a questioning scowl. Upperdine leaned back in his chair, apparently pleased to be the center of attention. "I returned from the trail with many surprises for Genoveva."

Upperdine briefly recounted the Lights' travails, the women now openly following his conversation. Benito listened solemnly, did not interrupt. Teresa occasionally clicked her tongue.

"Where is this unfortunate woman and her son?" Teresa finally asked.

"Well, that's the point," Upperdine said. "I offered her a room for the winter in your placita."

The table went quiet. Teresa stiffened. Even the boys knew to still their fidgeting. Thompson studied Benito, could not read his expression. He looked drained, his face gone slack. Thompson sensed his dilemma. The enormous inconvenience of hosting strangers while settling his family into a new home must surely give him pause. But Upperdine was their benefactor and the cost of incurring his displeasure might also prove great. Thompson hadn't a clue how Benito might manage. In the short time he'd known him, first by the works he'd begun, and now in the flesh, this Mexican had managed to incur his respect, mild ire, and, now, sympathy.

"When is she due?" Teresa interrupted the silence.

"Not long, I think," Genoveva answered.

Again the silence returned, the room stuffy with tension.

"Only if it is no imposition," Upperdine added.

"They are welcome," Benito said, finally, his tone accommodating if overlaid with a note of resignation.

An audible gasp startled them all. Paloma, flushed, pushed from the table with such violence that her chair toppled to the floor.

"*Esto es imposible*," she sputtered.

"Sit down," Benito said. "And speak English in the home of our host and his guest."

"*¡No!*" Paloma shouted and continued her outbust until Benito stood and slammed his fist onto the table. His slackened face turned hard, his eyes searing. "You insult our host. And you dare dictate who I might invite into my own home? My home."

Paloma hurled her napkin to the table and stormed from the house. Benito turned to Upperdine.

"I apologize for my daughter's outburst. Her behavior is unforgivable."

"She's had troubles," Teresa said.

"Unforgivable," Benito said.

"Enough," Upperdine said, raising his hands, palms extended. "The girl's worn out. Her emotions are frayed. Let's talk no more of it. Sit. Finish your coffee."

They sat for a moment, and then Teresa said, "Señor?"

Benito nodded, once, sharply, and Teresa followed after Paloma. Genoveva ushered the boys to the hearth where she produced a box of wooden blocks decorated with colored letters. "Play," she said. "Write your names for me." Then she hurried to join Teresa.

"I'd best be to the field," Thompson said, rising. He went quickly to the door.

14

Upperdine and Benito remained at the table when the others departed. Shortly, Genoveva returned, gathered the boys and led them outside to help feed the chickens and collect eggs. Upperdine watched them go and reached for the coffee pot and poured himself and Benito another cup. "You've had a long journey," he said.

"A long journey," Benito repeated.

"But uneventful?" Upperdine asked.

UNEVENTFUL? BENITO THOUGHT. A FEARFUL wife sick for home before even losing sight of the Plaza.

From the hilltop, Benito sat on his haunches and looked back across the valley of his ancestors: the Plaza del Arroyo Seco two miles distant rising from the treeless plain; the fields cultivated in wheat and corn; the orchards climbing the slopes in neat rows like misty green clouds against hillsides rusted by the early sun. Beyond, rutted badlands stretched out into the far distances, the gullied flanks of hills, the deep arroyos and wind-carved faces of bare, red rock.

Teresa stood beside him, weeping quietly. Paloma, dressed in black mourning costume already dusted red at the hem, stood away from the others, dour. The two boys played with a scorpion they'd found under a rock, tormenting it with sticks.

"Can we keep it, papa?" Benjamin asked. "We'll show it to Severo when we get home."

They didn't understand. He shook his head no, stood, and turned from the valley and walked to the cart.

"How do you know this is the right decision?" Teresa asked.

Benito thought of the Plaza, the slow decay, the buildings and the residents both reflecting a faded vigor: the whitewashed adobe graying, cracking; the moustaches of the men graying; the marginal fields gray with alkaline and dust. A fading world. The fifth son of a modest farmer, the land divided between so many over the generations that it now provided meager subsistence for many, prosperity for none. Other than a garden plot that in good years provided food and a sack or two of surplus peppers to trade in Taos for sugar, he'd inherited one of the apple trees and the two east-pointing lower branches of one pear tree. The ancient pear tree had produced a stingy yield in recent years and he knew that soon it would fail completely and he would have even less to pass on to his offspring.

"There is no other choice," Benito answered.

Of course there was another choice. They could remain and hope for the best. They could, like the others, make do, eke out subsistence from their private garden and their share from community fields. He wanted, dreamed of, more.

Until this past spring, before the trouble, he'd been hopeful for the future of his daughter, Paloma. After all, he had much say about who might court her. He was respected, the Plaza looked to him for leadership. She would marry well. But the two boys, what of their future? They were born long after they'd given up hope for additional children. Benito and Teresa had married in '34, and almost immediately they were blessed with a pregnancy, and almost as quickly cursed with a miscarriage. Twice more, and then came Paloma in '40, feisty and temperamental from her first day, conditioned in the womb to assert her existence. The Ibarra family celebrated, Benito's stern father smiling over the child, his mother encouraging Teresa, "There, see, a blessing. Now, it will come easier, the others, the boys." Years passed, nothing. It was as if Paloma had drained all fertility from Teresa's body. Then, during her fortieth year, Paloma nearly of age, Teresa became pregnant and delivered without complication a boy, Benjamin. And another, Alejandro, barely a year later. When her cousin Genoveva sent invitation to join her, a field and a plot on which to build in exchange for help with the crops and the animals, he'd set his mind.

"No other choice," he repeated, as much for his own reassurance as for Teresa's.

UNEVENTFUL? *A BITTER, HATE-FILLED daughter, incautious, with unpredictable temper.*

They approached Santa Fe in the afternoon of their second day on the trail. As they entered the plaza, Paloma grew even more withdrawn than had been her disposition of late, her back stiffened and she walked with her eyes focused straight ahead, without seeming to notice the commotion swirling around them. Past the siesta hour, a quiet sun gave off soft light, buildings beginning to cast shadows onto the open courtyard. Food vendors and assorted peddlers congregated under the covered sidewalk of the governor's palace and attracted a bustle of citizens, women flirtatious in immodest, colorful dresses with fitted waists, men carrying silver-tipped canes and outfitted in tailored suits, a few American officers in full uniform, polished buttons and waxed moustaches. Military rulers and property owners, Benito thought; patrons, men and women of wealth and influence, puffed and proud. Their vainglory insulted him; same flesh as he, same blood, yet elevated to gods by virtue of birthright and possession.

Benito hurried his family through the square, past charcoal sellers, a Navaho offering silver bracelets and pottery, fandango parlors, a mercantile. At the far end of the plaza they approached four American soldiers tossing coins into a ring drawn in the dirt and rolling dice. As they passed, Paloma stopped abruptly, turned to face the soldiers, and spit at their feet.

"What the hell," one of the soldiers said.

"I believe she likes you," another said, poking the first in the shoulder.

"I got a coin here, for your favors," from the third. "Come sit with us."

Benito took Paloma firmly by the arm and pulled her away. The first soldier came up to Benito and blocked his way.

"See here. I believe we done asked your girl here for her company."

"You must forgive her," Benito said. "She is not herself."

"Cerdo!" Paloma hissed. The soldier did not appear to understand, but the tone of her voice caused him to sneer at her.

"She don't sound too friendly toward us, does she," he said.

"Please," Benito said, motioning for Teresa to take Paloma's arm and move away from the soldiers. "She is not of right mind. She wears the widow's gown." Benito cast his eyes to the ground and shook his head. The rim of his hat blocked his face and out of the corner of his eye he noticed Teresa edging the family away, heard the creak of the cart wheels. He slipped his hand to the small of his back and felt the hilt of his knife. Hopeless, he knew, but he'd draw, if it came to that. The soldier glanced at Paloma and looked back at his friends who had lost interest and returned to their game of dice. The soldier frowned at Benito and dismissed him with a wave of his hand.

"Well, get on, then, Mister pepper-gut," the soldier ordered. "Go learn her some manners."

Benito took the burro's lead from Teresa and moved them away. Near the plaza gate, they drew water from the community barrel and allowed the burro to drink for a few minutes from the trough.

"You are a foolish girl," Teresa scolded her daughter.

"Pigs," Paloma answered. "The Americans are pigs, and they disgust me."

Benito had to restrain himself from grabbing his daughter and shaking her. He came up close, hissed. "I was forced to degrade myself because of your outburst. Do not put me to the test again!"

UNEVENTFUL? A MAN TRAVELING ALONE *with two women and two young boys.*

"Quickly. Follow me." Benito guided his burro from the trail down the steep bank of an arroyo, slipping on loose rock and fine sand. He led them fifty yards along the floor of the arroyo to a thicket of saltbush that grew tall and dense. He tethered the burro as deep into the underbrush as he could force it and hoped the cart was hidden from view. He positioned the others beside it and waited.

On his previous trip alone, Benito had developed a keen sense for identifying fellow travelers from their dust sign. Men on foot kicked up low whiffs and almost always were more interested in putting miles behind them than in conversing or in causing trouble. Benito learned to distinguish between the fast moving, thin trails raised by Indian ponies and the denser column kicked up by cavalry horses. Thick clouds rose from mule teams hauling cargo wagons. Something in the dust rising in the closing distance told him to flee the trail. He shoved his boys deeper into the undergrowth and removed his hat and folded it under his belly and peeked out from the thicket. There, in the dry bed of the arroyo, Paloma's headscarf, a black signal flag starkly visible in the white sand. He sprinted from the cover and retrieved the scarf and wedged himself into a gully eroded into the ditch bank. Sparse cover. He reached overhead and scooped dirt into his hair, down the back of his shirt and trousers, and he angled his head slightly so that he could watch the trail from one eye. He worked his shoes into the sandy bed of the arroyo until little of the dark leather showed. He attempted to quiet his breathing, relax into the side of the hill. A tug at his pant leg caused him fright. He looked down. Benjamin, peering up at him. "Papa?"

"Quiet." Benito took Benjamin and pulled him into the crevice tight against his thighs, small body pressed against the bank. He put his right hand over the boy's mouth and positioned his thumb and forefinger against his nostrils and prayed he would not have to do it. To clamp shut. "Not a sound," he whispered.

He heard the jangling of tackle, creaking wood, the rub of leather on leather, iron on iron. Two riders came into view astride tall horses thick across the shoulders and haunches. Both riders wore Texas hats and were well armed: pistols at the belt, long knives, and muskets hanging in scabbards from the saddle. Trailing them, a team of four horses pulled a wagon driven by a huge black man with a bald head that shone with perspiration. The man's forearms looked as large as Benito's thighs. The bed of the wagon held three people bound hand and foot: an Indian dressed almost comically as a white man: dark trousers, a white shirt and red vest, and a black bowler; a Negro male slumped against the back gate seemingly asleep or unconscious; and a young Negro female in a calico dress torn at the bodice to expose one breast.

Benjamin squirmed. Benito's hand closed more firmly on his son's mouth. Every instinct, every muscle twitch urged him to run, but his

mind cautioned him to remain still as rock. One of the lead riders
pulled up, and the wagon halted and the other rider circled back
and sat his horse facing the arroyo and looked down the bank and
across the dry streambed. It seemed to Benito the rider stared
directly at him for an agonizing length. He dared not even blink.
The rider took a water bag from around his saddle horn, pulled
at the cork, and tilted it into his open mouth, still searching the
arroyo. He stopped the bag, returned it to the horn, turned his
horse, and signaled the wagon forward. Benito did not move for
several minutes, so frozen by fear and caution. He felt his son
jerking and realized he'd been pinching his nostrils, and he relaxed
his grip and whispered for him to hush and they remained against
the wall of the gully until Benito no longer could hear the wagon or
the horses. He eased from the bank and saw a hint of dust kicking
up in the middle distance. Only then did he pull away completely.
Benjamin emerged from the crevice like some desert insect, covered
in dirt. Benito took him into his arms, but when he began walking
he felt as though he were melting and his legs almost gave out and
he had to set Benjamin down and reach a hand to the bank for
balance. His every muscle had been tensed for what seemed hours,
although perhaps only a few minutes in chronological time, and
they no longer wanted to work. Benito waited until his legs felt
reliable and then led his son back to the others crouching in the
saltbush thicket. When Teresa saw him approach she jumped from
hiding and ran to Benjamin and drew him close and dusted him.
The child began to whimper but did not cry.

"Who were they?" Paloma asked.

"I don't know. Texas slavers, I think," Benito said.

"What were they doing up here?"

"Business."

"Those people in the wagon?" Teresa asked.

"Runaways perhaps. Perhaps just innocents in the wrong place at the wrong time. Who knows?"

"What makes you say that?" asked Paloma.

"The Indian. Dressed in missionary clothes."

"Where have you brought us?" Teresa challenged. "What place is this where we have to hide like lizards?"

"UNEVENTFUL," BENITO SAID TO UPPERDINE. "*Sí*, thank God. A busy road and our great good fortune to travel it unmolested."

"The trail is abuzz of late with low fellows," Upperdine observed. "I believe it is this rumor of gold that is spreading east. Bringing out prospectors of all sorts. Some just green farm boys out to get rich, some old forty-niners, and some foul types, opportunists of the worst kind, just out for the pickings."

"Perhaps it will blow over with winter."

"I don't have a good feeling about it."

"Tell me," Benito asked. "Your friend, Thompson. He knows the land?"

"He's a farmer," Upperdine said

"From the states? From the East?"

"Yes."

"It is much different there, I'm told."

"All I know is that I put him on the land and he has taken to it." Upperdine leaned close to Benito, his voice low but intent.

"He's a troubled sort. I don't know why I should give a fig for him, why he should concern me one way or the other. I seen plenty like him out here in the wilderness. Wandering souls. Groundless. Spirit out of fix."

"So, he may stay, or he may move on?" Benito asked.

"Who's to say," Upperdine said. "But make use of him. There is much to do."

15

Following the noon meal, Upperdine retired for a nap while Benito collected a rake and a pitchfork from the tool shed and hitched an ox to the flatbed wagon fitted out with the hayrack, and walked to the field. He was bone-tired, but not yet ready to face his daughter. From a distance, he watched Thompson as he moved along the rows. Benito judged him to be still in his twenties, perhaps six or seven years older than Paloma, although he was a poor judge of age. To Benito, people either were young or old, and time on earth had much less to do with it than the trials one faced getting from one year to the next. From a distance, Thompson had appeared young to Benito, clean-limbed and spry. Up close, he appeared much older.

He wished to take a measure of this man to whom John Upperdine had become attached. John was a trader, a shrewd businessman and a boisterous fellow. He'd made acquaintances up and down the trail, friends and more than a few enemies. Yet he rarely held strong emotions for anyone. He liked some men, disliked others, but it had always been in his best business interests to keep arm's distance. He always conducted trade with an eye to his own advantage with whomever he dealt. He'd never think to favor a friend, or to exclude an enemy. Better to keep even-tempered with both. Benito thought this uncommon interest in a stranger's well-being would eventually prove beneficial to John's spiritual constitution, but he could not help but wonder how this person's arrival might affect his own relationship with the Captain.

Benito walked to the lower end of the field and tested the cut grass, twisting the stem base, tasting it for moisture. Convinced it was ready to row up, he began raking the cuttings into stacks and piling them onto the wagon with his pitchfork. Deep into the day Thompson kept at his cutting while Benito raked and loaded. September, summer slow to ebb, the sun continued to throw heat, sweat soaked their garments. But, as the day wore on, the field turned golden in the soft light and a breeze stirred. The birds trilled in the thickets by the river. Grasshoppers chirred. Benito straightened, stretched, and thought, good work. Fodder for the cold season, for the animals. And, for hours, he'd forgotten his troubles with Paloma, hard labor leaching the anger from his pores.

When the wagon brimmed, he led the ox back down the trail to the barn and positioned the wagon below the door to the haymow. As he climbed into the bed Thompson came up beside the wagon.

"The field yields well," Thompson said.

"It does," Benito said.

"Rains must have fallen at opportune times," Thompson said.

"Must have," Benito said.

Thompson pointed off toward Benito's field and the irrigation ditch. "I appreciate your plan in case the rains don't come when needed."

Benito regarded Thompson. "*Sí*. We have a saying. Water is the blood of the land." And, after a moment, he added, "You've completed much in my absence."

"You laid out a good plan," Thompson said. "The crops not yet ripe, the grass wasn't ready to cradle. I had nothing better to bide my time."

"Still, I am in your debt," Benito said, uncomfortable with the notion.

"Your ditch filled idle time," Thompson repeated. He nodded toward the hay. "If you want to pitch it up, I'll work from inside."

For the next hour Benito tossed the fodder into the opening of the haymow while Thompson distributed it. When they were finished, Thompson climbed down from the loft. Bits of dried grass clung to his wet shirt and matted hair. They both went to the trough and drank deeply, sharing the ladle that hung from a peg on the well beam.

"I have to collect some goats and chickens Genoveva has been kind enough to watch after during my absence," Benito said.

Thompson glanced up at the sky. "A little of the day remains. I'll cut a while longer."

"Supper with us tonight?" Benito asked.

"You must be worn thin from your travels," Thompson said.

"It will be a simple meal," Benito said.

Thompson hesitated and then said, "Thank you, I will," and started toward the field.

In among John's livestock, Benito had grazed a handful of goats, one buck, the rest does. A dozen hens with his mark dyed on their crowns pecked and scratched among John's flock in the yard outside the coop. Already in this new land he had amassed greater wealth than he could have hoped for in New Mexico, although much of it through Genoveva's beneficence. Brood stock provided the beginnings and Benito's husbandry the increase. He left the chickens for the boys to collect in the morning, cut out his goats. His legs felt leaden, his body drained of energy, emotionally and physically, but he revived as the placita came into view. He turned the goats into the pen adjoining the outer wall and then stepped back and inspected anew his home.

He walked the outside perimeter, the three tall walls, the fourth partially built. He ran his hand along the textured surface of the adobe.
Solid, well constructed, he patted it as he might a favorite dog. He
entered the plaza through the opening he would soon door off and
stood beside the water trough and slowly turned a complete circle.
The cottonwood tree outside the partially completed wall cast a long
shadow upon the dirt of the square. The lines of the walls and the rooms
extending inward from them were smooth and round and pleasing to
the eye. Smoke rose from two chimney stacks, and he imagined Teresa
working at the hearth and the stranger at the other, preparing meals,
settling into the routine common to every time, every place. Teresa
had walked to their new home while Benito had been in the field and
already the smell of tortillas cooking drifted in the wood smoke. When
he entered their rooms, Teresa was bent over the cooking stone.

"It draws well?" Benito asked Teresa, pointing to the fireplace.

"Yes. Very well."

Benito looked about. The boys played with carved toys in the
corner, block wagons, a horse, figures Benito had fashioned from soft
pine last Christmas. His daughter was not present.

"Paloma?" Benito asked.

"In a state," Teresa said. "In the field. Down by the acequia. Pacing."

"And the others?" Benito asked. "The Anglos?"

"Hanna, she came over when we arrived," Teresa said. "With her
son, Joseph. She presented me with a tablecloth. Embroidered. Linen."
Teresa flipped the tortillas on the *comal* and stirred the beans in the
pot. "I like her."

"When is she due?"

"I don't know."

"You didn't ask?"

"She doesn't speak. Captain Upperdine explained."

"I thought, maybe."

"No." Teresa moved the pot to the table and Benito tested the seasoning with his finger. "But," Teresa continued, "she brought me her gift and she set about helping. Sweeping, replacing the mattress ticking, the things Paloma should be doing."

"Give her time," Benito said.

"Time is dear," Teresa replied, and removed the tortilla from the stone and added it to the others in the basket.

By evening, clouds had drifted in from the west and the low sun streaked them burnt orange. Benito watched the dark silhouette of Thompson coming across the field toward the placita and then detour to the river. Thompson's frame appeared stooped, belonging to an older body, a man who had been the better way through life and was contemplating folding back into himself. The work of the day over, he seemed to Benito to move hesitantly, as if unsure how to react to this time of repose.

A short while later Thompson entered the compound, his face ruddy and his hair damp from the river. Benito greeted him at the well.

"A pleasant evening. Shall we sit outside?"

Indeed the evening was pleasant, a cool breeze swirling in the plaza, but his purpose in asking had more to do with fear of his daughter's reaction to an American at the table than with agreeable weather.

Benito brought a small table and two ladderback chairs from inside, and they sat talking carefully, of weather and of crops, neither man comfortable yet with the other. Benito noted with approval that Thompson rose when Teresa brought their meal. While they exchanged pleasantries, he saw Paloma enter the compound and, keeping to the wall, make her way inside. The two men ate *machitos* of fried pork fat wrapped in Teresa's tortillas, and a thin stew of dried corn and beans reconstituted in a simmering broth of water spiced with crushed peppers from Benito's garden in New Mexico. The peppers from his own small garden here on the Purgatoire were not yet harvested and dried. Benito drew water from the well, cold and sharp with the taste of minerals, and as a homecoming toast poured a small portion of pear brandy brought in a wineskin from Plaza del Arroyo Seco. The brandy tasted of summer, a tart sweetness. They sat in the lavender dusk and ate, sopping the broth with tortillas. The chickens hunted insects left exposed in the dirt of the bare plaza. The burro ambled to the trough and watered. Later, Benito explained to Thompson, he would picket the burro with some fodder and keep the goats penned for a few days until accustomed to their home surroundings. He did not want the burro wandering onto the familiar trail or the goats straying back to Upperdine's larger herd.

"Much has gotten done, just this one day returned," Thompson said, pointing to the animals, to the tools stacked inside the lean-to, a colorful blanket strung out to dry. "It feels of a whole."

"The far wall needs completion, of course. Tomorrow I will start on a chicken coop." Then, thinking of Paloma, added, "And, if the weather holds, another room."

The brandy seemed to make both men drowsy. They sat in silence as the fading light attuned their hearing and accentuated the sounds that went unnoticed during the bustle of the day. Breeze stirring through shortgrass, the far-off gurgle of the river, the click and trill of night insects. Thompson slumped forward, elbows on knees, and went quiet. Benito wondered if he might have dozed off.

Suddenly, Alejandro and Benjamin bounded from the quarters and ran into Benito's outstretched arms. Thompson straightened and combed a hand through his hair and a light came to his eyes, it seemed to Benito.

"I can do a cartwheel," Benjamin said. "Do you want to watch?"

"They speak English?" Thompson asked. The boys had been quiet and shy during the noon meal, neither speaking above whispers.

"Yes," Benito said. "From their beginning, I knew where their future lay. Paloma as well, but she often refuses."

"I would like to see a cartwheel," Thompson said, smiling at Benjamin.

Benjamin stepped away from the table into the open plaza and arms and legs extended like spokes from the hub of his frame, spun vertically once, twice, before sprawling in the dirt, turning to Thompson, grinning proudly.

"Well done," Thompson said, and clapped his hands.

"Off to bed, now," Benito dismissed the boys with a wave. The men watched the boys run back into the house. They sat in the new quiet. Almost immediately, a darkness came over Thompson; he seemed to melt into the evening, became almost like a ghost. Had Benito been a superstitious man, he'd of thought to poke him, to test his substance, but he was not such a man, and soon Thompson seemed to come alive once again.

"I'd like to continue with the ditch," Thompson said.

Benito did not answer straightaway. What were this man's motives? Why was he attempting to indebt him? "The field is small. Enough for one man to work."

"I don't wish to share your field," Thompson said, evenly. "The ditch is a way to earn my keep. Until I decide where to go from here."

"You seem at ease farming. Why look further than this valley?"

"Different soil. Hard enough to break a plowshare," Thompson said. "I know about black loam, but not this. What might grow here? No water. All sun-baked and wind-blown. Another world, almost." He finished his brandy and stood and stretched. "Today, I felt good mowing. For the most part. I thought back only a few times." He shook his head as if clearing it of some unbidden memory. "But I don't know."

Benito stood with him. "Stay a while, then. Work in the fields and on the acequia if that is your wish."

They parted. Benito watched until Thompson blended into the darkness and then turned for his quarters. Paloma stood outside waiting for him by the door.

"Where do you expect me to sleep?" she asked.

Benito pointed to the adjacent room. "There."

"The boys are sleeping in there."

"Yes. You will share the room with them for now."

"You promised me my own quarters," Paloma said.

"Yes," Benito said, struggling for patience. "But temporarily you must share." He glanced toward the room occupied by Hanna Light and her son, Joseph.

"I refuse. I will not tolerate—" Paloma began.

"Enough," Benito said, his voice low and tired. "You will do as I say. I did promise you, but conditions have changed. I've agreed to host John Upperdine's guests, and you will honor my decision." He felt the blood pulsing. He hesitated, dizzy, and after pausing for a moment, added, coldly, "Carlos is not with you. You do not require a room of your own." Paloma recoiled as if Benito had struck her and spun on her heels and retreated into the room.

Benito remained outside, staring into the darkness, regretting his harsh words. He asked himself, do I deserve respect? What in my life commands it? My station? He walked the inner walls, absently counting, thirty strides square, and gradually he comprehended that the land under his feet was his land, the rooms his rooms, as well the walls, the livestock, and the field beyond, a minor kingdom. The realization brought him comfort, revived his optimism. He might actually set the course for his family, establish his heritage.

He retired to his rooms. Inside, Teresa slept. Heat still radiated from the hearth. The night had cooled and the warmth brought drowsy comfort. Weeks of travel had bowed him. He felt exhausted from the long day. But the warmth seeped into his bones like a soothing balm,

and before taking his place beside his wife of so many years, he went to
his provisions sack and retrieved three small candles and a hammered
copper cross mounted on a slab of sandstone. He arranged the pieces in
the corner of the room adjacent to the fireplace and lit the candles, and
then remembered the Santo. He reached into his bag and found the
carving of Saint Christopher, patron saint of emigrants. He held the
carving and thought back to the Plaza del Arroyo Seco the morning
of their departure. He'd led the burro to the north gate and tied the
rope to the post and entered the chapel while his family waited beside
the cart. Gypsum flakes had been added to the white plaster that
coated the inner walls of the chapel so that they sparkled wherever the
morning light flowed into the window and touched them. He walked
to the rail and knelt before the altar. Before him, on the lower shelf of
the altarpiece, were six *bultos*, one of which, St. Christopher, he alone
had carved from a cottonwood root. The statuette was crude, nothing
like the magic the itinerant *santeros* could achieve, but he'd gotten the
hands right, perhaps a bit out of proportion, large, but gracefully folded
in prayer at the saint's chest. And somehow, the eyes also, sorrowful and
expressive. And the green robe stood out pleasingly against the faded
red backdrop of the altar screen.

He made the sign of the cross and looked up. The image of the
Holy Mother returned his gaze from the top panel of the altarpiece.
Veiled in black, her head inclined slightly toward him in benediction.
Benito asked for her blessing over his family during their journey. He
stood and began to back away and then, on impulse, reached across
the rail and removed the figure of Saint Christopher from its shelf
fronting the altar screen.

Retreating down the aisle, he noticed that the old woman grand-
mother Melita had entered and taken a seat on the back-most bench,
veil covering her head, but her eyes were upraised and alert. She
watched as he approached. He saw her glance at the carving in his

hand, and then she looked into his eyes and he could not interpret whether her expression constituted a blessing or a curse. He laid his hand on her shoulder as he passed and exited the chapel and led his family from the plaza.

BENITO SET THE STATUE BESIDE the copper cross and knelt down before the icons and gave thanks for a safe journey and for finding Captain Upperdine and Genoveva healthy. He prayed for peace to descend upon his daughter and upon himself as well. He thought about the new people to the valley, the Anglos, but did not know what to pray for concerning them. So, instead, he asked for guidance, for the light of God to show the path forward. That he, Benito, his servant, might follow. He prayed for an easy yoke, a light burden.

At length he rose and went to the bed and eased onto the mattress beside Teresa. The ticking rustled under his weight and accepted him into its folds and all was quiet. Teresa stirred, and he could tell by her breathing that she had awakened.

"Your placita." Benito whispered.

"Yes," Teresa said.

"Do you like it?"

"It is a wonderful place. So much room."

"Is it a home?"

"Coming here," Teresa said. "Did you notice?"

"What?"

"For three days before we arrived we passed no plaza, no village, no houses at all. No one."

"But Genoveva is here. Paloma. The boys. The others."

"Yes, they are here."

"Is it enough?"

"Will others come? From our Plaza?"

"Yes, others will come, others will follow us."

"When?"

"Soon."

"Why? What is here for them, to draw them away from their history?"

"Land. Land is here, and a future for their children. They turn from their past to face their future. They must follow. They have no other hope."

They lay together, Benito wishing he could say something more to comfort his wife but knowing that there was little more to add. In time, the valley would come to feel like home to Teresa, he felt certain. As season passed into season, as the rhythm of life in a new country settled into their bones, the memory of old ways would fade into a soft nostalgia rather than the acute ache it now was. He forced himself to believe this.

Outside, night grew still, the animals bedded. The ever-constant wind moderated, a light, swooshing lament. Teresa's breathing evened, her body slackened into the ticking, and Benito relaxed into the warmth.

16

Thompson slept late the following morning. He was unused to waking to a lighted room, and for a moment felt exposed and self-conscious. He'd dreamed during the night, himself the proprietor of a fine placita, the rooms, the outbuildings, the fields, much grander than anything in the valley, finer than Benito's, finer than John Upperdine's, an expanse of field and grazing land. Full awake, he refused to dwell on his night visions even for a moment, but rose from his sleeping robes with resolve. After a breakfast of two cold biscuits and a ladle of water, he walked to Upperdine's, yoked a pair of oxen, hitched a wagon, and loaded a plow and additional harnessing. He led the team upriver, past the placita a half-mile over a small rise where he'd noticed a promising stretch of level ground tight against the river. He hoped spring run-offs would not wash it, but he could not imagine this land experiencing significant flooding. He rigged the plow to the team and began breaking a small patch. Only a few hours' sweat, but tough going, sod-busting. Low-growing grass with tangled roots pulled at the plow, frustrated his intention for straight rows. Still, the plow felt natural in his hands, the animals massive and plodding, the land yielding, if grudgingly. The furrows extended not more than seventy-five paces in length and half that in width, a large garden, really. Midday, Thompson already had the team unhitched.

"Preparing the soil for spring?" Benito asked, coming up beside him. Earlier, Thompson had seen Benito at work outside the placita, but had not stopped to visit. Benito must have noticed him as well and become curious of his intentions.

"No. I plan on sowing presently. An experiment," Thompson answered. "Obadiah Light, Hanna's husband, brought a strain of seed sent from the old country."

"The old country?" Benito asked.

Thompson retrieved a pouch from the wagon and showed Benito the wheat seed. "His vision, to plant out here. Russia wheat. Spread in the fall. Lies dormant, soaks up the winter snow, spring rain. Harvest before the heat of summer."

Benito examined the seed. Held it to the light. Bit it in two, tasted.

"Looks like any other wheat," he said. "Can we ask the land to work both summer and winter?"

Thompson stooped and picked up a clot of dirt the size of his fist.

"I don't know if anything will take in this soil, regardless of season." He attempted to crumble the clot but it fell from his hand in hard knots. "I checked Captain Upperdine's equipment. We lack a harrow."

"John is not by nature a farmer," Benito said. "Our tools are limited."

"But without a harrow—" Thompson started.

"There are ways," Benito interrupted. "We've a respectable crop in the field." Thompson noted irritation in Benito's voice.

Thompson had taken note of the corn, and already had raked the hay, the product of Benito's effort. He shrugged in acknowledgment.

"Leave the land set for a few days," Benito gestured to the newly broken field. "Glean the stones. Then drag it with a cottonwood log." He motioned with his arm. "Crossways to the furrows and finish down their length. Then cast your seed."

Thompson nodded. "Makes sense," and, after a pause, "thank you."

Benito helped Thompson load the plow into the wagon and they walked together as far as the placita.

"What made you decide to plant?" Benito asked as they parted. Thompson sensed that Benito had been mulling the question since inspecting the seed. Did Thompson weigh a future in this valley, seek to establish a foothold? Or, perhaps, to curry favor with Hanna Light? With Captain Upperdine?

"I felt I owed it to Obadiah Light," Thompson said. And what he said was true, as far as it went.

"Yes," Benito said.

They parted, Benito to work on his chicken coop, Thompson to return the wagon and fodder the oxen, an afternoon at the acequia, digging. Later, a thick slice of moon risen, Thompson retraced his steps to the low rise overlooking the wheat field. The moon cast the upturned soil into light and shadow, the furrows like a windswept pond. He'd thought to call on Hanna that evening to tell her of his plans with Obadiah's seeds, but did not. He'd been so protective of her and Joseph on the trail, felt such responsibility. But since she took residence in Benito's placita, he was content with his privacy. Unfair, perhaps to the Ibarra family to impose upon them, to have strangers within the walls of their compound, where, Thompson knew, Benito would feel accountable for them. Hanna, so fragile, and Joseph, as brooding and moody as Paloma. Perhaps they reminded him too much of his failings, perhaps he feared Hanna growing too dependent on him at a time he did not wish for closeness. Whatever the reason, Thompson valued the isolation of his cabin away from the rest.

He studied the field, listened to the silence of the night, and watched stars emerge from their dark womb, a rebirth each evening. He owed this field to Obadiah, yes. But something more, something Thompson could not fully articulate to himself and would never attempt to explain to anyone. At work on the land, he felt almost of a whole with it, the soil his substance, the seed his sustenance, the budding shoots his spirit. The emotions embarrassed him, made him feel somehow vulnerable.

17

Harvest upon them, almost before Benito thought possible. He'd finished the chicken coop, worked on a lean-to shed, and made sturdy the goat pen after his only buck and two of his does breached the rails and wandered along the river course until Benito finally had to give up a day tracking them down. They did not have many acres in crops, only him last spring to sow and to tend Captain Upperdine's trail stock. But a second section of grass needed cradling and the acres in corn stood ready. And, Genoveva's expansive garden. He'd hand-watered the garden and the corn that past spring before he'd left for Plaza del Arroyo Seco, hours trudging the cart from the river to the field, buckets brimming, empting, refilling, beginning of day to ending. There'd been little rain. But now, harvest called. He'd not yet finished the adobe, hadn't time to start a room for Paloma.

The women began putting up garden produce while the men finished the haying and began cutting and shocking the acres planted in corn. After drying in the field, Benito and Thompson gathered the shocks and stacked them beside Upperdine's storage bins and each evening after supper, weary, they all collected around the growing mountain of stalks to shuck and strip the corn by the dim wash of a lantern. The dried corn went into baskets and burlap sacks, stalks and husks were chopped and pitched into the wire and wood-slated storage bins to be used as fodder over winter. Cobs were saved for kindling. After just a single evening's work, they all suffered cramped hands and bloodied fingers.

Most evenings, Captain Upperdine easily tired of the labor and much preferred entertaining them with ditties sung by trappers and with yarns about the old days. He'd pace the yard, moving alternately within and beyond the reach of lantern light.

"I come out here with the freighters when I was no more growed than the boy here," Upperdine pointed to Joseph, who straightened and watched Upperdine intently. "Put on blustery airs so the others might think to take my measure, but mostly they just laughed. They brought me along because they needed a hand." Upperdine paced, and drank from the cup he seemed always to have in hand during evening hours. "Worked me into the routine from the get-go. Pulled night watch right off. Nobody needed to prod me awake. Every time the wind stirred, every titmouse moving through the grass was a grizzly or a prairie wolf or a savage. When I pulled early watch, I couldn't hardly calm back down until about daybreak, and when I pulled late watch, couldn't sleep at all beforehand. I was wore thin before even a week in the barrens."

"So one night, I stationed up, hunkered down, and the night was real warmish, and I dozed a little. But even in my sleep, things seemed too still, too calm, and I jerked awake. Not five paces away they'd come up out of the dark, five, six Red Men, moving among the livestock, selecting the best of the horses. They watched me take notice, kept their eyes on me as I stood, but didn't seem none too alarmed. I just stared at them, couldn't move a muscle. Tried to shoulder my musket, but it weighed a hundred pounds. Thought about the long knife in my belt but couldn't move. Stuck in place. Couldn't call out. No voice."

Upperdine drained his cup and the others continued with the work and waited while he searched for his jug. The night fell quiet for a while, the scratchy sound of brittle husks being pulled from ears and tossed onto the fodder heap. Then Upperdine returned and took up where he'd left off.

"It seemed they'd seen my sort before. They just watched me out of the side of their faces while they went about their business and then one of them motioned to another, hands moving all this way and that, and this savage edges close. I see that he is no older than me and the same fear showed in his eyes, except that he willed hisself forward. He's got his hand on the hilt of his knife and he's all jittery and dancing, and I can't move. He gets to within six feet or so and then he just leaps, like a deer clearing a log, and before I can even register it, he come up on me and taps me on the top of the head with his open hand and runs back to the others and they are all smiling at him. They pick up the leads of the horses they done cut out and start back through the field, and all a sudden a shot rings out over my right shoulder, so loud my ear goes numb and them Indians scatter into the dark."

Upperdine paused and looked off into the shadows and several sets of eyes involuntarily followed his gaze, searching for danger. "There was shots ringing out and men shouting and Indians giving up their spoils and running for their ponies and after all that chaos we ended up losing but a single horse. Only one. But enough that I worked the entire trip without pay to make up for it."

Benito watched Paloma to see if she might react to Upperdine's story, if her expression might show any hint of compassion for a young man put to the test and rendered immobile by fear. But if she was affected at all, she did not show it. She just continued with her work, as though not listening to the story at all.

"How come they didn't kill you outright?" Joseph asked Upperdine.

"I don't know," Upperdine said. "Thought about it over the years. Figure maybe I was just no proper test for them. No honor to be gained by putting me under." Upperdine chuckled and plopped down cross-legged beside Genoveva and the young boys and absently picked at an ear of corn.

Benito studied Joseph, how he had perked up considerably at John Upperdine's stories. Joseph was a boy just bursting to become a man, and Benito also noticed him displaying uncommon eagerness to join the work group in the evenings, sitting close by Paloma, shyly glancing from the corner of his eye, watching her hands at work, stripping the husks and shelling the kernels from the cob. Once, Benito watched Joseph attempt to engage Paloma in conversation, but she turned away with a dismissive gesture.

Most of the dried kernels would be used for *posole* and to grind into meal for the tortillas. But a portion Upperdine set aside to experiment with fermentation, having once sampled a local distillation in Taos and determined to duplicate it. Last year, his efforts resulted in a gut-churning concoction unfit for consumption, good only for sopping the hogs or for sale to the most desperate and thirsty of lowlifes passing by the new fort. But he claimed to be inching closer to that magic formula, that this year his confidence was high. Genoveva scolded his wastefulness, but did not begrudge his folly.

Benito silently questioned Genoveva's generosity with the corn. The field yielded fairly, but this winter there would be additional mouths to feed. He'd worked to exhaustion the previous spring putting as many acres as possible into production, planning on his family's arrival. The unexpected presence of Thompson and the Lights imposed an additional burden on the stores. Benito had discretely raised the issue with Upperdine, who had dismissed his concerns.

"Thompson will bring in meat," Upperdine had said. "If our grain runs short, he'll make up for it with game."

"Grain keeps through the winter," Benito had countered. "Meat can spoil."

MORNING OF THEIR THIRD DAY hauling corn from the field, Benito stood at the end of a row, stretched the muscles of his lower back, and assessed the dwindling number of shocks. They should have the remaining corn loaded by day's end, forenoon tomorrow at the latest. Another few evenings of husking, and the storage bins would be full. More than a decent yield, he thought. He removed his hat and mopped his head. The humidity had come up during the day and he noticed a dark cloud on the horizon. He hoped rain would hold off until the crop was safely stored. He studied the sky for an answer. The cloud seemed to undulate, to change shape before his eyes, to grow and shrink, darken in mass, a dense ball, and then lighten and thin out. He heard a horse advancing and saw Captain Upperdine galloping toward them. Thompson and Joseph came from their wagon and walked to Benito and stood beside his cart waiting for Upperdine.

"Gather in the corn, boys," Upperdine called from his horse as he drew near. "Stack as high and as fast as you can."

Benito and Thompson looked at one another in confusion and then at Upperdine, unsure how to respond.

"That's what we're fixed on," Thompson finally answered.

"Hurry. We have two hours at most," Upperdine shouted, pointing to the west.

"Grasshoppers."

The three regarded the cloud with a grim comprehension.

"Son of a bitch," Thompson said.

Speechless, Benito watched the swarm for a moment longer before leading the burro at a run toward the next row of shocks. He called to Upperdine over his shoulder, "Have the women collect what's remaining in the garden."

Within a half-hour, sweat-drenched, Thompson, Benito, and Joseph delivered full loads to Upperdine's barn loft. Hay and other fodder occupied normal capacity, but they stacked corn to the ceiling and when they could wedge not another stalk, they began tossing shocks onto the barn floor, leaving Joseph and the young boys to stack it. The women saw to the garden, hauling in under-ripe melons and pumpkins, pulling bush beans and pepper plants up by the root, throwing everything they could gather into the house.

With each trip to the field, the swarm advanced. Benito calculated the remaining minutes, urged his strength-drained legs forward, palsied with fatigue, down the rows. He filled his cart and ran the burro to the placita and, after unloading, he and Teresa took a few minutes to chase the goats from the pen. He was unsure how the grasshoppers might harass his animals but wanted to give them opportunity to seek what relief the low hills might offer. He covered the well with a tarp and weighted the tarp with stones and hoped Upperdine thought to do the same. Arriving back in the field, he continued gathering shocks. His back ached. His shoulders and arms as well. Dizzy with fatigue, his ears buzzed. He stood for a moment to regain equilibrium, to catch his breath. His dizziness abated but the buzzing intensified. He shook his head and looked up. The cloud loomed, the air vibrating with the whirling onslaught. Benito threw bundles of corn stalks haphazardly onto the cart. Deafening, the high-pitched din coalesced into a single voice as the swarm advanced low overhead, fully blotting the sun, casting an ominous twilight over the land. His cart half-full, Benito turned for the placita as the first insects alighted.

They spent that night trying to sleep in shifts but not sleeping, really, listening to the hum outside and inside, to the pop of grasshoppers dropping from the chimney vent into the fire that Benito had stoked. He, Teresa, Paloma, and Hanna occupied the placita. Thompson and the boys remained at the main house with the Upperdines. Teresa had pleaded with Benito to retrieve the boys, but he thought they would be frightened by the insects. On his arrival earlier from the field, grasshoppers had fallen from the sky like hail, pelting him and amassing on his hat, eating through the sweat-soaked brim until it literally fell from his head. By the time he had reached the compound, his shoes were caked with the crushed bodies of insects and a stench rose up from the ground where they stacked like cordwood against the walls and over-flowed the trough. No, leave the boys with Captain Upperdine and Genoveva, he'd told Teresa, and she glared at him in silent assent, accusing, as if it were through some sin of his that the plague had been visited upon them.

Sometime around midnight, grasshoppers chewed through the window coverings and began flowing into the room, swarming over the tortilla basket. The women pounded them with brooms while Benito shuttered the window with planks.

Morning, the wind that normally rose with the sun remained still. Benito lay on his bed listening to the sound from outside, the incessant clicking of mandibles as grasshoppers in numbers uncountable moved about the placita and beyond, stripping the valley of the Purgatoire. No one had slept. Eyes focused on the roof beam, Benito tried to find reason for hope. Apart from sore muscles, a few cuts and scrapes, no one had been injured in their rush to salvage what they could of the harvest. As far as he knew, the pests were not harmful to the animals, carried no disease. They inflicted no permanent damage to the soil or to the grasslands; they could not stop the river from flowing, the sun from shining. No, they could have been visited by far worse a curse. Had the locusts arrived a month earlier, the crop too green to pick, nothing could have been saved. Yet, still, in the core of his feeling, he could not help but question whether the insects had been some kind of theological judgment on his emigration from the Plaza, a foretaste of trials to come. He could not allow himself to dwell on such thoughts. He rose and went out into the morning.

Everywhere, insects crawled, carpeting the enclosed compound a half-foot deep. His chickens moved among and over them, pecking, gorging. He inspected his storage shed, found the door held firm and he confirmed that for the most part what he had been able to cram inside remained unmolested. But outside, the hay bin sat empty, not a blade remaining of what had been left unprotected; and beside the bin, a pitchfork rested on the fence, its handle gnawed to the iron shaft by the grasshoppers attracted to the sweat-infused wood. His boots crunched as he walked across the placita, insects popping. Teresa and Paloma came to the door and watched with unbelieving eyes the scene before them. Paloma had left a lace shawl hanging to dry from the line and, scanning the courtyard, she looked at it now in horror. She marched across the courtyard and pulled the shawl from the line in tatters, shook off the grasshoppers, ran to her father, slipped and almost fell in the squash of insects. She held the rag to Benito's face, screaming, crying "Look. See what you've done?"

The fields denuded, the hillsides reduced to stubble, Benito crossed a naked, desolate landscape on his way to the Upperdine house to collect his boys. Birds everywhere, a feast. In his field, a coyote brazenly grazed on the grasshoppers, casually glancing up as he passed within three yards, its stomach distended, unable to flee even had it wished to. Benito inventoried the damage as he walked, an uncomplicated assessment. Nothing remained in the field.

MIDMORNING THREE DAYS FOLLOWING THEIR arrival, the locusts rose in a mass, hung like a low mist over the valley, and drifted southeast with the prevailing wind. Dead grasshoppers crushed under the feeding swarms littered the countryside, rotting in the sun. Birds, raccoons, skunks, all came into the fields day and night, but they could not eat fast enough and a great stench rose from the ground. Benito shoveled three cartloads of the insects from his courtyard and buried them in trenches he'd dug along the rows of his fruit trees. The trees, barren of leaves and fruit, gave the orchard the feel of midwinter. Benito prayed the trees would recover, and he fertilized with the remains of their tormenters.

Afterwards, Benito's chickens laid eggs with red yokes that smelled of the insects on which they had gorged, and the two boys and Paloma gagged the first time they tried to eat one. But Benito knew hard times were ahead and he refused to waste the eggs, so Teresa experimented with pepper flakes, goat cheese, anything to make them palatable.

Over the course of another few days, they cleared the areas surrounding their living quarters and the winds carried off the stink. Benito and Thompson retrieved the salvaged corn from indoors and they all resumed the work of preparing it for grinding. They toiled in grim silence, the adults among them fully aware of their lack. They'd all endured hungry winters, times of famine and scarcity, and the possibility again loomed on the horizon, dark and foreboding as the locust swarm. Grasshoppers had found their way into Upperdine's storage shed through knotholes in the planks and from beneath the ill-fitted door. Several bags of grain had been lost before Thompson noticed the incursion and plugged the entrances. On final tally, Benito calculated they had saved perhaps one-half of the harvest. Bitterly, he thought of his labor that past spring. While Upperdine had been on the trail, he'd worked to exhaustion, sowing more acres than he thought possible for one man. And now, half lost to pests. He'd brought his family, his young boys north for this? On the Plaza del Arroyo Seco, in times of trial, the community would have come together as one to pool their foodstuffs, suffer and survive together. No one would have greeted summer with fat on their bones. But the Americans he knew little about. Genoveva, he trusted and loved. John he respected. The others? Who knew how they would react to hardship?

Teresa understood Benito's worries, intuition and years of marriage conspired against his intent to keep private thoughts private. When they had completed the harvest, when they had surveyed the bags of meal, the sacks of dried pumpkin and squash they'd wrestled from the grasshoppers, calculated the dressed-out weight of the hogs and the ox they would fatten for slaughter, with what no one had a clue, when Benito and Teresa had returned home and slumped onto the porch step, discouraged and disillusioned, she put the question to him.

"Perhaps," she paused, and continued, "perhaps best to return home. Maybe try again next year."

Benito bristled. Home, she'd called it. After all his work to build the placita, it stung that she still considered the Plaza home. And he hated to hear spoken the thoughts he'd been silently debating.

"It is not possible. No."

"You spoke before even thinking through what I've suggested," Teresa said.

That was inaccurate. Benito had been mulling the option since the first grasshopper dropped onto the brim of his hat. But hearing Teresa proclaiming the Plaza "home" had set his mind. If they sought winter refuge in the Plaza, they would never return. One branch on the pear tree. How does one branch divide between two boys? Or, should

Paloma never marry, two boys and one daughter? Here? Chickens, goats, good water, three rooms and more to build. A field, a garden. Return to his one branch on the pear tree?

"Never," Benito repeated, more to himself than to Teresa. "I will be buried here, on this land."

18

They met at Upperdine's the following week to decide how the harvest would be split. After an early supper, light, just a thin soup and tortillas, as if already training their stomachs for shortage, Captain Upperdine stood and leaned heavily against the table.

"We'll require rationing," Upperdine said, a foregone and obvious conclusion to Benito. But the Captain had assumed the role of trailmaster in time of crisis, so Benito knew enough to not interrupt.

"Way I see it," Upperdine continued, "only fair way is to split it up according to bodies. Now, the two young ones we'll count as one full growed man, so that means Benito gets a four-tenths share, two tenths for me and Genoveva, one tenth to Thompson." Upperdine paused to glance at Hanna, her swollen belly. "Two and a half to the Lights and the final one-half to next spring's seeding."

Finished, Upperdine looked from Benito to Thompson for approval. Benito remained silent, staring into his folded hands. The Ibarra family would take its allotment and make do.

"I don't require a full share," Thompson said.

"That won't hardly do," Upperdine said.

"I won't starve," Thompson answered evenly. "Next spring, we have the Ibarra acreage as well as yours to put into production. We need additional seed corn."

Thompson's tone was matter of fact, rational, and to Benito's ear perfectly logical. The man thought like a farmer, and Benito considered Thompson's foresight a virtue, but he also saw in his selfless gesture a certain ambition for the future that put Benito ill at ease. *We need seed corn,* he'd said. What were Thompson's plans? What were his deepest desires? Was he even conscious of them?

"It's settled, then," Upperdine said. They rose from the table and the women, who had not spoken during the meeting, cleared dishes and later followed the men out onto the porch, the collective mood subdued, and listened to the distant chatter of insects, and other night songs, a bird calling, the high-pitched grunting of a frog. Benito thought how pleasant these familiar sounds compared to the terrible clicking of the locusts. Teresa began humming a slow, melodic tune, a lullaby, soothing and a little sad.

Hanna smiled and swayed gently, and massaged her stomach. Her eyes wandered from the porch and she pointed to the bare shadow of a shrub, leaves stripped by the grasshoppers. There, a chicken egg in the tangle of low branches, and she stepped from the porch and bent to retrieve it and stood abruptly, dropping the egg, splattering it. She turned toward Genoveva. Hanna nodded to her, and Genoveva went to Teresa and whispered something and the two women led Hanna away, toward the placita. At the edge of the lamplight, Teresa turned and motioned to Paloma.

"Come, you can be of help as well."

Paloma looked with apprehension at her mother but rose and followed them into the night. Benito, too, had noticed the communication and accompanied them back to the placita, and drew water for them to heat, and collected clean rags. He set the rag bundle and one final bucket of water just outside the door where the women could retrieve them when the time came. With his thumb he made the sign of the cross above the lintel and then he rejoined Thompson and Upperdine and the others, who were completely oblivious to the pending delivery. When informed by Benito, Thompson jumped to his feet and started for the placita.

"Where do you hurry?" Benito called into the dark. "These things take time."

Benito roomed his sons in with Captain Upperdine. On the porch, he found Joseph still sitting, back against the wall, legs extended out, hat pulled down over his eyes.

"Coming?" Benito asked.

Joseph at first ignored him, but when Benito did not leave, he lifted his brim to look out at Benito with one eye. "I'll just make do here."

At the placita, Benito built a small fire beside the well and sat close beside it. Sometime late, the door of Hanna's quarters opened and Paloma took up the last of the water. From inside came inhuman sounds: deep, extended lowing; sharp keening; breathing like the snorting of a bull. Benito watched Thompson grow more agitated as time passed. He paced the courtyard, and as the moaning increased in volume, his pace quickened until he broke into a trot around the perimeter of the three standing walls, finally vaulting the partial outer wall out into the night and then back into the compound, lap after lap until, finally breathless, he slumped down beside Benito.

Benito remained perched on the edge of the water trough, whittling. The shavings accumulated at his feet. He thought about the demands of birthing. A difficult undertaking. After Paloma, he had not desired additional children, had not wished additional trials for Teresa. Benito was the fifth male of his father's seed, the first three born by his mother's sister. She had given birth to his brothers in the old way, her wrists bound with a leather strap hung across the roof timber. She pulled up as the contractions came, pulling, pushing, pulling, pushing. After her third son, the bleeding would not stop. She lay in bed, blood soaking through the mattress stuffed with corn husks, dripping onto the dirt floor beneath. After two days, drained white, she died. His fourth brother and he were the products of his father's new wife, the younger sister of his first. Time and again, growing up, he observed what childbearing demanded of a woman, the trade, how a small spark of life passed from the mother to each child she bore until, sooner or later, her inner flame seemed to dim and grow cold.

A few sharp cries sounded from the women's quarters, and with the frail light of morning a baby's yelp, sputtering at first, growing into a plaintive wail before softening. And so, Benito thought, an infant comes into the frontier. Thompson and Benito approached the door of the birthing room and heard Teresa's soothing reassurances and a baby's gurgle. Paloma came to the door and reported that all was well and asked for fresh water.

Benito brought the water and the men fell to chores, Thompson to attend the stock while Benito made coffee and stoked the fire in their quarters and heated broth in the kettle. He carried three cups of coffee and a cup of broth on an earthenware platter to Hanna's room and tapped on the door with the toe of his boot. Teresa answered, looking at once both weary and buoyed.

"You remembered the *atole*. Good." Earlier in the week, Teresa had made a batch of the cornmeal drink for Hanna to soothe her spirit and to fortify her following childbirth.

"She's endured a difficult night."

"All is well?"

"*Sí*. The niña has taken to the breast and the mother produces."

"The niña?"

"*Si*, a girl child."

"When may we welcome her?"

"They are both resting. This afternoon, perhaps."

Teresa took the platter from him and motioned for him to wait. She returned with a bundle double-wrapped in a flour sack. Benito accepted the flaccid package and took his pick ax and went up into the breaks above the floodplain and scarred the hardpan as deeply as he could and buried the afterbirth.

The men returned near sundown, John Upperdine leading the others, young Benjamin and Alejandro lagging shyly behind. They entered the room and found Hanna sitting in bed with the child asleep at her breast. The men huddled awkwardly near the door until Thompson came close to Hanna and looked down at the baby, nodded, touched the baby's cheek and backed away, head bowed as if in prayer.

Teresa had kept the fireplace fed and the room felt hot and stuffy, and Benito noted a dull odor suggesting decay. Hanna, although drawn, looked serene, and the baby had good color. The men inched forward and stood timidly talking in whispers.

"She's small," Alejandro said.

"I seen catfish bigger," Upperdine agreed.

Hanna noticed Joseph come into the room and motioned to him and he approached the bed and appraised the baby impassively. The infant, still asleep, began working her mouth in suckle.

"What's her name?" Benito asked. The others regarded him blankly. He moved beside Hanna and took her hand in both of his, cradling it like a chick, and looked into her eyes.

"The mother names her child," he said. "Mrs. Light?" All silent, waiting. Benito's adjuration hung in the air, Hanna's muteness becoming almost a physical presence in the room with them.

"Destiny," Hanna spoke at last, her voice raspy from disuse, and weak. Then, again, more forcefully, "Her name is Destiny Light."

"So it is," Benito said and backed away as the others gathered around Hanna and repeated Destiny's name, laying hands on her and remarking on her beauty. Benito, from the corner, noticed Joseph edge from the bed toward the door and ease out into the dusk.

19

Thompson worked together with Benito into autumn. They grubbed additional land by the river for plowing the following spring. They dug potatoes that had been spared despite locusts having eaten the leafy plant above ground. They walked the river and upstream several miles, unmolested by the insect swarm, they discovered a thicket of plum trees, heavy with fruit. They chinked Thompson's shack against the elements. A growing urgency pressed them throughout shortening days.

Thompson accompanied Benito up into the rises to collect dirt for adobe bricks. The right dirt, Benito explained. Too much sand or too much clay and bricks would not cure. They scraped the crest of ancient hills, dirt that had absorbed the memories of ancient worlds; such dirt would make adobe that harbored secrets from the past, Benito said, wisdom of the earth.

Time grew dear, temperatures dropped, a chilling time that soon would signal a close to the season for brick-making. Deep frost tinged grasses bronze and red.

"Best not to lay adobe after November," Benito instructed Thompson. Outside the placita, they dug a pit and sifted the dirt through wire mesh. "Discard any rock larger than a musket ball," he commanded. They mixed earth with water and rolled their pants up over their knees and went down into the pit and stomped the dirt into a thick mud and then added a bit of mulched straw. The young boys scrambled to help.

They packed the mud into wooden forms and turned them out to dry flat for three days and after set them on edge for three days more, Benito praying for heat from an autumnal sun growing more fickle. Bricks in the Mexico style: four inches thick, ten inches wide, fourteen inches long, thirty pounds each.

Warmth held, and the bricks cured.

"I think we'll make do," Benito said one day. He ran his hand over a brick they'd just finished turning from the rack. "An abundance. Enough both to wall off the placita and build Paloma a room of her own."

Thompson looked forward to learning how bricks would be laid and cemented in place. He marveled that such simple elements could be put to such use. Except that, when he and Benito began work on the wall, every other brick crumbled in their hands or cracked under its own weight when they picked it from the stack.

"Something is wrong," Benito said.

"I'd guess as much," observed Thompson, dryly. "You said they looked ripe the other day."

"Yes."

"So?"

"I don't know. Different slant to the sun here. Colder nights. Perhaps not all the bricks were properly mixed."

"I followed your instructions," Thompson said, stung by the accusation.

"Foreign soil," Benito said, perhaps to himself. He seemed distracted. "Last summer, they all cured perfectly. Earlier in the season. Who knows?" They surveyed the broken and worthless bricks with disgust. Wasted labor, lost time.

Thompson realized Benito too had much to learn about this new country. Lessons remained, an insight that concerned him greatly. With the loss of crops, the coming winter months, margin for error shrunk. They could ill afford misjudgment. He watched Benito carefully inspect the bricks, set aside the properly cured, tally the results. As the rubble pile grew, Thompson watched Benito's face harden, his priority crystallizing. He needed the final wall to protect his chickens from predators and his goats against weather when it turned ugly. Thompson sensed Benito's hopes for a peaceful coexistence with his daughter during the closed winter months crumbling with the bricks.

In following days, Benito concentrated on the wall while Thompson, more keenly interested in preparing land for spring, returned to the acequia, working on the secondary ditches before the ground froze. Joseph sometimes joined one or the other, swinging a pickax or splitting firewood. He lacked enthusiasm. More often, unannounced, he went off by himself, following the Purgatoire upstream or down, or, borrowing one of Upperdine's horses, riding into the plains. Joseph took to horseback naturally and had developed in just a few months into a graceful rider. Thompson thought perhaps the freedom allowed from riding eased Joseph's restlessness but also may have served as an outlet for his unfocused anger. The jarring pace, the pounding hooves, a release.

Autumn remained mild; the weather held. They worked through days of crystal blue, the sifted light and migrating clouds shading the prairie first brown, then rust and ocher. They remained at work long as they could each day, until darkness and hunger drove them from the field. They ate, famished. Occasionally, Genoveva insisted on their company during the evening meal. As autumn deepened, John Upperdine, like Joseph, had grown more restless, spending days afield, at Bent's Fort or at one or another Indian encampment trading, visiting, passing news and gossip. So occasionally, although Genoveva understood the pull of the season, the short time before endless nights and frozen days overtook them, she desired their company. At those times, Thompson might take his rifle and walk the riverbank and return with a jackrabbit or a brace of mallards they roasted over the outside fire pit. They buried onions in coals to bake. Afterwards, they visited until drowsiness overcame them.

The final wall rose slowly and once enclosed, the placita looked fully complete. Adobe made from the valley of the Purgatoire held less red in its pigment and more yellow than that of their ancestral lands, Benito explained to Thompson. But still it pleased the eye, a soothing, soft shade. Walls rising from earth, rooms flowing from walls, a claim for permanence. A number of bricks remained after the last wall went up, but insufficient in quantity for Paloma's room. With the help of Thompson and Joseph, Benito carried the bricks outside to the southfacing wall. With his spade, Benito traced a semi-circle in the dirt radiating perhaps fifteen feet from the wall. He began digging a shallow trench following his outline.

"I'll collect a shovel and help," Thompson said, starting back toward the gate.

"No," Benito said. "It is not necessary. I'd prefer to work alone."

"What are you building?" Thompson asked.

"*Un santuario*," Benito said, and at Thompson's expression added, "a chapel." He was able to finish the trench and lay foundation bricks and two additional rows before exhausting the remaining supply.

WEATHER FINALLY TURNED, COLD WINDS from the north stripped the trees, the grass turned brittle. They began collectively storing away

for winter. They picked apache plums from the thicket they'd discovered, and also sand cherries. Hanna especially enjoyed walking
the riverbank and side ditches, Destiny slung to her hip with a
serape tied over one shoulder. The women boiled the fruit into
glue-like paste, passed the mixture through a sieve, and poured a
thin coating of the liquid onto large platters which they slow-dried
beside the fire until the fruit looked and felt like the cured hides
of some small prairie animal. They strung the flat wafers on wire
and hung them from rafters to be reconstituted in boiling water
during winter. The few squash saved from grasshoppers they sliced
lengthwise and draped from tree branches to dry. They picked
hazelnuts and black walnuts and stored them in seed sacks hung
from the roof beams as well, away from mice and squirrels. Benito
took the burro into high desert to the west and collected prickly
pear and baskets of sage leaves.

Twice, Thompson traveled with Benito into the foothills of the
Mexican Mountains to collect firewood. They hitched a team of
oxen to one of John's open-bedded trade wagons and cut deadfall:
piñon, soft pine, and juniper. The first time out, while they were
still in the open plains, just west of the junction of the Arkansas and
Purgatoire rivers, Benito guided Thompson to a small rise known as
Sierra Vista and from there offered him his first sight of the Spanish
Peaks, three days distant, rising from the earth, jagged and tipped
in white like the canines of a fearful beast.

"I hardly know what to make of it," Thompson said. The green of
pine-covered slopes, the snow, overwhelming to him after months
on the prairie.

"*Si*. God's imagination is limitless, is it not?"

Thompson did not know how to respond. A permanency of sky
and rock contrasted with the transience of flesh, the capriciousness
of death, all so magnified in this place.

Nights cooled. A film of ice appeared in the water trough more mornings than not. Following several days of hard frost, they butchered an ox and two hogs that Upperdine had been fattening with mash remaining from his experiment with whiskey making. Beginning with the ox, over the course of three days, in turn each animal was tied to a short rope and brought low with a strike to the forehead from the flat edge of an ax. Upperdine took pride in his ability to dispatch his animals with a single blow. They flensed the ox and hung the carcass from the thick lower branch of a cottonwood to bleed out. Propping open the inner cavity by inserting a fencepost between its hind quarters, they then removed the innards, the liver and heart, the tripe and sweetbreads. Once the ox carcass was lowered for processing, John used a saw to remove the head. He knocked off the horns and tied a flap of skin around the neck to keep dirt and flies from soiling the meat. The hogs, once bled, were scalded with hot water to soften the bristles so they could be scraped off. They collected pails of lard and another bucket of organ meats. The quartered ox along with its severed head, the hams and pork slabs were hung for curing and freezing in the cold shed dug into the side of a low hill.

The opening of the animals, the scalding of the hogs, the waste offal, the smell of animal fear and excrement all created a distinctly rank and distasteful odor during the time of butchering. Blood saturated the ground beneath the cottonwood on which they hung the animals. Bits of gristle and bone lay scattered about, and each morning they found tracks of plains carnivores circling the tree: wolves, coyotes, fox, and, on the last day, a grizzly bear.

"I should a expected the bear," John complained. "I'd a sat up waiting for him. Nothing like bear grease to keep you stout and healthy during the winter."

THE MORNING FOLLOWING THE LAST of the butchering, others began arriving at Upperdine's homestead. Alone, in pairs, they came from the north, from the Arkansas ford, and set camp in the near pasture. Traders from Bent's Fort and trappers dressed in animal skins and fur-trimmed hats. Midday, a small band of Indians crossed the Purgatoire from the east, Arapahoe and Cheyenne, the tribe Upperdine had married into so many years earlier. Tepees went up along the stream bank. Captain Upperdine greeted each group as they arrived and later he and Genoveva walked between camps, visiting, offering a taste of brandy, some tobacco. Thompson declined their invitation to join them, instead working on the acequia through the day, the ground not yet hard frozen, and the secondary ditches all but complete. Since the birth of Hanna's child, memories had resurfaced, his boys at Rachel's breast; the way a child's presence filled a room. Whenever he could, he worked alone. But he was also curious about Upperdine's guests.

After noon, Thompson met Benito at the placita and together they walked toward the encampment.

"What occasion do they celebrate?" Thompson asked.

"Harvest, the coming hibernation, the making of meat."

"How did they know to gather here?"

"They know. Somehow word gets around that John wishes to share in his good fortune, his bounty, and those who are able come to feast, to talk, to reminisce. A rendezvous."

"There is little to celebrate, this harvest," Thompson said. "What is it we plan on sharing with these folks?"

"The soft meat, whatever won't keep," Benito said.

Later that afternoon Upperdine called for Benito and Thompson to fetch the ox head from the cold shed. They loaded the head onto a handcart and wheeled it to the pasture where Upperdine had supervised the digging of a large pit in which he had built a fire. The men stood around the fire, watching the wood burn down until John signaled and Benito shoveled out the coals and Upperdine and Thompson lowered the steer

head into the pit and covered it with several inches of dirt. They lit a
large fire over it and hung a kettle on a tripod and boiled the innards
from the butchered animals. The heart, liver, and kidneys went into
skillets to fry over smaller side fires. The Indians kept off to themselves,
but John divided time between the two groups with equal hospitality.
The white men sat on their haunches telling stories of the past and
speculating on the future and cutting lengths of intestines from the
pot with their long knives. One trapper, Ezekiel Pence, had come west
from Kentucky in '28. Grizzled, scraggly-bearded, he'd known John
Upperdine in the old days, and he told stories in snatches.

"Rode down the Green River in a bullboat, faster than any horse
could run," Ezekiel told them. "High in the mountains, snow deeper
than a full-growed elk. Run into Ute bucks wearing strings of seashells
around their necks. Seashells."

"Snow that deep?" Thompson asked.

"Had to hole up in a lean-to for the better part of winter. Like a
bear. Couldn't move, lived on beaver plew."

"Pelt? You ate the pelt?" someone asked.

"Boiled in water, a little flavor leached into the water and I gnawed
the skin. Imagine. Plews going for three dollars. I'm masticating away
my fortune."

They toasted Ezekiel Pence's lost wealth.

"Them days gone forever," Pence lamented. "No beaver, no market.
Now, it's buffalo they favor. Have to go east, into the flatlands. But
I don't set much with barrens once mountains got to my blood. I'm
quit of it."

"If it's mountain life you crave," one of the traders broke in, "you
may still have a future. Gold. Trail's thick with prospectors. Most
of them green, poor fitted, and full of bluster." The trader cut a slice
of beef kidney and offered it to Upperdine with the tip of his knife.
"Saint Louis papers say there is not a doubt but that riches await for

the claiming. They say a man with experience, a man what knows the mountains, fortune is his for the price of a pick and a shovel. I aim to see about it."

Upperdine chewed the kidney and shook his head. "It's seldom anything comes free and easy." He pointed toward the tepees near the grove of cottonwood by the river. "Arapahoe say white men are setting up diggings over their winter camping grounds. On the Platte, near where it joins Cherry Creek. They know what gold is, know the white man values it, and say there is little to be found there. They laugh at the whites who've arrived. Most have no buffalo robes for winter and the few that have horses don't guard them well."

"Disclaiming the presence of gold would serve their purpose," one of the traders said.

"They worry about having their grounds overrun. I see no good to come of any of this," Upperdine said.

"Still, the tide of emigrants flows, and no savage can stem it."

They talked on, eating and drinking as night fell and a chill set in. The fire died down and they banked it and sat a while longer. John intended to keep hot embers over the pit that entombed the steer head until the following day. Finally Thompson rose and stretched and backed away from the coals. Benito followed and they walked to the placita in the dim light of the waning moon. They passed the Indian camp and Benito raised a hand to an old man squatting by the fire and the old man raised a hand in return.

"Indians are nomads, best I can tell," Thompson said. "I don't see how they get a notion that they own camping ground along the Platte."

"They have no notion of owning land," Benito said. "But, they claim rights over hunting territories."

"I don't understand how a man could not wish to own land," Thompson said.

"You've stated you have no wish," Benito said.

"I have a wish, but no right, and little means," Thompson said. "But here, there is such abundance it makes me reconsider, some days."

"I see no sin in coveting land if for honorable intent," Benito said.

"And what do you consider honorable?"

"For family, for livelihood. Not for power. Not for empire."

Thompson left Benito at the placita gate and went to his shack on the bluff. From his overlook, he watched the fires glow along the streamside and from the meadow. Captain Upperdine seemed energized with the company. Even Benito and Genoveva appeared to relish visitors from outside the valley, fresh news and different faces. But Thompson felt no curiosity about the world outside his range of vision, no need for companionship. The field below seemed uncomfortably crowded. He turned from it and looked out into the black night.

Forenoon the following day, Thompson rejoined the meadow assemblage. The Indians were there among the white men, and relations seemed guardedly cordial. They'd gathered to unearth the ox head and determine the merit of Captain Upperdine's handiwork. John directed the exhumation. The head came out of the pit looking like a great charred gargoyle, clouded eyes staring accusingly.

"Captain, I believe you've created a monster," one of the mountain men gibed.

"There's beauty below the surface," Upperdine said. "Wait and see."

Upperdine untied the flap of skin at the neck and slit it toward the head, exposing roasted meat so tender it barely hung from the bones. He pulled the meat from the neck and cheeks with tongs and piled it high on a large serving board and he removed the tongue and sliced it into thin strips. They passed the board and sampled the meat and ate and talked as the morning wore on. Noon passed, the light weakened, and clouds crept in from the northwest, bringing flurries. They stoked the fire and pulled buffalo robes around their shoulders and continued to eat and to talk and to smoke. Thompson grew impatient with the idleness and excused himself from the gathering. Benito stood and together they walked out into Benito's field. The acequia complete, Benito demonstrated the workings of the floodgate and, as they walked the length of the ditch, how to cut the water into the field with a spade once the rows had been furrowed and the seed cast. There was not sufficient flow in the stream to actually irrigate his field, and the time was not right, but Benito wished to give Thompson some initial instruction.

"Over the winter, the acequia will collect debris. It must be cleared before we irrigate. And early spring grass burned off."

"I can handle that," Thompson said.

They continued together to the placita and sat under the overhang outside the living quarters as the day ebbed. Snow fell through a luminescent sky, thin clouds, unsubstantial, lighted from above by the rising moon. Thompson extended his arm past the shelter of the eaves and watched as the flakes melted on his open palm.

"They say rain follows the plow," Thompson said. "I believe no such thing."

"Makes a good story," Benito said. "If only it were true that plowing disturbs the balance between earth and sky so that rain followed."

"Speculators luring folks from the east with promises of easy cultivation," Thompson said.

"*Si*, I believe so."

"They are bound for disappointment."

"Yes."

"You know this land," Thompson said. "What will take, what won't. How much a chunk to carve out for crops. You've set out your boundaries."

"*The lines are fallen unto me in pleasant places*," Benito said, remembering a line from his Book.

"Psalm sixteen," Thompson said.

Thompson had spoken so softly Benito asked him to repeat what he'd said. Thompson was unaware he'd spoken aloud.

"You remember your scripture," Benito said.

"My father," Thompson said. "An Anglican priest."

"Ah, yes."

"I was wondering," Thompson said, "the irrigation ditch. You have planned for fifteen acres. They will produce well, I predict." Thompson rose and began pacing under the eaves. "But if for fifteen, why not for thirty? Sixty? A full section? There's more bottomland that can benefit from the irrigation scheme."

"And who would dig the acequias? Who would work those acres?"

"Well," Thompson paused, forming his thoughts. "Men. Field hands. We . . . You could hire field hands."

"I've heard this before, grand plans, a head full of dreams." Benito answered. "Peons to work the fields, tend the flocks. But peons also require attention, nursing and clothing and feeding. I'm no patron. I don't want the responsibility for workers, for large herds. I want only enough. No more."

"I'm not envisioning an empire," Thompson protested. He couldn't appreciate Benito's reasoning. "Just working the land to our greatest advantage. Realizing its full promise."

Something in Thompson's voice, a firm conviction, perhaps, caused Benito to stand also. "Let me tell you something," Benito said, stridently. "This soil is stingy, and temperamental. Sometimes she is generous, more times sparing. She will spurn you on a whim. Pamper her with water and plant crops that do not tax her greatly and she may smile on you. Demand too much, and she'll reject you like that, poof."

Benito now also was excited, walking rapidly to the end of the overhang and back. "Wait here," he said, ducking into the house. He returned and opened his palm to Thompson and pointed. "Peppers, corn, beans, some melons. This is sufficient." He tossed the four seeds at his feet, and looked across the plaza to the coop. "Some chickens. A few goats with hillsides to forage. In time, a few churros for wool." Benito spread his arms out before him. "This is enough. If greed outweighs respect for the land, if you attempt to enslave her, bend her to your ambitions, you become the one enslaved. What you believe you own instead owns you." Benito had come near and pointed his finger in Thompson's face. Thompson felt scolded, and embarrassed. He stepped back. Benito started to say something more but did not. He smiled weakly, shrugged, and retreated indoors.

Thompson collected one of the seeds from the courtyard and studied it as if he were assaying the worth of some precious gem. He'd not heard Benito string together so many words in the time he'd known him. Benito had struggled to convey his feelings and Thompson struggled to understand, but could not. Benito's relationship to the land seemed so alien to his own, so subservient. As with mountain men and Indians, to Thompson's thinking, Benito's ways belonged to a past age. But, it was none of his concern.

AFTER MORNING CHORES, THOMPSON WALKED to the pasture and found it vacated by Captain Upperdine's guests, smoldering fire rings, ovals of matted grass, the grooves of tepee poles dragged across the damp riverbank the only sign of recent occupation. He turned from the rendezvous site and followed the river upstream at a leisurely pace, enjoying the new day and the renewed solitude. Snow had ended sometime during the night and had not accumulated in the fields. A trace in the hollow of a cottonwood trunk, a patch of white between shadowed boulders, scant evidence of winter's first calling. But the morning was brisk, his breath frosted, grass crunching beneath his boots. A sword of mallards exploded off a quiet river pool, southbound, a ruckus of wings and repetitive, rasping squawks. Thompson stood in the naked field watching, clouds burnished orange by the early sun. The birds disappeared behind a stand of cottonwoods, rose into view farther downriver, climbed into the sky, wings a blur of motion, and slowly shrunk from sight. Benito came up behind Thompson and they stood together.

"Feels like a day for travel," Thompson broke the silence.

"It does," Benito replied.

Thompson felt the urge. He wondered where the old trapper, Ezekiel Pence, was off to and where the Indian band had set course. Unlike Upperdine, he was a man by nature bound to the land. Yet on mornings like this he felt the pull of the trail, could understand Upperdine's restlessness. He stood with Benito and watched the ducks and inhaled the cold morning into his lungs. His stroll had taken them close by the patch of ground Thompson had sown in wheat.

"Come look," Thompson said, and pointed out the new growth carpeting the cleared section. "Sprouted early last week."

"I don't see how it can survive winter," Benito said.

"Lies quiet, they say. Sets to again when the ground warms."

Thompson knelt and took a shoot between his thumb and finger and felt its suppleness. Alive and green and ripe with promise.

"With good fortune, a start for Hanna and Joseph." Thompson said. "It shouldn't prove too burdensome for the boy to tend this plot."

"You do not plan to stay through summer?" Benito asked.

"I don't know," Thompson said. He hesitated, but went on. "Working this section," he motioned with his arm. "It was hard. When the blade first bit into the earth, I felt like I was reclaiming something I'd lost. But memories came, slowly, and then in a rush, and I almost abandoned the plow in the field."

Benito did not ask what memories could be so powerful, and Thompson was glad about that.

"Eventually you'll figure your course," Benito said. He blew into his cupped hands and rubbed warmth into them. "Come. Let's see if Teresa has made coffee."

Approaching the door to Benito's rooms, they stopped short at the sound of conversation from within. Harsh tones. Genoveva and Teresa talking, a loud exclamation from Paloma followed a sharp retort from Teresa and Genoveva's soothing murmurs, placating and conciliatory.

"I don't understand the language," Thompson whispered. "But I get the idea now would not be the most opportune time to inquire about breakfast."

"Let's sit and talk a moment," Benito said and led Thompson away from the door. He told Paloma's story.

20

When the Ibarra family set out from Plaza del Arroyo Seco, there was to be another person joining them: Carlos de Vargas, a young man from a neighboring village, a weaver who also owned a small but growing flock of sheep. At age twenty-one, someone with promise. Paloma's betrothed. The past summer, Paloma and Carlos, chaperoned by Teresa, traveled to Santa Fe seeking the priest's blessing for an abbreviated engagement so they could marry upon Benito's return from the Purgatoire. The day hot, dusty; American soldiers loitering outside the tavern, drinking; a girl dancing a fandango, her slim waist cinched with a bright sash, her skirt fanned, ankles flashing; a lewd comment as Paloma walked by, a challenge from Carlos; a response from the soldiers. One of them grabbed Paloma's arm and pulled her close and attempted to engage in a clumsy two-step. Paloma slapped the soldier, he pushed her roughly, and Carlos charged him, striking him full in the face, splitting his lip. The others came quickly to the aid of their companion, knocking Carlos to the ground. He got to his feet but one of the Americans pulled his revolver and held it to Carlos's face, full cock, daring him to advance. They made him watch while they passed Paloma one to another, hands groping, fondling, raising her dress, mocking Carlos, his manhood. They tore her undergarments, exposed her flesh to Carlos, think you can handle that, boy? Teresa hurled herself at the men and was tossed to the ground as well. An officer passed and noticed the disturbance and dispersed the soldiers. Teresa still sprawled in the dust, Carlos bleeding from the head and nose, Paloma, in tatters, nearly naked, hysterical with anger and shame. No apologies offered, a warning from the officer for Carlos to keep his place.

Relating the story, Benito's voice lacked emotion, but he continually wrung his hands as if attempting to wash away the events as he spoke them, cleanse the stain of recollection. Thompson listened, expressionless, elbows on knees, head lowered, eyes focused on the ground a short distance in front of his feet.

"No harm came to them?" Thompson at length asked.

"None to the body."

"And no satisfaction demanded of the soldiers?"

"When I returned, I met with the elders of Carlos's village. I traveled to Santa Fe with a delegation and approached the commander of the American garrison, seeking redress. He blamed the incident on the fandango dancer. She enticed his men and enflamed the passions."

Thompson reached down and picked up a pebble and sat up and tossed it across the courtyard in the general direction of a hen.

"The villagers talked of revenge," Benito continued. "I argued against it."

Thompson looked at Benito and Benito could sense his question.

"No good could come of it. No satisfaction, nothing righted. The American soldiers possessed overwhelming power, cold eyes. They lacked nobility. Sometimes it's best to put evil to our backs and move on with life."

"Good advice, perhaps, but difficult to follow," Thompson said.

"True," Benito allowed. "Paloma's bitterness remains. She hates Americans. She feels betrayed by me and disgraced by Carlos. In her anger and humiliation, she accused him, questioned his courage, his honor."

"And Carlos?" Thompson asked. "How did he respond?"

Benito shook his head. "Quit his loom. Abandoned his sheep. Disappeared."

"Where to?" Thompson asked.

"Into the badlands, I suspect." Benito looked up from his hands and waited until Thompson turned to him. "Shame is an unforgiving master. It can drive you far from home."

"I know shame," Thompson said, and Benito saw remembrance welling behind his eyes, sorrow and remorse. Thompson started to speak and stopped and shook his head slowly back and forth as if dismissing the thoughts that rose in his throat, denying them voice, forcing them back into some inner vault.

"I suspect at some point all men feel remorse," Benito finally said.

Thompson shrugged.

"And here," Benito motioned with his hand. "Is this a place of banishment or of second chances?"

"Depends on the day," Thompson said. "Some days I wake up and walk outside and it's like I'm standing at the gates of hell. But other times I seem a part of the valley. I feel almost at home."

"What about this place makes it feel like home?"

"It's difficult to put into words," Thompson said. "The endlessness of its want, perhaps."

"Yes?"

"The river wants for flow, the land for rain. The sky for days almost seems in want of clouds. Without clouds, there is nothing to define the sky. The horizon wants for end." Thompson paused, and it seemed to Benito that he waited for validation, for permission to have these notions. Benito gestured with his hands, go on.

"My cabin," Thompson said. "On that rise no more than twenty feet above the river."

"Yes."

"When I look east, on clear days from that vantage I can make out a stand of trees surrounding a spring out in the plains."

"I know that place," Benito said.

"Once, I walked there. A day and part of the second morning it took." He shook his head in disbelief. "Almost a day and a half."

"Yes," Benito nodded. "This is a vast, empty place."

"And that emptiness gives me comfort. Some days. I don't know why."

"It is good to find comfort wherever one is able."

"But such a peculiar succor."

"Comfort, nonetheless," Benito said, "and that is a start."

21

Days shortened. Each new snow lingered in the shadows. Ice thick-
ened along the riverbank and in wagon ruts. Winter constricted
the world—low skies pulled horizons near, walls closed in, rooms
shrunk to the size of a tomb.

Benito noticed Teresa withdraw inward. One morning, carding
wool by the fire, he watched her hands go still. She took up a fluff
of wool from the paddle and studied it, absently pulling at the fine
threads as she stared into the flame snaking between two lengths of
piñon. Benito knew she was remembering the Plaza, the women who
would gather to card and spin and share coffee and gossip. In the
months since they'd arrived, no word from Plaza del Arroyo Seco, and
little free time to wonder. But now, winter, a time for reminiscence. He
looked about the room, empty save for him, the quiet crackle of fire
and the wind slashing against the window shutters the only conversation. He struggled to find some words of encouragement, something
to brighten her spirit, but nothing came. He pulled on his jacket and

went outside. A wan sun offered feeble comfort. He walked. Fog hung above the river—a heron glided through the diaphanous ether. He returned to the placita. Across the courtyard his sons tossed table scraps on the ground for the chickens and collected eggs from the coop. He went to Paloma's door and knocked. Her room shared a common wall with Benito and Teresa's and originally had been connected by an archway inside. But when Paloma was made to take in the boys, she insisted the archway be plastered over and a separate entrance be installed opening onto the plaza. Benito had little spare time for additional work, but decided acquiescence offered the greatest opportunity for familial harmony. He knocked out and framed an outer opening and used the reclaimed bricks to wall the interior.

Benito rapped again more forcefully and Paloma opened the door but did not motion her father inside.

"Your mother requires your help in preparing the wool," Benito said.

"I am helping her," Paloma replied. She opened the door wider and pointed to her hearth, the stack of raw wool and the carding paddles on her chair.

"I think she'd like your companionship as well," Benito said.

"The only time I have to myself is when the boys are at chores," Paloma answered without apology.

Benito felt helpless. If he ordered his daughter to Teresa's side, her company surely would prove worse than no company at all. And he had no idea how to appeal to Paloma's sense of duty. Unable to comfort his wife or to command respect from his daughter, he pulled his jacket close and pushed open the gate of the compound and went to the goat pen. He busied himself sinking posts to expand the enclosure to accommodate the kids that his does soon would drop. The frozen ground made digging almost impossible. But he needed the challenge. Paloma's self-imposed isolation was unhealthy both for her and for the family, and her simmering, open hostility toward the Americans could eventually prove dangerous in this new country. He must somehow persuade her to move past her misfortune. He remembered her before. Always strong-willed, she nevertheless was respectful and devoted to Teresa and to him. How to turn back time? Benito believed their future happiness depended on it, but he lacked a solution. He worked through the morning, the labor an eventual balm for his irritation and worry.

Alejandro and Benjamin joined Benito presently and they too lightened his mood. They took turns carrying posts and scratching with the pick. At noon, Benito returned with the boys to the placita and was buoyed at the sound of light chatter coming from the room when he opened the door. He found not Paloma but Hanna visiting with Teresa. Disappointed, Benito nodded to them and hung his jacket on the door peg while the boys scurried to one corner of the room to play with clay marbles that Thompson had molded for them from adobe mud earlier that autumn. Hanna helped Teresa by the hearth with the midday meal, and learned from her as well. Benito sat at the table and watched them.

Following the birth of her daughter, Hanna had refused the usual laying-in period and daily seemed to gain strength both physically and emotionally. Destiny riding her hip, she visited almost daily with Teresa, offering help with chores and peppering her with questions about ways of the Plaza. Reserved at first, fearing how Paloma might react to Hanna's presence, Teresa gradually warmed to the visits and now openly welcomed Hanna's friendship.

"And this, what is this called?" Hanna indicated the flat stone sitting on the hearth.

"A comal. For the tortillas."

"How do you make tortillas?"

"Corn. Water. A pinch of limestone ash. Simple," Teresa smiled. "But for every woman, a little different. How much of this? How smooth the *masa*? How hot the stone?"

"Do they keep well?"

"*Si*, but whenever possible fresh every day. No table is complete without tortillas, and a cold tortilla is really nothing at all. Serve fresh. Serve warm."

Teresa took Hanna's elbow and led her to the pot where the corn had been soaking and demonstrated how to skin the kernels and grind the pulp into masa using the *mano* and the *metate*. Good, thought Benito. A purpose for Teresa, and a distraction. With their backs to the room, talking, the two women did not hear the door creak open. Benito turned and motioned with his eyes for Paloma to come, sit. Paloma stood at the door for a moment watching Hanna and Teresa, glanced darkly at Benito, and left.

THE WINTER SOLSTICE APPROACHED, NIGHTS that seemed to flow one into another without break. Benito began chores before first light and ended in the murky afternoon darkness. Sunk deep into that interminable season, the celebration days arrived almost without notice. There was little to celebrate. Corn stores ran short and some days they went without bread, without tortillas. A ration of meat, some onions perhaps. Never starving, but persistently on the edge of hunger. On La Noche Buena, Thompson stopped by and presented the boys each with a hand-carved whistle, which they delighted in. Beneath his smile, Benito noticed in Thompson a solemnity, and he seemed distracted, his thoughts somewhere far off, and he refused to sup with them.

On Dia de los Reyes, John Upperdine arrived at the placita like one of the wise men bearing gifts. With ceremony, he handed Teresa a covered basket and beamed as she unveiled a mound of fresh lemons and oranges. She marveled at the fruit and examined each piece individually, each one a heavenly orb in miniature, admiring its color and the firmness of its flesh. Even Paloma became animated for a few moments before resuming an expression suggesting she'd tasted the fruit and found it sour. Teresa could not imagine such a bounty appearing at her table, and later, in private, Benito advised her to accept the gift without delving too deeply into how the fruit had been procured. He knew John Upperdine to be a shrewd and sometimes ruthless trader, and he had no doubt that the transaction had a history best left undocumented. But Benito gave thanks for the smile he saw come to Teresa's face, a short respite from the challenges of winter.

Two weeks following the New Year, Benito led his cart to Upperdine's house with a load of kindling the boys had collected from the river bottom. He found the Captain checking tackle on a pair of horses hitched to a light freight wagon.

Thompson emerged from the barn shouldering a bag of sugar, which he loaded onto the wagon. Benito took inventory of the freight: two hams from the cold storage, a keg of whiskey, pouches of tobacco, several glass panes arranged in a box with straw padding, and a stack of hand-milled lumber the length of the wagon bed. How Captain Upperdine came to possess such items never ceased to confound and impress Benito. He silently eyed the hams. With corn supplies low, they had been consuming more meat.

"A journey?" Benito asked.

"An exploratory trip," Upperdine answered. "To the mining camps along Cherry Creek."

"I thought you stated that nothing good would come of those settlements," Benito said.

"Nothing will," Upperdine said, "for ninety-nine out of every one hundred ill-equipped, scruff-necked prospectors and for one hundred out of one hundred Indians." He patted the bag of sugar approvingly and smiled. "But for a merchant, that's another story."

Upperdine climbed onto the wagon and took up the reins. "I expect to move smartly and return before the month is out." He pulled a buffalo robe around his shoulders and slapped the reins against the animals' haunches, and the wagon creaked from the yard and followed the river trail downstream.

"I offered to accompany him," Thompson said. "He declined. Said he was meeting up with some of his old boys out from Bent's Fort."

"He does grow anxious when duties or weather keep him home-bound for long," Benito said.

"He's not a natural landsman," Thompson said.

"No. Land for him is a means to an end, not the end itself."

"Yet he's laid claim to a large tract."

Benito looked over at Thompson, paused and breathed deeply as if to begin a story. But he said only, "Yes. An impressive holding."

"But not impressive enough to keep him," Thompson said.

"John is drawn to the trail," Benito said, "and that is partly why we've been invited here. To keep Genoveva company."

"I thought the land for the placita was offered in exchange for your service."

"*Sí,* everything is an exchange for John. A field to ensure my continued assistance, but also his wife's contentment."

TRUE TO HIS SCHEDULE, UPPERDINE returned on the last day of January, invigorated of spirit and full of news. He summoned Thompson and Benito to dine with him and when they took a place at the table, he emptied a purse full of gold flakes on the plate in front of him. Thompson moved around to sit beside Upperdine and they both leaned close over the plate to examine the small mound, Upperdine with a self-satisfied grin, Thompson wide-eyed with surprise. Thompson took up a pinch of gold and let the flakes drift down through the flickering light from the hearth fire.

"So, the prospectors have found success," Thompson said.

"Hardly." No sizable deposits, Upperdine explained. A little placer gold, yes, and rumors filling the air like flocks of pigeons. He described the camps strung along Cherry Creek and the South Platte as shabby clusters of huts and tents inhabited by ragged men desperate for supplies and willing to part with the whole of their meager earnings for basic necessities.

"Many have ate their own mule. Will have to walk home."

"So, how were you able to sell your wares?" Benito asked.

"A few of the experienced ones, the veterans of forty-nine, knew what to look for, actually sifted a few nuggets from the gravel. Others have backing from the states. They were excited to see glass windows and plank boards. Rushed to outbid one another for bragging rights. Eggs, a dollar a dozen, and more, and I thought to bring none."

"Tobacco?" Thompson asked.

"Two dollar a pound."

"Whiskey?" Thompson asked, his voice rising.

"Handed out a goodly amount free," Upperdine said. "Grease for the hub, so to speak. Loosens the purse strings. The rest, whatever the market would bring. A nickel a cup, sometimes ten times that, depending on the mood and the luck of the miners.

"But the glass panes," Upperdine shook his head in disbelief. "Those glass panes brought them to frenzy."

Thompson and Upperdine talked on after the evening meal. At length, Benito excused himself and walked back to the placita. The night sounds quieted, only his footfalls on the frozen earth. What men were these, he wondered, who rush into the territory, his territory, shovel and pan valued over the plow. Men fueled by greed and false expectations, turned mean by disappointment and hunger. And what of Upperdine and Thompson, flushed with ambition at the sight of gold dust sparkling in the firelight, shining in their eyes?

22

Mid-March, a cold day of blustery winds and intermittent snow, Joseph presented himself at Benito's door. Ice braided the hair left unprotected below his hat, and the white tip of his nose suggested frostbite. He held a brace of jackrabbits by the hind legs. Benito motioned him inside and Teresa ushered him to the fireplace.

"Look at you, no sense to be out in this."

Benito understood why Joseph needed to be outside. Daylight reclaimed a few minutes each day, but no rhythm yet to the season. Clear skies, restorative warmth followed by ice storms pounding the tableland like fists. They all fidgeted to be out and beginning the work of spring. Even Benito's animals showed restlessness: his does, low-slung bellies and swollen udders, had kidded, and now were anxious to graze.

Joseph went to the corner where Paloma sat at a chair, churning butter from goat's milk. He watched her for several moments while she pumped the handle, the sinew in her forearms defined, her upper body bending to the task. Waiting for notice. She ignored him.

"Paloma," Benito said. His harsh tone caught her attention and she paused, looked up.

"Thought you might like one of these." Joseph held up the rabbits. The two young boys came up beside Joseph and stroked the soft fur underbelly. Paloma turned back to her work.

"I do not care for rabbit," she said. "Stringy."

"Soak it in milk. I could skin one out for you if you like," Joseph said.

"What I would like is for you to take those rodents from my sight," Paloma said.

"Paloma," Benito said.

"Father, this boy is pestering me."

Joseph stepped back, his face blanked, shutting down. Benito approached Paloma, bent near and hissed in her ear. "I will not have this rudeness, do you understand?" So intent was he on the reprimand, he did not notice Joseph back from the room and retreat into the sleet.

The following morning when Benito cleaned the goat pen and carried a bucket of droppings to fertilize the field, he came upon the torn carcasses of two rabbits. They had been decapitated, their heads stacked one on top of the other, and their bodies mangled, chopped. He toed the body of one and thought about the troubled boy and about the dark moodiness threatening to overcome everything decent about his daughter. He did not know the boy well and feared he had little guidance to offer him. But he did know his daughter, or had known her, and resolved not to surrender her to melancholy without contest.

After three days of pelting hail and battering winds, the quarrel-some weather lifted, skies cleared to an intense blue, sun warmed the fields, and gentle breezes carried the scent of budding sagebrush. March grass tentatively sprouted through last season's brittle stubble,

pliable shoots not yet sufficient to support the livestock of trade caravans or wagon trains. But the promise of renewal. Benito checked the
skies, noted the direction of the wind, and loaded the cart with ax,
saw, and a bundle of fodder for the burro.

Inside, he found Teresa and Paloma making tortillas, the rhythmic
slapping of masa from hand to hand, the flattened discs hissing on the
stone. Cornmeal supplies had diminished and Teresa made tortillas
only four days a week. Other days they made do with stale leftovers
or went without. Benito took a hot tortilla from the basket and folded
it and ate slowly, watching them.

Mother and daughter working together, as it should be. But not
conversing, not connected. Benito ached to hear the banter that
greeted him daily from the Plaza when he returned from the fields.
The boys playing with their cousins, the young women whispering
between themselves while seated at their mothers' elbow, learning the
work. Where had the companionship gone? The belonging? Why did
Paloma refuse even to attempt opening to her mother, reestablishing
their bond? On impulse, Benito addressed his daughter.

"Accompany me?"

"Where?"

"To gather wood."

"I'd rather not."

"I need your help."

"Take the boys. They love to be with you."

"I want to collect upstream from the Arkansas ford. They'd soon
tire."

"Too far for me as well."

"We'll camp one night only, return tomorrow before noon."

"Surely you don't expect me to—"

Benito suddenly found it difficult to breathe and his vision blurred.
The disharmony she created simply by her presence in a room, the

pressure of her brooding, and her invariable low-grade disdain worked like thumbs pressing into his temples until he felt his head might explode. He slammed his palm on the table, a resounding crack, his hand instantly numb.

"Quiet," he sputtered. "Not a debate. Go."

Paloma rose from the hearth, gave her mother a pleading glance, and went to her room to change. Teresa continued to work the masa. "To what point?" she asked.

"I don't know. Alone perhaps we can talk without reservation. I don't know."

Benito took a stack of tortillas and wrapped them in a flap of cloth. Paloma returned dressed in trousers and a wool shirt, her hair tucked under a man's hat. She took her jacket from the peg and shrugged it on and went outside without a word to either of them.

Benito led the burro from the placita, Paloma following behind the cart at a distance. He walked back to pull shut the gates and heard the latch engage. The sound reminded him of leaving the Plaza del Arroyo Seco for the last time, the gate at the outer wall swinging shut, the hinges squeaking like a high moan and the latch catching with a clanking finality. His grandfather had helped reinforce that gate and rebuild the section of wall around it following a Comanche raid three years before Benito had been born. Benito would not look on that gate again, he'd not have that gate to remind him of the life and times of his father and of his father's father, and of the fathers who had gone before.

They passed through his field and on toward the Arkansas River. The land appeared much the same as it did in New Mexico Territory, but for the first time it felt unfamiliar under Benito's feet, and for a moment, only a moment, loneliness crept over him. He would miss the forays into the hills with friends to collect piñon nuts, and the companionship of the field, to the right and to the left, his brothers and his cousins bowed over the rows. Peppers would grow in this new home, but they would taste altogether unlike those that earned him renown on the plaza, lacking the heat and the earthy flavor produced by that particular marriage of soil and climate.

They reached the river and forded upstream from the confluence with the Purgatoire and set camp beside a pool that collected clean water and ate a midday meal of pickled eggs sprinkled with pepper flakes. They did not talk. After eating, they followed the course of the river, collecting deadfall. Wagon trains had yet to converge on the trail and firewood was plentiful. With his ax he hacked the limbs into manageable lengths that Paloma loaded onto the cart. After two hours, Benito stopped to rest, tied off the burro, and led Paloma up the embankment to the broad mesa. He stopped and she stood beside him and he motioned with his arms.

"Turn in place," he instructed Paloma. "Tell me what you see."

Paloma glanced around. "Nothing. A waste. Ugly brown nothing spreading into nothing."

"People?"

"No."

"Plazas? Towns?"

"Of course not."

"Water?"

"The river. Out there, a desert."

Benito moved to face her. "Correct. A harsh geography. But, there," and he pointed in the direction from which they'd come, "a stretch of land with willing soil, an acequia that soon will flow, neighbors to help and in return to offer help. A home."

"Neighbors?"

"If you give them a chance."

"Overrun with Americans. It's already begun. How can that place be home? They spit on us. Pepper-bellies, they call us. Greasers."

"You exaggerate. Our neighbors treat us with respect."

"The boy is dark. He lurks. I don't trust him."

"And John Upperdine, your uncle, so generous to us," Benito continued.

"Papa, please. He's no saint. I've heard Mother and Tia Genoveva talk. I know why he's so anxious for the trail, why he is hardly at home, why he depends on you to manage his fields and his animals."

"You are young. You do not understand as much as you think you do." Benito took her shoulders in his hands and turned her to face him. "I know the Americans. I am not quite the foolish old man you take me for. I know their ambitions. But there are places here, land they are too lazy or too ignorant to make use of. They have no interest, and that land will be our home."

He studied Paloma for some sign that she understood, but her expression refused to disclose her feelings. At an impasse, they went quiet and looked out over the yawning plains.

"They touched me," Paloma said at last. "The soldiers."

"I know."

"Their hands," she said. "Their eyes."

"Yes."

"They opened me for the world to see." Tears were running down her cheeks. "They touched, they stared. Others saw."

For the world to see, the words struck Benito. Her world. Carlos. And Teresa. The two, wanting to shield their eyes but unable to. And it dawned on him that the chasm between Paloma and Teresa must have something to do with shame. A shared humiliation.

"Don't let the soldiers ruin you," Benito urged.

"Carlos," Paloma said.

"Yes," Benito said.

"I loved him so."

"And now?" Benito asked.

"How could I? Someone who allowed me to be treated so?"

"What would you have had him do?" Benito asked. Paloma did not answer.

"Die for you?" Benito asked.

Paloma, after a long pause, "Yes."

The wind picked up and a keening rose through the branches of the cottonwoods beside the river.

"It must be complicated for you," Benito said.

"How so?"

"To at once love someone and wish them dead."

Paloma stiffened. "No matter," she said. "It is finished."

"No," Benito said. "Sadly, it is far from done with."

THEY RETURNED TO THE RIVER bottom and filled the cart and had started back to camp when Benito noticed the tracks in the firm sand of the riverbank. Ponies, six perhaps, unshod, hoofprints still damp and well-defined. Too soon in the season for Indians to leave winter range, he thought. A hunting party? Had they noticed his cooking ring and bedrolls? The tracks led out of the river and upslope. When Benito arrived at his camp he cautiously walked the perimeter of the clearing and found no sign of Indian presence. When he returned, Paloma was arranging kindling in the cook fire.

"Not here," Benito said. "We're moving."

Paloma's expression challenged, but before she spoke, she seemed to catch herself. "Why?"

"Too open," Benito said. He casually mentioned the pony tracks, careful to mask anxiety. Paloma nodded at his explanation and gathered up the kindling and scattered the stones of the fire ring. Benito decided to re-cross the river, putting it between them and the Indians on the trail. In the distance he picked out a stand of cottonwoods that grew just upslope from a willow thicket. The brush would offer concealment and he would be able to hear the approach of any riders. A tall bluff at his back would protect them from that direction. He chose not to backtrack to the ford. The river, not yet swollen by snowmelt, ran shallow and slow. He walked upstream for a quarter-mile until he came upon a gravel bar that extended far into the river, and with Paloma on the cart he guided the burro, soaking only his trousers to the waist and keeping the provisions and his daughter dry. Still, the March breezes blew cold, and he decided to chance a small fire to boil coffee and to dry his clothes. They drank the coffee and ate dried fruit and reheated tortillas. Full dark, Paloma curled beside the embers. Benito wrapped himself in one of Teresa's woolen blankets and sat propped against a cottonwood and stayed awake as long as he could, listening for splashing hooves and the rustle of branches.

He woke before dawn and sat up, alert, aware of a change, listening. No ponies. But the wind had shifted during the night and now came hard from the northwest, carrying a bite. First light brought a sideways snow. They broke camp with urgency and made for home. Normally, they'd be traveling the far bank to the ford downstream, an easy trail. But Benito dared not chance a crossing in this weather, so they traveled slowly over un-trailed ground, the stream bank steep in places, boggy in others.

The storm built, whipping gusts, plummeting temperature. Snow covered the rocks of the streambed, a treacherous sheen of ice. Paloma slipped, caught herself, and her hand came up bloody. The cold stanched the bleeding nearly before it began.

"We need to climb from the river bottom," Benito said to Paloma. "Reach firm ground, level going."

"But where?" Paloma asked.

Benito searched the steep banks for an opening, any hint of a game trail, footpath. He knew the ground flattened near the ford, but it was miles downstream.

"We'll leave the cart." He unhitched the burro and loosely secured their provision bag across its withers. He and Paloma pushed the cart into the scrub to hide it from Indians, and they started up the embankment. They traversed the slope downhill, feet slipping with almost every step. The more sure-footed burro set course straight for the crest of the bank, pulling at its lead, keeping Benito off balance. Benito at first tried to guide the burro and, failing, tried to turn loose the strap, but he'd wrapped it around his hand and wrist when they'd begun their assent, and the straining burro tightened it until it dug into his flesh. Benito planted his feet uphill and yanked desperately on the leash, felt it go taut, and then slacken, the burro's flank filling his vision, felt its weight slamming against him, a cracking in his midsection when initially he hit the ground, a tumbling, and then nothing.

BENITO OPENED HIS EYES AND looked up into a gray sky that seemed somehow close to him, smothering and heavy. All was quiet, as if the snow had insulated him from the surrounding world. "A misfortune," he thought to himself, "I must see to it." He braced his hands in the snow to either side and attempted to rise, but he had no strength and his legs refused his will. He lay back and the snow wetted his face. He felt blood pooling in his mouth and he turned and spit and a tooth came out with the blood. He looked about calmly, dazed, and assessed his situation. Snow. Some blood on the snow, not a great calamity. Paloma?

"Paloma," he called and pushed against the cold earth again and with great effort managed to rise to a half-sitting position and craned around, looking up the bank. There, Paloma striding, then sliding down the bank, slipping, pants torn, arms flailing, digging her heels through the snow, searching for purchase in the riprap. He watched, eyes going in and out of focus. Kneeling beside him, he felt her hands gingerly exploring his head, his neck. "A lump, like a hen's egg," she said, examining her hand, "and bleeding."

"The burro. Is he injured?"

"I don't think so. I don't see him. He's wandered."

They both rested a moment, their labored breathing condensing, carried away by the wind in drifting tendrils, swirling with the flakes that continued to fall. Benito again tried to rise and again he fell back. He looked down at his legs and Paloma followed his eyes and gasped. His right leg at the thigh bent almost perpendicularly from his body. He reached into his pocket and removed a folding knife and held it out to her.

"Cut the trouser. Let me see the leg."

She did as he directed and he looked down at the leg. The bulge of the bone was clearly visible but had not broken the skin.

"Good," he said. "You must set it."

"I cannot."

"Who, then?" She did not answer. Benito dimly realized he was in shock and that both it and the numbing cold helped buffer him from the pain. But the pain would soon break through. In the end, pain always finds a route.

"Listen to me," Benito said, his breathing shallow and rapid, words coming in quick bursts. "I may lose senses for a while." A pang like a blade piercing his ribcage forced him to suck in his breath and go quiet for a beat. "Straighten it best you can," he continued, fighting for words. "Can't be gentle. Find something to splint with." He sensed himself fading. "Understand?"

Paloma nodded.

"Find burro. Collect food before snow covers. Find shelter."

"Yes," She said.

"Now, move to my leg. Brace your feet. That's right. You must lean into it. Now. Pull."

PART THREE

HOME,
1859

23

Thompson went to the well at daybreak, found the water in the trough free of ice, and again his hopes stirred. Spring came in fits and starts in this new country. He fidgeted to be in motion, free from constraints of abbreviated days and fickle climate. Mostly, he wished to be rid of idle time spent dwelling on past lives, past transgressions. He would have liked to have been invited to accompany Benito to gather wood, even if it meant sharing a campfire with Paloma.

Restless, he walked to Upperdine's homestead and found the Captain in the tool shed, inspecting locust-damaged tackle. Even Upperdine's round, full face had thinned over winter, and Thompson noticed gray streaks in his beard, which he'd let grow during the cold season. Harness straps draped his shoulders like a shawl, and, stooped over a bench straining to work punch pliers, he suddenly appeared old to Thompson. Upperdine looked up at his approach.

"Thompson. I've been meaning to visit you."

Thompson nodded a greeting. "Repair work?"

"Those damn pests ate right through the leather." Upperdine tossed a strap onto a small heap of discarded tackle. "Some is salvageable. I've been pecking at it all winter."

"You have need of it soon?" Thompson asked.

"I'm off with the new grass."

"To guide?"

"To Denver first. Some trading. Then to Westport."

"The trail."

"Yes." Upperdine must have heard something in Thompson's voice. "You interested in joining up?"

"I don't know. I'm about sick of the view out my cabin," Thompson admitted.

Indeed, Thompson had thought about the trail, relived his journey time and again. Initially, he could not imagine willingly retracing those steps, revisiting that history. The act of recalling the most mundane detail, the dung beetles children played with at evening camp or the bloom of a cornflower in the damp soil of a wagon rut would cause other, darker memories to worm to the surface from some deep pit where he'd buried them. But lately, he'd begun to harbor a morbid attraction to the trail as if compelled to test his memory, to learn what remained of the nightmares.

"Winter will do that to a man," Upperdine said. "Perhaps spring will arrive for good and your mind will turn to planting."

"Perhaps." In truth, Thompson also faced the coming spring with apprehension. The field held memories as well.

"But if not, you can be of use," Upperdine said. "You have experience. Benito is established now and can look after my affairs, and his."

ANOTHER NIGHT WITHOUT A HARD freeze brought to life a few strips of green that hugged the base of outcroppings where porous rock radiated the sun's heat. Thompson walked out into Benito's field.

In Indiana, he'd be turning the soil by now, but here the ground remained partially frozen. He walked to the river. No sign of runoff, the water a murmuring rill, ice still thick on the bank, the pool below the acequia's diversion dam shallow and still. Irrigation waited on the thaw. Everything waited on the thaw.

Walking back toward the placita, Thompson noticed the wind shifting into his face, coming hard from the northwest. It carried the feel of weather, a damp chill. Yet another turn, Thompson wondered?

John Upperdine rode the trail from the river and overtook Thompson as they neared the goat pen. "May need to move the new kids and their does inside tonight. Fixing to pepper."

"For sure?"

"Nothing for sure out here. But I do believe so."

"Will they be all right?" Thompson asked, thinking of Benito and Paloma. Upperdine apparently had been wondering the same.

"I suspect so," Upperdine said. "Winter's tolerable here compared to elsewhere in this territory."

Upperdine turned his horse and Thompson continued toward the low rises to the west. The sky directly above remained partially clear, patches of blue showing through scudding gray clouds. But to the west, a dark curtain advanced rapidly, dust carried by stiffening gusts. He stood watching the storm approach. The clouds above, a dark shadow engulfing the plains below. Grit irritated his eyes. He felt the temperature drop suddenly as if he'd walked from the warmth of the day into an icehouse. A spit of sleet, then a curtain dropping. The horizon closed. A cold sting against his face. Another. As he began to retrace his steps, the storm overtook him. Lightning flashed from thunderclouds that expelled snow and hail with the force of grapeshot. Nothing one moment, a white wall the next. He moved downhill, following the contours of the land, but could not see an arm's length in any direction. The air white, the ground white. Land he'd walked for months now a slick unrecognizable nothingness. He sensed the river, almost walking off the embankment before catching his step and working upstream until instinct directed him to turn away, toward the placita hidden somewhere in the boil. He tramped into the force of the gale now, counting steps, thinking the walls should come into view, willing them into view, and they materialized, a vague presence rising from the earth. He made his way to the gates and entered the compound and there snow swirled around the walls like a whirlwind. Thompson felt his way, keeping one hand on the wall until he came to the raised porch and the doorway and he tumbled inside. His face numb, frost painting his eyebrows, ice shards clinging to his hair, he fell to the floor with the sound of breaking glass when he shook his head. When had he lost his hat? A quarter-hour only, a few minutes exposed to the storm and already he'd lost feeling in the tips of his fingers and his feet were numb.

Teresa and Hanna jumped from their chairs where they had been knitting. Teresa grabbed a blanket and Thompson pulled it close around his shoulders.

"You were out in this?" Hanna asked.

"Walking. Got caught, it came fast," Thompson said, and seeing the worry in Teresa's eyes immediately regretted it.

"It is bad out, si?" she asked.

"I've seen worse," Thompson lied. "I'm sure they will be fine. Just hunkered down in the shelter of trees until it blows over." He went to the fire and endured exquisite pain as his flesh warmed and circulation returned. He glanced around the room, and then remembered. "The goats."

"It's too late," Hanna said.

Thompson hesitated. He still could not feel his nose, and his ears stung. In truth, the storm had frightened him, its ferocious onslaught.

For long moments he had lost his bearings completely and now, standing beside the hearth, he understood how easily he could have miscalculated his steps. One wrong turn and done.

He had no desire to return outside. He was not accountable for the Ibarra animals and he regarded Benito irresponsible for leaving them unattended. Why should he put himself at risk because of Benito's poor judgment? What did he owe these people? The wind outside howled, the warmth of the hearth pulled him close.

During his hesitation, Teresa had pulled on her coat and wrapped her head and face in a long woolen scarf. As she started for the door Thompson felt a flash of anger at her, at Benito, at the situation.

"Wait," he said. He drew the blanket more tightly around his shoulders, thrust his bare hands into a pair of Benito's mittens and pulled on one of his hats. It fit tightly. Taking a rope from a hook beside the door, he stepped past Teresa into the blizzard.

Again, Thompson followed the wall to the gate and around the outer perimeter until he came to the goat pen. Some of the herd had been caught in the hills and would have to fend for themselves but nannies with their kids had been left in the pen and Thompson could make them out huddled in the near corner, does sheltering their kids, backs to the wind, snow covering their flanks like a layer of fleece. Their bleating sounded muffled and distant in the dampening snow. He leashed what he thought to be the dominant nanny. She allowed him to pull her along, and the others followed, nose to tail. Looking back, he noticed two of the kids lifeless in the snow, on their sides, legs stiff. He opened the pen, and immediately one of the trailing does led her twin kids out into the field and in less time than it took to call out to her they had disappeared from sight. The remainder followed the lead nanny through the placita gates. Thompson herded them into the living quarters.

While he shivered by the fire, the others took blankets and flour sacks and rubbed down the goats. Thompson watched, taking inventory. Four nannies and five kids. One-half the newborns and a nanny lost to the storm. Six goats unaccounted for somewhere in the scrub. Last year's crop decimated, Benito's herd threatened, his family hungry, would the Ibarras hang on? Could they? Even if Benito and Paloma survived, would their will be broken? Thompson recalled passing the crumbled ruins of Bent's old adobe fort on the Arkansas and imagined the Ibarra placita a weathered and abandoned skeleton and inexplicably found himself saddened by the possibility. What was their loss to him? What was his stake?

THE STORM DEPARTED AS QUICKLY as it had arrived. The following morning Thompson stepped out into a pre-dawn morning as quiet as a meditation. The wind still, the morning star hanging low in the east. Spread out before him, a silent, white world. He trampled a path to the water trough, broke through a half-inch of ice, and led the goats from the living quarters out to water and to feed on coarse fodder he spread on the snow. Although the storm had blown in with ferocity, it lacked the mass and endurance of a winter blizzard, and in open spaces where the wind had not banked the snow against wall or hillside, less than a foot had accumulated. The storm would not live in the memory as anything extraordinary. But it had posed grave peril for one caught in the barrens unaware or ill-prepared.

After seeing to the goats and chickens, he encouraged Teresa not to worry, and he broke a path to his shack above the river. He hastily collected his woolen coat, mittens, and spare hat, pulled on high boots, and continued on to Upperdine's homestead.

Captain Upperdine was already afield when Thompson announced himself from the front porch. Genoveva called him in and poured him coffee.

"John was up at first light," she said. "Saw to the animals, then rode west to high ground, to search for sign before deciding where to begin," she explained.

"When were they due back?"

"They were a day late even before the storm hit."

Thompson finished his coffee and Genoveva began to pour a second cup, which he waved off. "The Captain will not start out directly?" he asked.

"Not unless he catches something in the distance through his glass. He said as much."

Thompson went to the corral and saddled a horse, mounted, and nudged it forward, following the first set of hoofprints in the new snow. Still an awkward rider, he bounced in the saddle. Two miles out, he met Upperdine returning from reconnaissance.

"Any sign?"

"Nothing."

"What do you think?"

"I think we should gather what we can in our saddlebags and set out directly."

"Set out for where?" Thompson asked. He could not imagine hunting for a single cart in so vast a wilderness.

"They shouldn't be far," Upperdine said. "Benito told me his route. He planned to be out only a day or two, collecting deadfall upstream from the ford."

WITH FULL SUN CAME THE glare. After only a few hours of riding, Thompson's eyes stung and became irritated by his constant rubbing. Determined not to slow Upperdine, he kicked his horse forward even though his vision filled with starbursts. Snow like sun reflecting off a mirror. Upperdine rode ahead and Thompson followed his trail, but had constantly to correct his course because of his blurred wandering. Shortly, Thompson felt a tug on his reins and became aware of Upperdine pulling beside him, bringing their horses to a halt. Upperdine retrieved two woolen scarves from his bag and handed one to Thompson.

"Wind it tight around your eyes," he demonstrated. "Two turns. Now, create just a slit to see through." Thompson followed Upperdine's instructions and the two continued on. The pain in Thompson's eyes eased a little. They came to the ford and crossed to the north side and slowed the horses to a walk and looked for tracks until darkness prevented them from searching further. The horses began to stumble from fatigue and slick footing. They made camp beside a patch of brittle grass that had been shielded from the brunt of the storm by a thick stand of willows. They build a smoldering fire that provided only the memory of warmth and ate a cold supper that Genoveva had packed for them. They ate in silence. Upperdine seemed perplexed and withdrawn, and Thompson was unwilling to give voice to his own misgivings. He wondered, not for the first time that day, why he was here, why he had felt compelled to join Upperdine in the search. What assistance could he possibly provide that Upperdine alone could not? He served only to impede progress. And to what end? Benito should not have wandered afield with his daughter during this unsettled season. He knew better. But he'd gone nevertheless. Some overwhelming desire to repair his daughter, to restore balance? Whatever irritations Benito stirred in Thompson, his motives seemed rooted in family, and for that Thompson held grudging admiration.

Unused to long rides, Thompson's legs could hardly boost him into the saddle the following morning. Thankfully, a thin cloud cover lessened the glare and provided relief to his eyes. They encountered no one on the trail nor did they discern any evidence of recent use. The snow melted through the day, and the trail slogged. A thin layer of mud glazed still-frozen ground. In the cold aftermath of the storm, the earth had become an inhospitable, primeval ruin.

"Snow, and now the melt," Upperdine observed. "I don't think any sign at all is left."

"Could they have come this far?" Thompson asked.

"I doubt it."

Midday, they watered the horses from the river. The ground was clear, in places, snow remaining stacked on the windward banks, the prairie a stark, piebald mix. Thompson could scarce imagine a less inviting land, and he wondered again about the constitution of a man who voluntarily searched out such a place to stake his future.

"We'll ride another hour," Upperdine said. "And then backtrack."

Around a wide turn in the river, they came upon a rough lean-to extending from a hollow gouged from the riverbank. Two men stood by a narrow side stream that emptied muddy water into the Arkansas. One shoveled gravel into a cradle-like contraption, while the other agitated it with a rocker arm. A third man lay wrapped in a wool blanket on the ground beside the lean-to. To the side, a burro grazed on stubble around his picket.

The two prospectors looked up from their work as the riders approached and the four of them took measure of one another. Thompson judged them to be green and not long on their own, younger than him by more than a few years. Farm boys out to seek their fortune. Upperdine reined his horse and nodded to the boys and they nodded back.

"Storm hit you hard?"

"Some. But we had shelter." The one holding the shovel extended the haft in the direction of the dirt cave. "Didn't much bother us."

"Any movement on the trail since it blew over?"

"Just you."

Upperdine's eyes scanned the boys' camp. "This don't seem a likely claim if its gold you're looking for."

"Our thought was to follow the river upstream, into the foothills," the boy at the rocker arm said. "We just killing time here until our pard is fit for travel."

Upperdine looked over at the man lying on the ground.

"Poor health?"

"Got hisself bit on the hand by a raccoon a while back. Never did heal right. Festered up."

"How in hell did he manage to get bit by a raccoon?"

"Varmint scrounging around camp for scraps couple weeks back. He set his mind to feed it, missed his hound back home. Seemed tame, that coon. But it up and took a chunk out of his hand."

"Canine fever, I expect," Upperdine said. "I've seen it before."

"What's to be done for him?"

Upperdine studied the man in his blanket, his blotchy face, glazed eyes. One leg twitched convulsively. "You might consider shooting him when it gets too bad."

The two boys looked up at Upperdine to see if he might be joking, and one started to say something, his mouth opened, but then he pursed his lips and sucked at his teeth, and they both looked off away from him.

"Save him considerable suffering, if the time comes," Upperdine said.

Thompson looked at the boy on the ground. Sixteen, seventeen maybe. Life over before it got a good hold. He looked about, a stark and desolate place to die. Would the boy call for his mama when the time came? Had his own boys whimpered for their papa? Thompson involuntarily shuddered.

Upperdine raised his hand to the two men and turned his horse and Thompson followed.

"That's a harsh pronouncement you made," he said to Upperdine.

"Do no good to coat the words with molasses," Upperdine said. "The boy is set for bad times, and the others ought to prepare for it."

"What if you're wrong?" Thompson challenged.

"Good for them," Upperdine said. "They'll cuss me for causing them worry and pass the jug around." They rode on for a minute, and then Upperdine said "But I ain't."

After covering another quarter-mile, Upperdine abruptly reined, cussed under his breath, and turned back toward the prospectors' camp. He approached the miner cradling the river gravel.

"That burro," Upperdine said. "How'd you come by it?" They both looked over at the burro.

"It's ours."

The second man came around the machinery and stood with his partner, both fists wrapped around the haft of his shovel. Upperdine casually let his hand drop to the grip of the pistol tucked into his waistband.

"I did not inquire about ownership. I know whose property it is. My question is, how'd you come by it?"

Thompson rode up with his rifle resting across his lap, unsheathed and at full cock. The two diggers stood silently, eyes darting between the two riders as if assessing their options. Thompson had no heart for this. The two prospectors seemed innocents, young men in search of a fool's dream, bumpkins unfit for this land, and he was certain the two at least would soon return to their family farms in South Carolina or Georgia, or wherever, provided they survived long enough to be shed of their wanderlust. But Upperdine had recounted story after story of shallow graves filled with unwitting boys who let misunderstanding escalate into argument. He stood guard, prepared to do whatever he must. The horses shuffled and snorted and pawed at the loose gravel of the streambed.

"It wandered into camp," the boy with the shovel finally said. "We fed it."

"When?"

"Yesterday. All drawn out. We fed it."

"What direction did it come from?" Upperdine asked.

"Downstream," the boy said, pointing. "From the south bank."

Upperdine reached into his greatcoat and drew out a silver coin and tossed it to the boy. "For your trouble."

The boy nodded. "All right. That seems fair."

Upperdine led his horse to the burro and took up its tether. He turned his horse and looked back over his shoulder at the boys standing by the stream, wet, mud-caked, fagged out.

"If you stay here long, best move camp up slope. Your dugout will be washed out within the month by the spring floods. You may have little notice."

"Obliged," one of the boys answered.

Again, Thompson and Upperdine took leave, and with the burro in tow, forded the river where a wide bar and gently sloped banks allowed easy footing.

"Benito changed his plans and crossed the river," Upperdine said. "I should a knowed when we didn't come across his sign."

"But where?"

"I'm guessing close by," Upperdine said. "If they'd been near the junction, the burro would have made for the placita."

They retraced their route, except this time from the south bank. In places the land rose beside the river into steep bluffs, and thick brush near the water obstructed their views. Twice, Upperdine fired his musket, hoping for a return signal. He knew Benito did not carry a musket, but something, a shout, smoke from a stoked fire. Nothing came. They moved slowly, dismounting and clamoring down embankments to search the thickets and the backwaters. They moved downstream almost to the ford and back again. The shadows lengthened and at full dark, fearing they might miss some evidence of passage, they stopped. Cold seeped beneath Thompson's coat, the icy stars, darkness a malevolent presence. Upperdine walked along the river, and returned. They ate tortillas, jerky, slept little, and at dawn were mounted. To Thompson, Upperdine seemed indecisive now, confused, often turning in his saddle and looking back from where they'd come. His shoulders slumped; his eyes squinted into the distance. Forenoon, he reined his horse.

"They must be nearer the ford. They'd not of come this far."

"How can you be certain?"

"He came to collect wood. We passed by thick growth coming here, winter downfall. He'd of stopped long before."

Thompson followed Upperdine, again covering ground they'd been over, grimly scanning near and middle distances. Midday they dismounted and let the horses and Benito's burro graze and water for a few minutes. A hawk circled above, a dark shadow gliding over the patches of snow and rock. Thompson followed the flight of the hawk and his eyes caught something, a flash of color unnatural to the landscape that drew his attention.

"There."

Downslope from the trail, at the base of a bluff where underbrush grew thick, a flap of red cloth, a thin column of smoke.

They rode to the bluff and spotted the cart with its awning fashioned from one of Teresa's blankets.

"Hullo," Upperdine called. Paloma's head darted above the awning and she stepped out from behind the wagon and answered his call.

"Papa is hurt."

The two men dismounted and descended the slope clumsily, the footing still treacherous. Benito lay wrapped in blankets, feverish, shivering under his covers, sweat beading at his forehead. A tendril of smoke rose from a sputtering fire. Paloma had cut his boots from his feet, and swaddled them in cloth stripped from her blanket. His right leg from thigh to knee was swollen to the size of a ripe watermelon. Juniper branches splinted the leg.

"Took a spill, did you?" Upperdine asked.

"I've made quite a mess," Benito said. He tried to make his voice light, unconcerned. But his eyes reflected agony, his breathing raspy and shallow, and his face beaded with sweat.

"Got it set?"

"Paloma did as well as she could." Each sentence an effort.

"Did bone break through?"

"No."

"Can he travel?" Thompson asked.

Upperdine shook his head, no.

Benito's awareness ebbed and flowed. He seemed to drift at times to the other side and his face would relax, his breathing turn shallow and thin. Then a forced determination would distort his features and he would return to the here and now of pain and discomfort. He dozed, a troubled half-sleep, mumbled what sounded like ancient incantations. Thompson listened, mesmerized, and thought, another world? He's there now. For an instant he felt an almost irresistible urge to ask Benito, are they with you? Are they safe? Do they remember me? Condemn me?

Paloma did not leave her father's side. Thompson and Upperdine stoked the fire when Benito shivered and banked it when he burned with fever. On the morning of the second day in their makeshift camp, Benito's delirium increased and Upperdine unfurled him from his blanket and packed his torso in snow dug from the banks that still hugged the north facing slopes. Benito convulsed from cold and the jerking of his leg caused him to cry out.

"You're hurting him," Paloma protested, but weakly.

"His leg is hot to the touch and all swolled up," Upperdine said. "He'd improve his chances without it."

Paloma did not understand. "Without what?" she asked, and then after a moment she comprehended and sucked in her breath. "No. You cannot."

"Would you have him die?" Upperdine asked, gently. Thompson noticed Paloma's eyes glistening. She bit her lower lip and turned from them.

"Will it come to that?" Thompson asked.

"I don't know. Sometimes the poison works itself out. But if we wait too late, taking the leg won't matter."

Benito's eyes fluttered and he opened them, struggled to focus. "I think we'll leave the leg be," he whispered. They all turned to him. So, Thompson thought, good, he is still with us.

"As you wish," Upperdine said, putting his hand on Benito's shoulder.

Thompson thought about the options, and found himself in agreement with Benito. Could a man work the fields on one leg? His boys were not yet capable of heavy labor. Thompson had known a man in Indiana who'd had his leg pinched off mid-thigh in a logging mishap, but he had five sons and three daughters to take on the load. Paloma and Teresa? They'd do what they could. But it would be difficult. Easier to return to family in New Mexico Territory.

For another two days, Benito floated in and out, too weak to move, Upperdine sitting with him, pulling a wineskin from somewhere in his pack, squeezing the liquid first into his mouth, and then offering a taste to Benito. Paloma hovered, silent. Thompson paced. Food gave out, and for a day they made do with only melted snow.

Before dawn on the fifth morning, Thompson heard a turkey gobbling in the distance and he sneaked out into the brush and shot it. While it roasted over the embers, Benito awoke, alert, hungry, and ate more than he had for days, slept soundly the remainder of the day and through the night, and upon waking the following morning, said to John Upperdine, "I am ready to be rid of this place."

"Well, then, we'll see to it."

They placed Benito in the cart and harnessed the burro. Paloma rode Thompson's horse while Thompson led the burro. They followed the river downstream until the bluffs fell away and the bank gentled sufficiently to allow them access to the higher ground. Every rock, every jolting bump elicited a soft moan from Benito, the jostling of the cart a constant agitation. Finally, they reached the junction with the Purgatoire and made good time, Benito resting more comfortably on the established trail.

A few miles on, the homestead and the placita. They all waited at the gate. Upperdine turned away for his house and Thompson led the cart to the gate and stood back and watched the procession. The boys jumped with excitement and before anyone could restrain him, Alejandro threw himself onto the cart to hug his father, who groaned in agony but refused to relinquish his hold on the boy. Teresa approached Paloma and placed her open palm on her daughter's cheek and, to Thompson's astonishment, Paloma did not pull away. Teresa appeared to Thompson to have aged a decade in the days they'd been away. Haggard, face streaked in worry lines and tears, she could easily have passed for one of the ancient ones. She bent to her husband, feeling his forehead, clucking her tongue, saying only "Foolish man." Thompson could imagine her thoughts, what herbs remained in the medicine sack, what blends to cool the skin and heal the leg. As he eased away from the homecoming to see to the horses, he caught sight of Hanna and Joseph standing by the gate. Her eyes looked swollen and she raised her hand to him and he sensed her watching him as he walked across the field toward Upperdine's stock pen.

Hanna came to him later, at his cabin, to call him to supper. She waited at the door while he gathered his jacket. He sensed that if he invited her in, she would come. He did not want that, was not ready. Would he ever be? He hurried out to meet her and they walked to the placita.

"We were all worried sick about you," Hanna said as they traversed the field between Thompson's shack and the placita.

"We were not far," Thompson said. "But a new crisis arose daily with Benito's condition, and it did not feel right leaving." After a few minutes, he asked, "How did you fare while we were gone?"

"Teresa is a stronger woman than even I credited her for," Hanna said. "As soon as the snow lifted, she had us out scouring the brush for the missing goats, and we were able to save them all. She helped Genoveva look after Captain Upperdine's stock as well."

"Is Teresa capable of maintaining the field while Benito is recovering?" Thompson asked.

"She's managed so far. But not without cost. She is exhausted, both from worry and from work."

"I could see as much," Thompson said.

"What of Benito?" Hanna asked.

"I think he will do," Thompson said.

"The leg. Will it have to come off?"

"Don't know. But either way, it will prove a burden."

"Lame?"

"For good, I expect."

"How will he farm?" Hanna asked.

The question remained with Thompson for days on end.

24

Buffalo grass appeared on the high plains, and Upperdine prepared to ride out to guide an eastbound freight train. He planned to return by late summer with an assortment of trade goods and a full purse, and perhaps another swarm of emigrants in tow. Thompson helped hitch the team.

"You'll not change your mind?" Upperdine asked.

"No," Thompson said. "I'll see to the fields." He'd gone back and forth about it, packed and unpacked, walked along the river and far afield testing his legs and his will. But, soon as he had set his mind to assist Benito with planting, he realized the land had taken hold of him again. The prospect both excited and frightened him. What memories might be turned to the surface by the plow?

"Well, then, see to my holdings," Upperdine said, clapping Thompson on the shoulder. "A share will be yours." His face, grown doughy over the winter, now flushed, as if he'd dipped into his poor experiment with Taos Lightning. His eyes shone. Thompson knew

Captain Upperdine took no interest either in planning or in planting his fields. He traded. The prospect of profitable exchange brought him visceral pleasure. Thompson harbored no doubts about Upperdine's destiny on the frontier even as he questioned his own.

"Safe journey," Thompson called and watched him go, and traveled in his mind back across the desolate track, back to Indiana and to those three graves beneath the persimmon tree. The trail carried in its ruts and grooves so much of his pain and history that it seemed almost a part of him, a long scar running the length of his soul.

Lost inward, the wagon had long passed from sight when finally he turned and found Genoveva on the porch, watching. She'd not been present for Upperdine's departure. Standing above him, she seemed regal, larger than life, her soft brown skin and black hair; her expression tranquil and untroubled. Thompson thought her a symbol of this country, at once both new and timeless.

"Coffee?" Genoveva asked.

"I have chores," Thompson answered, and then, "But, yes, thank you."

They went into the dining room and Genoveva filled first his cup and then her own. He sipped, and, glancing over his shoulder, said, "So, he's off."

"Yes."

"Will you be all right?"

Genoveva laughed, although without mirth. "Yes. I think I will be just fine."

Thompson thought it a silly question even as he asked it. Of course Genoveva would manage. She'd managed before any of them had arrived. Seasons of solitude, seasons of unending chores, of night fears and grinding sameness.

SNOWMELT FED THE PURGATOIRE RIVER. Winter's purl increased in volume and velocity almost hourly until it threatened bank and bottomland. Some mornings the sound of water battling over and around the rocks woke Thompson and he walked the few paces from his cabin to the bluff and stood mesmerized as the river coursed below. He'd known it only as a trifling ripple. Now, an angry boil.

Spring took hold, but grudgingly: warmth to soak the shirt; a sudden thunder-snow; calm, fragrant mornings; afternoon winds so fierce that once he actually was lifted from the ground. Wind billowed his open coat and for an instant his feet lost the earth and left him with an otherworldly sensation of floating, of being somewhere other than where he was, someone other than himself.

As had become habit, Thompson went to the placita each morning for Benito. Benito could not yet walk, and he found crutches cumbersome, so Thompson hitched the burro to the cart and Paloma helped her father from the house, and the men went out into the fields. Fifteen acres, secondary ditches dividing the field into three plots.

"I thought corn here," Thompson pointed. "And there, melons."

Benito shook his head. "Corn, over there," he countered. "Here, beans. In the third section, peppers." Benito explained the contours of the land, how the water would flow, pool, and soak; the most favorable patches for each crop; how they would alternate each year.

"Visualize the water from the ditches flooding the field," he explained to Thompson.

"I expect I've seen a field or two," Thompson said.

"You've seen ground so hard the water just sits on it, can't soak in?" Benito asked. "You've seen corn stalks grow tall as me and not put out one ear because of bad soil? You've seen an apple tree curl up and go barren not three feet from the bank of a stream because the roots can't reach?"

Thompson thought Benito smug in his knowledge and resented him for it, but also recognized once again how much he must adapt to this alien world. "I'll harness up tomorrow." They both sensed it was time. The earth fully thawed, the diversion pond filled.

"Come with me," Benito said, and they led the burro across the fields and into the placita. From the cart bed, Benito summoned his boys and pointed them to the tool shed. Alejandro and Benjamin listened to his instructions and rummaged through the shed and with effort dragged out what looked like the large knee-timber of a tree. One end of the crotched log curved upwards to serve as a handle of sorts and the other branch tapered to a point tipped in iron.

"A Mexico plow?" Thompson asked. It looked primitive and clumsy, like debris swept downcurrent with the floods and deposited on the bank.

Benito nodded. "We'll break ground in the old way."

"Backwards," Thompson said.

"Traditional," Benito said. "It serves well in this soil."

"It looks like something Moses would have used," Thompson said.

"Well, if it was suitable for Moses, it should be suitable for us as well."

"That is a backward tool and I will not use it." He much preferred the steady bulk of Upperdine's eastern plow, and in the end Benito deferred to him. What choice had he?

They began with Upperdine's fields. Benito insisted on accompanying him each day, sitting in the cart, watching, shouting advice, criticism.

"That line is crooked, true it up."

"We should be making better time."

"We?" Thompson asked. He tried to understand Benito's frustration, watching the fields take shape because of Thompson's sweat, the strength of Thompson's back. But at times irritation overcame his good intentions.

When Upperdine's fields had been readied, they turned to Benito's. Thompson had worked Upperdine's land for two weeks, but the first pass over Benito's ground felt altogether different. Upperdine's fields had been broken previously and the plowing went relatively smoothly. Benito's land was unbroken, resistant. And more. The plow cutting into the undefiled plain seemed a desecration of something primeval and irreclaimable. When the blade turned the furrow slice to expose the ribbon of alien yellow soil, Thompson had to pull up before reaching his turn. He slumped over the handles and began shuddering with grief and with longing for deep woods and black loam and Matthew and Daniel bumbling along beside him and Rachel at the hearth and in his bed. With his longing came the flood of guilt. He recoiled at the suddenness of its resurfacing, its intensity and burrowed permanence.

He concentrated on willing himself forward, the plow carving deep ruts. Why these emotions, at this time? He'd worked Upperdine's fields. He'd plowed and sown Obadiah's wheat. Then it came to him. The first a business endeavor, the second an experiment only, and a repayment of sorts. But this field, this land, Benito's claim, Benito's declaration of freedom. The beginning of his legacy. And, a complete growing season come and gone since Thompson had buried his own legacy, forfeited his past. He straightened, self-conscious, realizing he'd again halted the team mid-row. There, Benito, resting in the cart. Had he noticed Thompson's jerky movements? Thompson gripped the handles and shouted the team forward.

WITH PLANTING COMPLETE, THOMPSON WALKED to his patch of wheat and found that it too had awakened with the season. Pliant shoots grew dense and boot-high. Thinking back, he found it ironic that the health of the wheat had likely been ensured by the very storm that had threatened Benito and Paloma. The storm that had served to anchor him to the valley for the planting season. Had it been a warning, or a godsend? The wheat prospered. Thompson plucked a stem and held it between his teeth and tasted the sweetness, its potential.

Hanna should see this. Obadiah's dream bearing fruit. He walked to the placita and knocked on her door without answer. He checked with Teresa, who reported seeing Hanna earlier in the day. She had helped with the tortillas. Thompson thought to return to the fields, the endless harrowing of weeds, but decided first to stop at his cabin to bundle a midday meal. As he approached, he heard scraping sounds from within, and he entered cautiously.

Hanna moved about the room whisking a broom over the plank floor. Destiny rode at her hip in a sling, burbling. Hanna glanced up, unsurprised, at Thompson's arrival.

"Hanna?"

"I brought you dinner," Hanna said, pointing to a cloth package on the table. "Some tortillas and *carne seco*." She shrugged her shoulders. "But you weren't to be found. So, I stopped it by and thought to tidy up."

"That's kind of you, but you shouldn't trouble."

"You keep the place orderly. For a man. It's no trouble."

Thompson scanned the cabin. Indeed, what possessions he did own were neatly arranged. His rifle hung on two pegs wedged between the chinking on the wall beside the door. His cookware occupied one end of the hearth: cup and plate and fork stored in the kettle that sat on the iron pan. Kindling and a day's measure of cordwood stacked on the other end. One extra shirt and pair of pants and his winter coat on nails above his bed. Ax, spade, handsaw, and pick occupying the far corner of the room, the tools a loan from Upperdine in exchange for putting them to use. He thought briefly of the life he'd abandoned in Indiana, the contrast between current paucity and former abundance, and for a moment he went dark. When his thoughts cleared, he saw that Hanna had stopped sweeping and was watching him intently.

"I own little clutter," he said.

Hanna smiled. A rarity, he thought at once. Her lines softened when she smiled. She tucked a loose strand of hair behind her ear and lifted Destiny higher onto her hip.

"Well," he said, "I'd best be to work. Thank you." He picked up the food and turned for the door.

"Do you mind if I finish up here?" She looked at him, steady-eyed, a leveling inquiry.

Thompson hesitated. A simple question. Why did it seem more complex?

"That's kind of you," he nodded and hurried out. He was in the field and hoeing before he remembered he'd not mentioned Obadiah's wheat to her.

25

One day in mid-July, weeding, Benito limped over to Thompson. He mopped his face with his forearm and gazed off into the cloudless sky.

"Behind me," Benito said to Thompson. "Do not look. A glint from the brush on the river bank."

"Near bank or far?"

"Far, I think."

"Indians?"

"I do not believe so. If Indian, we probably wouldn't have seen them until they wished to be seen."

"Then who?"

"Highwaymen perhaps. Vagabonds. I don't know."

"I'll cross upstream," Thompson said. "And circle back, from above."

"Take care."

Thompson glanced at his grub hoe. A sturdy tool, a sorry weapon. "I'll do nothing foolish."

Thompson went to where Joseph and the boys were hunched over the rows, picking leaf beetles and cutworms from the plants. Joseph straightened at his approach, stretched his back.

"Take the boys to the placita," Thompson instructed.

"Why?" Joseph asked.

The question irritated Thompson. Lately, Joseph had taken to challenging nearly every request made of him, quarreling at the slightest provocation.

"Some activity down by the river," Thompson said. "Not sure who it might be or what their intentions."

Joseph searched along the banks. "Boys can get back on their own."

Thompson regarded Joseph; tall, lanky, beginning to fill in. His pants were too short in the leg and his shirtsleeves hung just below his elbows. But not yet a man. "Do as I say."

Thompson walked upstream as if inspecting the corn, and once out of sightline, crouched low and moved to the river and crossed at the gravel bar. On the east side, he scrambled up the bank and continued several hundred yards out into the plains and then turned and moved downstream. He could see the placita and the upper edge of the field that rose from the floodplain but had view neither of the riverbank, nor of Benito's exact location. He turned back toward the river and approached the high bank on hands and knees and studied the willow thickets upstream and down for movement. Nothing seemed out of ordinary. He looked across the river and saw Benito in the cornfield, but was unsure whether Benito saw him. Thompson remained motionless except for his head, which he moved imperceptibly as he searched. He wished the wind would rise to mask his sound, allow him to inch closer. But for the moment, it remained still. After five minutes he resolved to change positions. He began to edge away, but stopped when he saw Benito wave his cane in the air and begin marching to the river, moving deliberately to a position directly across from him. Benito reached the bank and called out.

"*Hola!* Hello! Who is there? *Quien es?*" He waited for response and called again.

Thompson noticed movement in the brush immediately in front of him. The willows parted and a man backed out, hunched low, carrying a machete in one hand and a metal tube in the other. Thompson watched the thicket for sign of others. No one. Could he be alone? The man backed to within ten feet of Thompson. Thompson stood, hoe at ready, like a musket at arms.

"What is your business?"

Startled, the man whirled around and raised the machete. Thompson was positioned on the bank above the man, the distance between them loose and sandy, and he felt confident of his ability to dodge any advance, so he held his ground. The man was young, ragged, hatless, and dark-complexioned like Benito.

"Do you speak English?" Thompson asked. "State your business."

The man eyed Thompson without answering. He seemed to be measuring the strides between them, but his eyes also darted to either side as if assessing escape routes. The man's reluctance for battle was obvious, but Thompson also sensed a dangerous edge to him, nerves frayed, eyes sunken and hungry. He wished he'd more carefully thought out the confrontation before engaging the stranger. He could not walk away, leaving this unknown threat so close to the homesteads. But he was ill-equipped to advance on him.

A splashing from the river attracted the attention of both men. There, mid-stream, Benito crossing, unbalanced, his movements made clumsy both because of his injury and because moss covered the river rocks. Spring runoff had receded but he'd not chosen a safe ford, the water waist-high in the pools, the current swirling. He floundered, and fell, and his bad leg gave him no purchase to right himself. The stranger raced toward Benito, machete in hand. Thompson started down the bank, slipped on the loose footing, and tumbled, hoe flying from his hand, body folding into a hoop, landing at the bottom of the embankment in a flail of arms and legs. He jumped immediately to his feet but, stunned, collapsed into a sitting position and sat for a moment, dizzy and disoriented. He again struggled to his feet, looked midstream, and there, the stranger stood above Benito, machete at ready.

"Wait!" Thompson called. The stranger turned at the sound. His free hand gripped Benito's shirtfront. He turned back to Benito and began dragging him toward the near bank. Thompson closed the distance, losing sight of them as he scraped through willows, tripping over low-growing tangles and flood-swept debris, and then he came suddenly upon Benito prone on the bank and the stranger kneeling over him, machete thrust into the ground at his feet. Beside the machete lay a telescope. Before Thompson could assess the situation, he heard a commotion to his right. Joseph broke through the brush a few feet from Benito and raised a pistol to the stranger's back.

"No," Benito screamed.

There sounded the sharp plink of hammer against cap followed by the dull fizz of bad powder, and before Joseph could fire a second time, Thompson wrapped him in his arms and turned him away. He felt the heave of Joseph's chest and saw the bloodlust shining in his eyes. Instinctively, Joseph fought Thompson's hold, a snarling from his throat, spit and a trickle of blood on his lip. Thompson did not dare release the boy, but he felt vulnerable to the stranger and his machete.

"Easy," Thompson said. "Let go the pistol." Joseph attempted to raise his arm, to re-aim, but after several seconds the futility must have registered and the resolve weakened, and he went limp and the pistol fell to the ground.

"Easy," Thompson repeated, as if calming a skittish colt. He slowly relaxed his hold on Joseph and retrieved the Allen pistol and turned to the stranger. Benito now stood beside the man and rested one hand on his shoulder for support, his crutch lost to the river.

"Are you hurt?" Thompson asked.

"No. I am fine," Benito answered.

Thompson found himself short of breath and he bent with his hands to his knees, still holding the pistol. He and the stranger eyed one another cautiously. The stranger's attention moved between Thompson and Joseph and he appeared on the verge of bolting for cover.

"Thompson," Benito said. "This is Carlos."

The name meant nothing to Thompson. "Carlos de Vargas." Benito said. "From near Plaza del Arroyo Seco."

It came to Thompson then. Paloma's betrothed.

"I'll be damned." Thompson said. "What the hell is he doing here?"

"I did not recognize him at first," Benito said. "Nothing to him but bones."

Although they all had endured a difficult winter at the placita, Carlos seemed to Thompson worse off by an order. Joseph towered above him, bulky by comparison. Carlos's hair hung straight in long tangles, and he wore a patchy beard.

"But what the hell is he doing here?" Thompson repeated.

"He helped me from the river," Benito said. "Then you arrived. We've not had a chance to visit." Benito turned to Carlos and they conversed a while in Spanish. Carlos's voice sounded soft and youthful, in sharp contrast to his appearance. Thompson thought him too frail to have lasted any length in the wilderness. His face was fine-featured, almost feminine, with a thin nose and deep-set eyes. Ragged clothes hung loosely from narrow shoulders.

"How did you find us?" Benito asked, switching to English. Carlos responded in kind, but with a heavy accent Thompson found difficult to understand.

"I asked at the village. I traveled to the mercantile on the Arkansas, and they directed me back."

"How long have you been here?"

"Ten days."

"Along the river? You set camp?"

"Yes."

"You are welcome at my home. Why didn't you present yourself?"

Thompson knew the answer to Benito's question as well as Benito did, and suspected he asked only out of courtesy and because he wanted Carlos to address the issue directly. Carlos looked away, stammered in English, "I. I." and reverted to a rapid Spanish. Thompson walked downriver a few paces, and motioned Joseph to follow. He searched for Benito's lost cane in the shallows.

"What did you think you were doing back there?" Thompson demanded.

"Just trying to help," Joseph said.

"But for bad powder, you might have killed a man."

"Wildman sneaks into our home, how do you expect to greet him?" Joseph asked. Thompson detected no remorse.

"He is an acquaintance of the Ibarra family," Thompson said.

"I know who he is," Joseph said. "Have to be deaf and feeble in the head not to know about Paloma's trouble." Joseph turned and studied Carlos talking to Benito. "Looks the coward to me. No man for her."

Thompson started at the loathing in Joseph's voice, a snarl, his face contorted in hatred and jealousy, and for a moment he was afraid for Carlos and for Joseph as well.

"You know nothing of such matters," Thompson said.

"Enough," Joseph said.

They continued milling downstream while Benito talked with Carlos for several minutes more, and then watched as Benito approached them while Carlos turned upriver toward his camp. Carlos had cut a staff for Benito, but the bad leg dragged uselessly behind him.

"Shame overwhelms him," Benito said.

"It should," Joseph said. The men ignored him.

"Did he say why he's come?" Thompson asked. Benito nodded.

"To see her, of course. Simply to catch sight of her through the telescope. To assure himself that she is well."

"That is plain wrong," Joseph said. "To spy on her with the glass, like she was game he stalked."

"We've spoken of it," Benito said, sharply. "It is done." Benito reached into the pocket of his trousers and held out the eyepiece from the telescope.

"He will not approach her?" Thompson asked.

"No."

"How long will he camp by the river?" Thompson asked.

"I don't know," Benito said. "He yearns, but will die out here before risking Paloma's final reproach."

"Would she condemn him?"

"She aches deeply. Perhaps."

"He should settle it," Thompson said.

"He doesn't want Paloma to know he is here until he decides on a course," Benito said.

"If he can't hide any better than he can fight, he'll be discovered soon enough," Joseph said offhandedly, out of the side of his mouth.

They made a shallow ford, but Thompson hesitated. "Can you make it up the bank?"

"I made it down on my own," Benito said. He stood for a moment watching the current ebbing and swirling, gathering his strength. "Some know this river as El Rio de Las Animas Perdidas en Purgatorio."

"Long name for a small stream," Thompson said.

"The River of Souls Lost in Purgatory," Benito said. He clutched Joseph's shoulder and began a hobbled climb.

So, that is why I feel at home here, Thompson thought. And Carlos as well, perhaps. He left them and retraced his steps and came upon Carlos's camp, a crude hut, willow branches arched over a stiffer cottonwood frame and interwoven with reeds and rushes. It blended perfectly with the surroundings. Carlos squatted beside a fire ring just outside the hut, striking a flint to ignite a mound of sun-dried moss. Thompson wondered about not detecting smoke during the past days and cautioned himself against complacency. Carlos looked up at Thompson's approach but continued hammering the flint against the harder rock. The moss sparked, and Carlos blew softly and cupped his hand on the backside of the moss bundle, coaxed the spark to a flicker, and motioned to Thompson. Thompson knelt and took up a handful of wood shavings and let them drop onto the moss and added his breath as well. The shavings caught, Carlos added kindling, twigs, sticks, and finally a few dried limbs, and soon a flame took hold and threw off heat enough to help dry his clothes, wet from assisting Benito. He removed his outer tunic and draped it across his hut, within reach of the fire's warmth. In his woolen undergarment, he appeared to Thompson even scrawnier, like a winter-starved coyote.

"Do you carry a firearm?"

"A pistol. But I have no shot. No powder."

"How have you eaten?"

"I had money enough to buy meal. And there are catfish in the larger river."

Thompson pointed to the bluff upriver on the opposite bank. "A cabin there, mostly hidden by the sumac and the scrub. Usually, I have meat enough. You get hungry, you come by."

Carlos regarded the bluff. "I would not wish to be seen."

"Just hang close by the underbrush. There's no view from the placita," Thompson said. "Paloma works the garden and the field midday, after morning chores."

"I know."

"Of course."

Within the hour, Thompson rejoined Benito in the field. "Will he inform Paloma?" Benito asked, nodding toward Joseph in the distance, returning to the placita.

"I don't think so," Thompson said. "Not until he figures a way to use the news to his advantage."

"Is he that cunning?" Benito asked.

"He's that desperate, I'm afraid," Thompson said. He turned and looked back across the river, and thought he detected smoke. A moment only, and then just the dull green of the willows, the brown expanse beyond, and he decided his eyes must have deceived.

At day's end, Thompson walked to his cabin and found Joseph sitting outside, waiting for him.

"I thought to collect my pistol," Joseph said.

"First off," Thompson said, "you have no need of it. It is useless as a hunting piece, and as you recently discovered of little value as a sidearm."

"It is mine. I want it."

"Secondly, it is not your pistol. It belongs to John Upperdine."

"You won't return it to me?"

"Joseph, does it even register with you that you attempted to kill a man?"

"What registers is regret that I failed," Joseph said as he turned to leave. His eyes still reflected the strange glint Thompson had noticed that morning, and his dispassion chilled.

Thompson entered the cabin and took the pepperbox pistol from his belt and disassembled it in the dull light. It was obvious why the piece had misfired, so clogged with dried mud and bits of leaf and twig. Luckily, the boy had little knowledge about sidearm maintenance. Thompson considered discarding the unreliable weapon, but instead cleared the barrels and wiped grime from the springs and mechanisms. He had no oil, but he rubbed the outer surfaces with a thin coating of grease. Then he reassembled the pistol and dry-fired it, watching the hammer raise against the pressure of the mainspring and drive down onto the nipple as the barrels rotated smoothly with each trigger action.

Obadiah had held this pistol when the border ruffians rode down on them, refused to raise it. Joseph had told him as much. Thompson was certain that is why Joseph so insisted on keeping the pistol, a symbol of his shame, of his anger. That day came back to Thompson in swirling flashes: the raiders turning and charging toward him hunkered in the buffalo wallow, the man raising his revolver, twisting almost sideways as he aimed, a puff of gunpowder from the barrel, the high-pitched sing of the ball past his ear. A sweet buzz. Deadly intent. And, later, after repelling the attack, coming into camp on Turkey Creek to find the mutilated body of the freedman, Ned, and Obadiah's vacant stare. He remembered thinking that the circle on Obadiah's forehead leaked far less red than he imagined it should. And the blood running down Hanna's bare leg, and the death-quiet that descended upon the camp once the violence ended.

Obadiah had refused to use the pistol. Could that explain Joseph's eagerness to pull the trigger? What if Thompson had returned to camp an hour earlier, might he have altered Joseph's future? He lay on his robes and stared at the ceiling for several hours before drifting off. In the morning, he collected his spade and his hoe from the corner and started for the near field to cut water from the acequia, and thought as he walked how much more comfortable the tools felt in his hands than the weapon.

26

"A boy," Thompson said. "Just sixteen."

"Still," Carlos said.

"And Anglo," Thompson continued. "Paloma barely tolerates him."

"She's thin," Carlos said.

"She is sturdy."

Thompson realized that even without a telescope, Carlos could not help but keep Paloma within sight. He must be taking chances. He imagined Carlos on his belly in the low grass, moving on his elbows, edging ever closer. Surely he'd seen Paloma in the fields with Joseph. Was he working up to something?

They walked together to Obadiah's wheat patch. Something in the air, the dry wash of the wind across his face, a scent of ripeness perhaps, triggered in Thompson the notion that the time for harvest approached. Out of sight of the placita and the irrigated fields, Carlos walked easily beside him. Settled in his camp and benefitting from Thompson's offer of food, Carlos had gained weight over the past month, and gone was the abject hollowness of his face. Thompson had grown fond of Carlos: his earnest devotion to the ideal of Paloma, so foreign to Thompson's own assessment of her in the concrete; his self-denial; his guilt, which Thompson painfully understood.

"Yesterday, she worked without a hat." Carlos made a motion with his hand covering his head.

"A bonnet," Thompson said. "She wears mostly what she pleases."

"Caution her about the heat," Carlos said.

Thompson laughed. "My warning would carry little weight, I assure you. Why don't you reason with her?"

Carlos went quiet.

They came to the wheat field, golden in the sun, the stalks brushing against Thompson's waist, heads bulky with seed and bowed. Heat of summer, Thompson thought, a strange time to harvest. He possessed little knowledge about this wheat other than what Obadiah had passed to him in conversation and what Benito knew from growing a different variety in Plaza del Arroyo Seco's community field. He picked a grain and tested it with his thumbnail. Firming up, it could be dented but only with considerable pressure. Let the wind dry it for another day or two, Thompson thought. A small field, but it would yield well. Obadiah's wheat indeed appeared suited to this land. Rain had been scarce and had not fallen at opportune times, and autumn harvest would suffer for it. But this wheat prospered. Obadiah had guessed correctly. Benito as well. With good fortune and proper management, this land could produce. He imagined acre upon acre spreading the full sweep of the valley. He'd require seed, land, tools. Was he seeing the future, or a fool's dream?

"Time to make ready," Thompson said.

"I wish I could help," Carlos said. He mimicked a cutting stroke with his right arm.

"Perhaps it's time," Thompson said. "Show yourself. You can't stay in the brush forever."

"I cannot."

"Then leave," Thompson said, his tone harsher than he'd intended. "Get on with your life." He watched Carlos for a reaction. Carlos remained impassive, eyes downturned.

"I cannot," Carlos said. "I cannot stay. I cannot leave."

"Benito told me something of your story," Thompson said. "A tough fix."

"I handled it poorly."

"Sounds to me like you did what you needed to stay alive."

"Alive for this?" Carlos said, pointing in the general direction of his camp.

"That one moment will consume you if you allow it," Thompson said.

"I have no control," Carlos said.

Thompson understood the feeling.

"That soldier's pistol," Carlos continued, "at my face?"

"Yes?"

"The barrel looked large as a stovepipe."

"I imagine so," Thompson said.

"I could not move. My bowels loosed."

"Go easy," Thompson said.

Carlos began to speak but his voice caught, and he raised his hands in surrender.

They turned from the field and retraced their steps toward Thompson's cabin. Just before it came into view, Carlos grew skittish and descended the river bank and went off into the brush. Thompson continued on and inside his cabin he retrieved a small pouch from the folds of his extra tunic and emptied coins into his palm, gold and silver, money remaining from Indiana. He began once again to relive those days when a knock on the door returned him to the present. He absently pocketed the coins and went to the door and found Hanna standing outside with Destiny slung at her hip.

"I'd not noticed you in the fields," Hanna said. "I wondered if you might be ill."

"I'm fine," Thompson said. "I was checking the wheat. It is ripe."

Without waiting for invitation, Hanna entered the cabin and took a sleeping Destiny from her hip and laid her on Thompson's bed and began cleaning. Thompson sat at the table and watched as she cleaned the hearth, the lines of her back and arms as she swept the soot-stained stones.

"There is some coffee left," Thompson said.

"That would be fine," Hanna said, not looking up from her work. He went to the outside fire ring and unhooked the pot from the tripod and poured coffee and brought it to her. Hanna straightened and put her hands to the small of her back and stretched. She reached for the cup and let her hand pause on his. A current worked through him, passing from his hand up his arm and down into his groin, and he angled his body away in embarrassment. He thought he saw recognition cross Hanna's face, the hint of a smile, but she did not say anything and returned to her work. Thompson wished both for her to leave and to stay.

Destiny stirred on the bed and began to whimper. "She's hungry," Hanna said, and went to her. With her back to Thompson she unbuttoned her dress and cradled the child in the crook of her arm. Thompson listened to Destiny's greedy suckling and was overcome with self-disgust at his own yearnings. He slipped from the cabin and walked rapidly, working up a sweat, attempting to distract his thoughts from milk-swollen breasts beneath the thin cotton of Hanna's dress. Without planning his destination, he found himself passing beside the wheat field and beyond. The coins jangled in his pocket, and he realized that he'd been pacing off acreage. A dollar and twenty an acre, he supposed. On a low swell where the fertile river bottom gave way to coarse scrub, he turned, and from that minor vantage he could look back over the valley. In the near distance, the wheat field; and further on, the placita walls and the irrigated fields beginning to flush with crops; and in the distance beyond, the Upperdine house, a small dark square. And then, a slow awareness: this place, home. A few months shy of a year spent in the valley of the Purgatoire, the seasons come full cycle, perhaps his anguish as well. Can grief be cycled with the seasons, he wondered? His? Carlos's? Can it be plowed under, worked deeper and deeper into the soil until it's finally buried for good? He did not know, only that the earth felt comfortable under his boots. The scabbed hills, the blank, raw-boned plains and expressive skies, the absolute otherness of this new world compared to his old, it all felt right.

27

"Hog fodder," Benito said. "My boys eat food meant for hogs, and you would deny us grain?"

It was true, Thompson admitted. The cornmeal had run low in June, and Teresa had collected dried husks from the fodder bin and crushed them and added the powdery mix to the remaining meal to stretch supplies. The tortillas tasted coarse but they filled the stomach.

Now they stood over the bags of wheat grain, twelve bushels, the yield from Thompson's experiment with Obadiah's seed. Together they'd cut the stalks, threshed it against the adobe wall of the placita, and winnowed chaff from grain. Twelve bushels they ended with.

"We need seed for planting come autumn," Thompson said, keeping his voice even.

"There is more than enough to replant your field and supply bread as well," Benito said.

"Bread would be welcome," Teresa said. The others remained silent.

"Wheat takes to this climate," Thompson said. "I, we need to expand acreage."

"Fair," Benito said. "You planted only a test section. What are your plans, ten, twelve acres?"

"Twenty-five, thirty," Thompson answered. He watched as Benito evaluated the grain, measuring Thompson's requirement against yield. Benito's expression darkened.

"We've had no bread since spring," Benito said. "Little cornmeal."

"The gardens are beginning to produce," Thompson said. "There's fresh meat. Surely we can trade for a few sacks of meal at the fort. Before long our own corn will be in." He looked to the others. Hanna alone returned his gaze. She appeared ready to speak, but Genoveva broke the silence first.

"A compromise," she said. "A share to all who helped reap, a double share to Thompson for his labor last autumn. He can keep his share in seed, and we can grind the remainder."

Thompson would have liked more, did not understand Benito's shortsightedness. He thought if he pressed the matter, Hanna would join the debate on his side. Was it not her seed, after all? But he felt partially responsible for having depleted it, for upturning Obadiah's sack into the river soon after they had arrived. He knew the dispute could split their small community and saw no good coming from such a division. And, even with seed available, he technically owned no acreage on which to plant. He nodded assent and looked to Benito, who inclined his head not to him but to Genoveva.

"A fair solution."

The following morning, Thompson returned to his cabin from early chores, built a small fire in the outside pit, and was reheating a pail of beans from the evening before when two men approached from the southwest, following the Purgatoire downstream. They were white men, lean-built and shuffling, one tall and long-whiskered, the other narrow-shouldered, almost boyish, clean-shaven, and with hair that hung down below his shoulders. The full-bearded man led a donkey loaded with what Thompson took to be mining gear: shovels and pickaxes strapped to the packsaddle; panniers knocking against the donkey's ribcage. Thompson considered retrieving his rifle from the cabin but decided against it because the two strangers had their weapons lashed to the donkey. They both lifted their hats as they drew near and Thompson moved his pail from the flame and set it on a stone of the fire ring and stood.

"It's good to come upon civilization again," the tall man said, waving his hat at the cabin. "We'd be looking for the junction with the Arkansas, and the trail east."

"You are not far," Thompson said. "A few miles downstream yet, but the path is clear and level."

"Obliged," the man said. He eyed the skillet, looked away, and rubbed his beard.

"You come from upriver, obviously," Thompson said. "Travel a ways?"

"We came west to prospect. The money men got all the Pikes Peak digs claimed. We went west into the mountains and south and followed this stream east, panning as we come."

"Success?"

"None to speak of. We have flat had our fill of the adventure."

"You eaten?"

"Oh, sure. A time back."

Thompson noticed them both purposely looking away from the beans, downstream, as if searching for the confluence. "Come sit. This will divide."

The bearded man glanced at his companion and motioned, and he tethered the donkey's lead to a willow limb and walked over to the fire.

"Obliged, again," the man said and offered his hand. "Edward Handy."

"Thompson Grey."

Edward motioned to his companion.

"This here is Olivia Handy, my wife."

Thompson quickly eyed her. Yes, a woman. Sun-darkened, leather-faced, hollow-cheeked, empty pouches for breasts, trail-worn.

"Mam," he said, tilting his head. "Excuse me a moment." Thompson went inside and carried out one of the table benches and set it by the fire. "Please, sit." He put the skillet back onto the coals and retrieved an egg from the basket he'd collected that morning and broke it into the skillet, and others, ten or so, and took his knife and scrambled the eggs with the beans and tossed in some dried peppers. He handed the knife to Olivia and she continued stirring the eggs while Thompson collected two tin plates from inside. He scooped eggs onto the plates and handed them to Edward and Olivia, and he ate from the pan with his knife. Olivia accepted the fork, and Edward ate with his fingers. Shoveling the food, the two prospectors without talk, without looking up until the plates were empty. Edward pressed his forefinger against the plate to tamp a morsel of egg and brought the finger to his mouth and sucked at it.

"How far to the trail, you say?" he asked.

"Couple of miles," Thompson said. "Easy ford this time of year."

"Well, then," Edward said, standing. "We are fortified for it."

Olivia stood as well. "You got more gold in that there skillet than we dug in four months on the streams."

"I don't follow you," Thompson said.

"Them eggs," she said. "Peddler come into camp month last, fresh eggs, fresh meat." Olivia spat in the dirt. "Men standing in line, just begging to give that man their gold flake for something other than salt pork and corn mush."

Thompson wrapped a handful of coffee beans in a strip of flour sack and handed the package to Olivia along with several strips of buffalo jerky. She nodded thanks and fell into step behind her husband and the donkey. Thompson watched them go, a bit more surefooted than when they had arrived. To the ford, and then set course eastward, perhaps to join up with a company headed by someone like John Upperdine. Return home. Missouri? Kentucky? Georgia? To a future of, what? They'd had a dream, followed it, and failed. Were they better off for the adventure, or worse? Perhaps the memory of having a dream at all would provide sufficient motivation to begin anew, or some measure of comfort in their dotage.

He mulled what Olivia had said. Eggs, as cherished as nuggets. What price fresh produce? Unsalted meat? He picked up the shell of a broken egg, examined it, and watched the two prospectors shrink to small, shapeless forms. A chance encounter, he reflected. An offhand comment. An opportunity?

28

The bear came from the riverbank early the following morning, with the lumbering deliberation of the unassailable. Haunches worked up and down, side to side, without haste, a hump-backed sway. Thompson stood outside his cabin, washing his face in a tin basin, preparing to shave, and through filmed-over eyes he thought he saw in the distance a wagon making slow progress across the untracked landscape. He instantly understood the improbability, swiped a cloth across his face, cleared his vision, and confirmed his suspicion. The prairie grizzly leisurely dug an onion from Teresa's garden, ate it, and another. A movement caught Thompson's eye, Benito limping from the orchard, waving his hat with one hand and hobbling toward the bear, staff gouging the earth, propelling himself forward as fast as his crippled leg could carry him. The bear lifted its snout and sniffed the air, head tilting as if listening to the birdsong, not a care in the world. It seemed to lose interest in the garden because of some random scent delivered with the breeze and it followed the adobe wall, occasionally pausing to rub its flank against the warm sandpaper texture until it reached the open gate, and disappeared into the placita.

Thompson scrambled inside for his rifle, banged his shoulder hard on the doorframe, and started across the field, progress slowed by his deadened arm and by corn stalks almost as tall as he. He broke from the cornfield just as Carlos exploded from the brush bordering the riverbank and charged through the pepper patch ahead of him. Carlos screamed as he ran, an unintelligible sound, some basic, primeval cry originating high in his throat, and the machete in his hand caught the sun, glinted as his arms pumped. Thompson noted the speed and a desperate forward-leaning stride. A single-minded, unwavering course.

"Wait," Thompson called, but Carlos did not acknowledge him. His hat flew from his head and cartwheeled among the peppers. Thompson raced after him, but knew he would not catch up, knew that Carlos would enter the gate first. As Carlos approached, a great baying sounded from within, a curling, deep-throated roar that caused Thompson to pull up. Carlos met the bear as it literally exploded from the compound, full gallop. Man and bear collided, uncontrollable force meeting fragile, malleable flesh. The bear continued forward across the fields and down the river embankment and into the brush. The human flew to the side, six, eight feet into the air, twisting, flapping like a cloth in the wind, thudding to the ground, a puff of dust rising, settling.

Thompson had not shouldered his rifle. The bear had emerged from the placita with such unfocused ferocity, Carlos had entered with such urgency, he'd never thought to take aim. The drama froze him, mesmerized. The power of the beast, the frailty of the man, the silent aftermath settling upon the placita. The bear disappeared into wilderness, the man lay motionless, and Thompson lowered the hammer on his rifle and approached the gates. He knelt beside Carlos and studied the gash along his scalp line, not deep but blood heavily flowing. Although unconscious, Carlos breathed evenly, almost peacefully, it seemed, a slight fluttering behind the eyelids.

"Does he live?" Benito asked, coming up beside Thompson.

"Yes. I don't think he's in terrible shape." Thompson stood and they started for the placita to check on the others, but were preempted by Teresa striding from it, followed by Paloma and Hanna. Joseph stood back with the two boys clinging to his legs. They were unharmed. Thompson noticed Teresa glance briefly at the man on the ground, assess his ragged appearance and rough clothes. Then she looked toward the field. "Has it fled?" she asked.

"Hell-bent," Thompson said.

Teresa returned her gaze to the injured man, studied him closely, looked quizzically first to Benito and then to Thompson and then back to Carlos. Recognition came into her eyes. She took Paloma's elbow and tried to lead her away, but Paloma pulled from her grasp and stood over Carlos, eyes wide, mouth agape, "Qué . . . ?" all she could mutter, "Qué es esto?" She turned and walked several paces back toward the compound and then returned and stood over Carlos, a look of distain as if disappointed the apparition hadn't melted away. She bent, peered into his face, stood, and repeated her pacing, brow forming questions she gave no voice to.

Teresa motioned to Thompson and Benito. "Gently," she said, "bring him inside."

"Do no such thing," Paloma said.

Joseph approached Paloma and pointed at Carlos with disgust. "He has no right to be here," nudging him roughly with the toe of his boot.

"Shut your mouth," Thompson commanded. "And step away." Joseph jerked his eyes from Carlos and glared at Thompson for a long moment before turning his back and retreating to the compound.

"You would have us leave him in the dirt?" Teresa asked her daughter.

"He left me in the dirt," Paloma said, her tone flat and distant.

"He was injured attempting to intercept the bear," Thompson said.

"No one asked his assistance," Paloma said. "Why is he here?"

"He came because he could not stay away," Benito said.

"Who invited him?"

"His heart."

"Well, his legs can return him."

Thompson came up close to Paloma. She diverted her eyes, but Thompson waited until she acknowledged him. "Think hard," Thompson whispered, "before you pass judgment. Carlos was willing to die for you. Perhaps longing to."

"A little tardy in his offer," she said.

"Would you really choose to live out your days as you have this past year?"

"You don't know what it was like," Paloma said under her breath, as if talking to herself.

"So. You are lost to the soldiers," Thompson said, not unkindly, with resignation.

Carlos stirred. Paloma looked down at him, started to speak, hesitated. "Enough," Teresa said. "Carry him inside." This time, Paloma did not protest.

Carlos regained senses slowly over the next few hours, periods of fuzzy-headed confusion alternating with deep slumber. Upon initially awaking, his right arm hacked the air furiously, his imaginary machete fending off the imaginary grizzly. He aggravated his head wound and the bandages began to seep. Teresa put her hands on his shoulders and pressed him down onto the mattress and hummed soothingly. He looked up at her without

comprehension but allowed himself to be tended to and comforted. He rested on and off and by evening realized his whereabouts, and now it was Thompson who had to sit with him, to
restrain him from leaving.

"Help me. I must go," he begged Thompson.

"You are not fit to be on your own. Tomorrow, perhaps."

"You don't understand."

"It seems there is much I don't understand today," Thompson said.
"Nevertheless, you need to rest, regain your strength."

Carlos sat up and looked about the room. He sucked in his breath
and wrapped his arms around his ribs and winced. "The bear?" he
asked, darkly.

"All is safe."

"The others?"

"Safe. Once we determined that you were in no danger, they
returned to their chores." Thompson knew what Carlos yearned to
ask and knew as well he never would.

"What of the bear?" Carlos asked again.

Teresa brought a cup of broth and handed it to Carlos and motioned
for him to sip and set a tortilla on the covers beside him. "You were
very brave," she said. "You drove it from the gates."

Carlos tasted the broth. "I do not remember."

"Very brave," Teresa repeated. "Eat. Then rest."

Carlos finished the soup and the tortilla and reclined on the
mattress and closed his eyes. The others drifted in from chores to
check on him, everyone except Paloma. Genoveva brought fresh
bread. Benito came late with the boys and Carlos thanked them
for use of their bed. When Teresa went to draw water from the
well, Thompson followed her into the courtyard. Across the plaza,
Paloma worked in the small garden they kept within the walls of
the compound.

"Will she see him?" Thompson asked.

"I don't know," Teresa said. "She is stubborn."

"She would deny herself a chance at happiness?"

"First she must allow herself to forgive."

Thompson took the bucket from Teresa and filled it, and they started back toward the house. "The bear," Thompson said.

"Yes?"

"It entered the compound and left in great confusion just as Carlos arrived."

"*Sí.*"

"What happened?"

"It started for the chicken coop," Teresa said. "We dissuaded it."

"How?"

"Pepper," Teresa said. "When the men are in the field, we always keep a cup of ground pepper and a corn knife close," she said. "For unwelcome visitors."

"Pepper?" Thompson asked.

"Pepper," Teresa said. "A cup of powder to the snout, the eyes, and they are discouraged."

"But to approach so close," Thompson said.

Teresa looked at him with confused bemusement. "What choice?" she said, and smiled.

They returned to the house and found Carlos asleep. Benito led the boys out to help herd the goats into the pen for the night.

"They will be nervous," Benito instructed the boys. "The bear's scent still hangs in the air."

Thompson collected his rifle and followed them to the door.

"You won't stay for the evening meal?" Teresa asked. She was adding onions, early potatoes and some wild greens to the broth she had prepared for Carlos.

"Thank you, but I should be off."

"I, as well," said Carlos, awakened, standing wobble-legged beside the bed.

"No." From the open door, Paloma pushed past Thompson. At the sight of her, Carlos' legs gave out and he sat back into a heap on the matting.

"You need rest." She came up and stood beside him. Not too close. "And you are filthy."

Carlos examined his worn trousers, the tattered shirt, but said nothing.

"You will stay tonight," Paloma continued. "Tomorrow we will wash your clothes. I will trim your hair."

"As you wish," Carlos said. His voice was weak, submissive.

Thompson eased from the house and across the courtyard. An uninspiring reunion lacking cheer, he thought. But, a start.

THOMPSON SAW LITTLE OF CARLOS during his convalescence. Paloma moved back into her parent's rooms and they quartered Carlos with the boys. He remained abed for three days and for a week following suffered debilitating headaches whenever he rose. Thompson noticed Paloma arriving late to the fields in the morning and leaving early in the afternoon.

"Are they reconciled?" he called to Benito one day as Thompson cut water from the acequia into the pepper field. Benito walked among the apple trees inspecting for insects. By some miracle many of the trees stripped of leaves by the locusts had regenerated that past spring and Benito coddled them if they were children who had emerged healthy from some horrific illness.

"Something is happening," Benito said, "but I am unsure what. I know only that each morning upon rising Carlos discovers some pain that prevents him from being fully up and about, and that Paloma does not dissuade him."

"How does he fare with the others?" Thompson asked.

"The boys won't leave him be. And Teresa used to regard him as family. Now, perhaps she's a bit more reserved in her opinion. But she is a forgiving woman."

"Does Joseph treat him with civility?"

Benito walked over to Thompson and removed his hat and scratched his head. "We've seen nothing of him since the incident."

"Nor I," Thompson said. "I'd just assumed he was helping out elsewhere. Mrs. Light's garden or with the goats."

"No," Benito said, and returned his attention to the trees.

THE DAY CLOSING, THOMPSON CALLED on Hanna Light. He'd kept from the placita these past days by intent. He was uncertain how the arrival of Carlos might affect the tenuous peace that existed between Paloma and her father, especially given the awkwardness of having the Lights occupying the room originally intended for her and Carlos. Thompson brooked little interest in social intrigues. Nevertheless, once he learned of Joseph's neglect, he felt compelled to check on Hanna and the baby.

The plaza was quiet when Thompson entered, Benito's family retired for the evening, smoke and the scent of piñon fire in the air. He knocked quietly on Hanna's door and waited on the porch. She answered but rather than join him outside, she swung the door open and turned into the room. He stepped inside. Fireplace embers offered faint light. She fed the embers with kindling and when it flared added a pine knob. Soon, a flickering illumination opened the space to full view. Well-kept, clothes folded on a stand in one corner, the kitchenware neatly arranged on the dry sink, white lace on the table, a pleasant, clean smell to the room. A quilt covered the bed, concentric octagons in vibrant colors. He could not take his eyes from it. He'd not been in a room with a quilt since Indiana, and the sight made his heart tighten in his chest. Destiny lay on the quilt, curled into a ball, sucking her thumb. He ached.

Joseph was absent. "He's away?" asked Thompson.

"More days than not," she said. "I rarely see him. Neglects the chores, keeps off to himself somewhere."

"Since Carlos arrived?" Thompson asked. Hanna nodded.

"Are you getting by?" he asked. "Do you need help?"

"No, thank you," she answered. "The garden is not too great a chore, and I'm able to help Teresa some. I do wish Joseph would take on more in the fields. We owe them."

"Them?" Thompson asked.

"Captain Upperdine. Señor Ibarra. I know we've been a great imposition." Tears welled; her eyes glistened but did not spill.

"Would you like me to talk to him?" Thompson asked.

"I'm afraid he's lost to reason," Hanna said. "I don't know him at all. I tried to be a mother to him after Obadiah died, but he wouldn't take to it."

"You've done right by him," Thompson said. "I'll talk to him."

"I'm not sure where to find him," Hanna said.

"I have my guesses," Thompson said.

"You are kind," Hanna said. "You are a good and kind man."

"Well," Thompson said, and started for the door.

"Mr. Grey," Hanna said, and he turned and she stepped close and took his hand. "Thank you," she said, and brought his hand to her heart and held it there for a time looking into his eyes. "For everything." When she did release his hand, he did not remove it from her breast. He caressed her, felt her heart beating, the warmth and swell of her. She closed her eyes and he also, remembering the feel, the connection between two people and then the baby stirred and their eyes opened and Thompson stepped away. Hand on the latch, he turned back.

"Do you think about them?" he asked. "The ones left behind?"

"Only in memory," she said.

"Do you ever ask what more you might have done?" he asked.

"I do not," Hanna answered. "I was there for them."

"But more," Thompson said. "Could you have done more?"

"There was nothing more. After the grief worked its way through me, I knew there was nothing more to be done."

"I suppose," Thompson said.

"Have you died in your grief?" Hanna asked. "Died and come out on the other side?"

"I don't know," Thompson said. "I don't know what that would feel like."

Hanna smiled and Thompson saw a measure of sorrow reflected in the firelight.

"If you don't know," Hanna said, "then you haven't."

THE NEXT MORNING, THOMPSON WENT to the river, forded at a shallow crossing and approached Carlos's old campsite. As he suspected, he found Joseph stooping beside the hut, a small fire, absently hacking a cottonwood limb with a machete. Thompson stepped from the thicket and Joseph looked up, seemingly unsurprised by his appearance.

"So, you know of this place," Thompson said. He sat on his heels next to Joseph.

"Wasn't hard to find once I set to it," Joseph said

"That's his machete," Thompson said.

Joseph continued chopping until the limb severed and he tossed one of the lengths onto the fire. "He left it in the dirt beside the gate that day with the bear. He wants it back, he can come take it."

"You here regular?" Thompson asked.

"Once he took up with them," Joseph answered, and suddenly animated, he propped the remaining length of cottonwood against the ground and cut the branch in two with a single violent stroke of the blade. "I never would of let them touch her," he said.

"You've said that you know of their troubles," Thompson said.

"I got ears," Joseph said. "Hanna is friends with Teresa. They talk." Joseph sunk the blade into the hard sand. "They would have been called to account."

"Easy enough to say without a pistol in your eye," Thompson said. Joseph spat in the fire.

"Look," Thompson said, "when the test comes, all we have is the moment. You can't go back, change things. Have to live with it, make your own peace, and move on."

Thompson stood and stretched and looked down at Joseph. "That time on the trail when the men came. Nothing you could have done." Joseph did not respond, continued hacking at the cottonwood branch with the machete. Thompson left the campsite more apprehensive than when he'd arrived. Joseph was a boy looking for a fight, any excuse to prove to the world that he was not his father.

Thompson recrossed the Purgatory and joined Benito in the field, moving down the rows, weeding and pinching cutworms and corn borers. Morning wore on, the work tedious and never-ending.

Toward midday, Benito called to Thompson, "Someone coming."

They both recognized the lead wagon, a six-mule team with Captain Upperdine astride the pole mule.

Thompson was not surprised at Upperdine's arrival. He had been expected shortly. Indeed, Genoveva already had readied their house for his arrival, filled the decanters with his pear brandy and stocked his tobacco tin. But both he and Benito were more than curious about a second wagon following behind Upperdine's, a light hitch pulled by two perfectly matched white jacks.

"A fine-looking team," Thompson remarked.

"Fit for a patrón," Benito said, "or a bishop."

"A single driver," Thompson said. "Wagon high on its springs."

"Light cargo," Benito finished Thompson's thought.

They cut across the field and met Upperdine just up-trail from his house. As was his nature after prolonged absences, Upperdine was buoyant, full of himself, effusive.

"Look at this place," he said, sweeping his arms. "You've created an oasis in the midst of the wasteland. Tall crops. My oxen and sheep, fat as ticks."

"We've had good fortune," Benito said.

"The pests have left us be, for the most," Thompson added.

"Nonsense," Upperdine said. "Give credit where due."

"Your journey was safe?" Benito inquired.

"The usual tests," Upperdine said.

Thompson and Benito both glanced at the trailing wagon and the man at the reins.

"Mr. Ansell Foster," Upperdine said. "From Zanesville, Ohio."

"Long way from home," Thompson said.

"Come to dinner. I'll explain everything."

"I'll see to the team," Thompson said, gathering the lead rein while Upperdine dismounted and walked back to Foster's rig.

THAT EVENING THOMPSON CALLED AT the appointed time, but nevertheless was last to join the dinner party. The women had dressed for company. Both Teresa and Genoveva wore shawls of fine lace that reminded Thompson of snow crystals he'd once viewed through a magnifying glass. Hanna owned nothing of matching refinement but had dressed carefully and had cinched her waist with a colorful belt of dyed cloth borrowed from Genoveva, he supposed. Even Paloma had troubled to arrange her hair up off of her neck in a fashionable twist. Carlos devoured her with his eyes. Genoveva apparently had relayed to John Upperdine news of Carlos, for the Captain accepted him at the table as an expected and welcome member of Benito's family.

Alejandro and Benjamin played by the hearth quietly with the baby. To Thompson's surprise, Joseph was present, his clothes brushed, presentable. A stranger coming into the territory always attracted interest. While they ate, Upperdine explained that he had met Ansell Foster in eastern Kansas Territory as he was forming up a westbound freight train.

"What news do you bring us of the east, Mr. Foster?" Genoveva asked.

"Nothing much of interest to the ladies," Foster said. "Politics, mostly. Bigwigs met in Wyandotte and drew up a new constitution for the Territory. Said it's sure to get us statehood."

"Free state or slave?" Joseph asked, loudly. It was the first he'd spoken and the only indication to Thompson he'd even been following the conversation.

"Free," Foster said.

"Will that stir up trouble again?" Thompson asked.

"Might," Foster said. "Ratification is certain by all accounts. Talk is the governor will form a militia as soon as the vote decides the issue."

"When is the vote?" Joseph asked.

"As we speak," Foster said. They went on for some minutes, Joseph more engaged than Thompson remembered ever seeing him. He wanted to hear any rumors of border clashes, any inflammatory news at all, peppered Foster with questions.

Partly to re-direct the conversation, Thompson finally broke in. "What brings you west, Mr. Foster? What is your business?" Foster appeared neither a prospector nor an immigrant. His frame was too slight for heavy work, and he wore eastern attire, a frock coat over a collared vest and a white shirt. A red cravat was loosely tied at his neck. He sported heavy side-whiskers, well-trimmed, and no beard.

A respectable gentleman, Thompson judged, and out of place as a silver tea service.

"I am a surveyor, Mr. Grey."

Thompson looked to Upperdine.

"Mr. Foster was laying out town sites, homesteads, farms, public lands, you could almost see the cities sprouting from his lines and stakes," Upperdine gushed. "I lured him here."

"To what purpose?" Thompson asked.

"Arkansas City," Upperdine said, and reminded them of his proposal to lay out a settlement on his holdings downriver, near the confluence. "A ready-built market for trade goods. We'll plat building sites on a fifty-acre grid, and fields in quarter-section parcels radiating out from it."

"Who will come to this Arkansas City?" Benito asked.

"Trail is thick with emigrants," Upperdine said. "Coming and going both. At present, mostly prospectors, discouraged ones flowing out, hopeful ones flowing in, and more and more with families in tow. I've already posted flyers in Westport and Council Bluffs."

"A town," Teresa said, her voice trailing as if attempting to formulate the idea. "People. Neighbors."

"Not our people," Paloma interrupted.

"Yes," Teresa said. "People just like us, in search of a new home."

"Is there land enough?" Benito questioned no one in particular. "The right kind of land, with water? Too many people demanding too much can wear out a place."

Thompson listened in stunned silence. He did not take in half what was being said. Land. Would they come? Would the choice cropland be claimed before he raised sufficient funds to lay stake? Lay stake? The notion hadn't occurred to him before this moment. Or, if it had, he unconsciously suppressed it. He remembered the collection of abandoned shacks on the convergence of the rivers when they'd first come into the valley. Could he acquire land ahead of the emigrants? And, even if somehow he were able, if he grew wheat, what might his market be? Would water flow prove sufficient to power a flour mill? Who would provide oxen or horses in sufficient quantities for the plow? Conversation buzzed without his hearing, without his being aware of the others at the table.

Upperdine blustered on for some time, the brandy flowing. Thompson sat with the others, but his mind drifted out into the valley, mentally laying out his acreage. A full section, steel breaker plows to turn the matted grass, and hired field hands. But even in his dreams, he knew he'd never be able to raise in one piece the money such ambitions required.

"I'll lend a hand," Joseph said. Thompson's attention focused back on the conversation. Joseph's head bobbed, a nervous eagerness.

"I do need someone to run the chains," Foster said.

"Well, then," Upperdine said, "the boy will assist you. When can you begin?"

"We'll have a look tomorrow," Foster said. "Begin laying it off."

Again, Thompson retreated into his thoughts. He heard the others but it was as if his ears were stopped. He registered only low, mumbling sounds, like the advance of a distant storm.

29

Thompson slept little. The events of the previous day weighed on him. He regretted his behavior with Hanna. His flesh had responded immediately to her touch, but he knew with certainty an emotional chasm separated them. She seemed anxious to move on with her life. A part of Thompson, however, remained in Indiana. Memories he held on to like a lifeline. A past he refused to let go.

But part of him also resided in the present and looked to the future. The arrival of Ansell Foster crystallized in him the desire for a stake in the valley; he felt he'd earned it, and he spent a good part of the night formulating a plan to secure it.

Early in the afternoon, from the field, Thompson saw Upperdine riding upriver toward his house. Thompson started out to meet him at the tack shed, but the Captain noticed him and turned his horse.

"Walk with me a ways?" Thompson asked.

"I'm used up," Upperdine said, glancing back toward his home. "To what purpose?"

CROSSING PURGATORY 265

"A business proposition," Thompson said, leading Upperdine. Upperdine grunted and followed on horseback. He was constitutionally unable to resist the lure of commerce. They reached the stubble of the wheat field and continued past for a quarter-mile. Finally, Thompson turned to Upperdine.

"This land, from the wheat field to here and up to that rise," Thompson said, pointing across the flat floodplain to a low crest.

"What about it?" Upperdine asked.

"I want it."

Captain Upperdine smiled. "This is, what, a couple hundred acres?"

"Closer to four hundred," Thompson said. "I've paced it off."

"I was not aware you are a man of such means," Upperdine said.

"I think this section will yield abundantly," Thompson continued.

"Benito grazes his goats on that hill," Upperdine said.

"Yes, but he has told me he has no wish to grow his cropland beyond the irrigated parcel he now holds."

"Still, this is fine natural pasture."

"Passable," Thompson said, "when rain falls. That is what gave me the idea that it might produce wheat as well."

"And Benito's goats?" Upperdine asked.

"Goats can make do on most any forage," Thompson said, brusquely. "His herd is small. Open range abounds." Even as he spoke, Thompson sensed, and as quickly dismissed, the minor betrayal.

Upperdine chuckled. "A future land baron, here. Corner the market on wheat." Then his expression hardened. "Do you have the funds? One-twenty an acre."

"I will pay over time, as the crops come in."

Upperdine chuckled again, but his tone conveyed no humor. "I'm not a banker, Mr. Grey."

"You've seen how wheat takes to this land. You know my work. My word," Thompson said. "Give me three years." He did not like looking up at Captain Upperdine, who had remained in the saddle. "I'll expand the acreage each year and be turning a profit in three."

"I have no doubt concerning your ambition," Upperdine said. "I recognized it long before you did. But this is a hard country and has broken better men than the both of us."

They fell silent, looking over the land. A muddled sky produced thunder. Upperdine turned his eyes upward.

"Wouldn't do to be hailed out," he said.

Thompson recognized the false promise of rain, the lack of humidity, did not answer. An antelope showed briefly on the rise but sensed them and dropped back out of sight behind the far slope.

"How much have you?" Upperdine asked. Thompson retrieved the coins from his pocket and opened his hand. Gold, and silver.

"That will see you twenty-five acres," Upperdine said. "A good start."

"A dollar and twenty is what the best land commands," Thompson said.

Upperdine regarded Thompson with narrowed eyes. "Forty acres," he said. "More than you could put up in crops. Take your pick of the land."

"Will you hold the acreage around it in reserve for me?" Thompson asked.

"I can't promise that," Upperdine said.

Thompson closed his fingers over the coins. "I'll give it some thought," he said.

"Don't think on it for too long," Upperdine warned. "My generous nature is vaporish."

ALMOST DAILY, THOMPSON FOUND EXCUSE to walk to the town site. From a distance he observed Ansell Foster set his ranging rod and direct Joseph to make perfectly straight the chain. Whenever they paused for Foster to make notations in his chart book or to change locations, Joseph approached the surveyor, animated. Several days into the effort, Thompson intercepted Foster returning from the site.

"Joseph working out?" Thompson asked, after pleasantries.

"Raw, but eager," Foster said. "The boy is inquisitive. To a fault."

"I'd not realized his interest in surveying," Thompson said.

"It's not so much the work he's interested in," Foster said. "He wants to know everything about Kansas. Who will run for governor? Who heads the militia? Any recent conflicts between pro-slave and abolitionists? Where? On and on, to distraction."

"He's left relatives there," Thompson said.

SLOWLY, THE PINS FOSTER AND Joseph had sunk into the ground began to define a shape to the town, building lots set along two bisecting streets. The town took form in Thompson's imagination, and he grew increasingly anxious. Captain Upperdine grew anxious as well, but with impatience. At the beginning of the second week of surveying, Upperdine rode out to Bent's Post to recruit additional crew for Foster. Midmorning the following day, Foster searched out Thompson, who was turning water into Benito's orchard. The last irrigation of the season. The river ran slow.

"Is Joseph about?" Foster asked, agitated.

"He's not with you, I take it," Thompson said.

"Been waiting half the day. Not a damn thing to be done without a chainman," Foster said.

Thompson left Foster at his cabin with a cup of coffee and went to Carlos's camp by the river. No sign of habitation, the fire pit cold. He rejoined Foster and together they walked to the placita and questioned Hanna. She'd not seen Joseph since they'd all shared supper upon Foster's arrival.

"He's timed it for Upperdine's absence," Thompson said.

"Timed what?" Foster asked. Hanna's face went blank. She knew, Thompson saw, but was unwilling to express her emotions.

"There will be a horse missing from Captain Upperdine's stock," Thompson said. "And tack as well, I fear."

"You confound me," Foster said.

"Joseph. He's off. Wyandotte. Or Council Grove, perhaps. Wherever he might find a militia to join."

CAPTAIN UPPERDINE RETURNED DURING THE evening with two men sitting in the bed of his wagon. They appeared ragged, red-eyed and surly. Upperdine, by contrast, was in high spirits. Hanna and Thompson stood with Foster and Genoveva on the porch to greet him.

"Got you some help," he said to Foster, and, turning to Thompson, grinned.

"Stood these men some whiskey. Now they get to work it off." Upperdine climbed down and motioned Foster aboard. "Take them to the site. They can pitch camp there with you." As Foster drove off, Upperdine called out, laughing. "Best keep them downwind until they sweat it out."

When the wagon had pulled away, Thompson said, "I've news," and watched Upperdine's mood darken as he recounted Joseph's theft.

"Which horse?" Upperdine asked, pacing the yard, enraged.

"The sorrel with the white blaze, I believe," Thompson said.

"Damn him, that's a fine animal. When?" Upperdine asked.

"Not sure," Thompson said. "Sometime yesterday evening, I'd guess."

"I can overtake him," Upperdine said.

"Wait!" Hanna said. Her eyes had been darting between Thompson and Upperdine. "Captain, I ask you, let him be."

"Be?" Upperdine shouted. "What kind of man would accept my hospitality, come into my home, and then steal my property?"

"He's a boy yet," Hanna said. "Impulsive."

"He's a man now," Upperdine said. "A man who has gravely miscalculated my nature."

"Please," Hanna said, and now she looked directly at Thompson. He felt her desperation.

"It's better that he's gone," Thompson said, and even as he spoke he believed it. "He's a troubled sort. Of a mind to avenge his father's murder."

"He'll never come across those men," Upperdine said.

"Close enough kin to them, I suspect."

"He has my horse. My gear," Upperdine said.

Hanna continued to hold Thompson with her eyes. He felt trapped.

"I'll pay for them," Thompson said, retrieving the gold coins from his pocket, holding them out. Upperdine examined the coins as if unfamiliar with the shiny trinkets.

"A fine animal," he said.

"You well know this is all I possess," Thompson said.

Upperdine looked across the yard toward his livestock, measuring worth against the inconvenience of giving chase. Finally he accepted the coins.

"If ever he shows himself, he'll be the worse for it," Upperdine said.

"He will not return," Hanna said. "Nothing remains for him in this place."

IN THE MORNING, THOMPSON DID not go to the fields directly. He sat outside his cabin on the stump and built a fire in the stone ring and made coffee and thought about things while absently whittling. A part of him felt released finally from any sense of obligation toward Hanna Light. He'd traded gold for Joseph's unhampered escape. Into what future, Thompson had no clue. Could he even make it unmolested to eastern Kansas? And if he did, could he find peace?

Thompson doubted it, but felt relief. If Joseph was destined for a life of confrontation and conflict, at least it would not play out here in the valley. Thompson had tried to help the boy, failed, but at least he'd brokered a resolution. A burden lifted. But with gold intended to secure his initial foothold in the valley. One debt to Hanna paid, but his craving for the land unabated for lack of funds. Thompson considered Upperdine's offer, turning it over in his mind, searching for any positive slant.

In the field below the placita he watched Carlos and Benito working the corn. Teresa dug in the garden beside the south wall of the placita, unearthing onions and carrots. Goats browsed the higher ground to the west. Benito had begun a future and Thompson envied him. His family would settle comfortably here, and as long as the river flowed, his field would produce. During the summer, he'd made bricks and built another room at the placita for Paloma. Already, expansion. But it was not Thompson's intent simply to homestead. He desired more, had his sight on supplying wheat to market. And for that, he'd require ten times the acreage Benito farmed. Twenty times as much. And, now he lacked funds for even a modest beginning; he lacked equipment; he lacked seed. But, if he could secure land, the rest would eventually follow.

His thoughts inward, Thompson failed to notice Genoveva approaching until she lightly brushed his shoulder. He started but quickly recovered.

"Good morning, Señora Upperdine," Thompson said, standing. "Can I offer you coffee?"

"Hello, Mr. Grey. Will you walk?"

"Of course."

They continued upriver exchanging small talk until they arrived at the section Thompson earlier had shown the Captain. Genoveva pointed to the wheat patch.

"This is a dry land," she said. "And yet it prospered."

"It did," Thompson agreed.

"Not much prospers in this country."

"Not without rain."

"You've thought it out."

"Obadiah's wheat holds promise."

"A plan for the future," she said.

"Fantasy, perhaps," he said. "A child's dream. Foolishness."

"The Captain will hold this acreage for a time," Genoveva said. "Until you can either raise funds or give up that dream."

Thompson heard the words but did not comprehend. He had no money, of course, but stood riveted by the proposition. "I beg your pardon?"

"The Captain will not sell the land you requested. Not for three years."

"That is kind of you to offer," Thompson said. "But I should come to terms with him."

"That is not necessary."

"I don't understand."

"The land is mine," Genoveva said.

Her words echoed in his mind. He remained mute, unable to form a response.

"The Captain and I have an agreement," Genoveva said. "I leave business decisions to him. But, in this case, I intervened."

"The land is yours?"

"Yes. Part of a land grant to my grandfather. I became heir to a tract. When the territory fell into American hands, I accepted the Captain's proposal for marriage. The prospect of retaining ownership seemed much improved by taking an American husband."

"A marriage of convenience?" Thompson asked before thinking through his words, and immediately regretted his forwardness. Genoveva did not show offense.

"We share affection," Genoveva explained. "The Captain courted me long before I agreed to marry him. The problem is that he too much loves his freedom, the freedom of the trail. He cares for me." Genoveva paused, glanced at Thompson and then out over the land. "But he also cares for his trail wife in Westport, his Indian wife. And others, I am certain."

Stunned, Thompson again fell silent for a time. "I'd taken a higher measure of him."

"Oh, he has fine qualities," Genoveva said. She brought a hand to his shoulder, tenderly, in comfort. "Evil men do exist in this world. Saints also, perhaps, although I've never personally encountered one. But most of us are both good and bad, don't you agree?"

"I suppose," Thompson said.

"The test of a decent person is to elevate our saintly instincts above our evil ones, yes?"

"You possess more lofty thoughts than I," Thompson said, and then, "Thank you for your kindness."

"You have a difficult path, still," Genoveva said. "Currency is hard to come by."

"A chance is all I could hope for."

"I do have motives," she said. "I fear Benito will continue to be hobbled into the future. I hope Carlos will be here to assist him, but that is no certainty. And the Captain of course has neither the skills nor the interest."

"Of course," Thompson said.

THOMPSON FOUND SLEEP AGAIN ELUSIVE that night. Genoveva's intercession bought time, but surely would alter his relationship with John Upperdine from this day forward. How to approach him? And how to make good on the opportunity presented?

When finally sleep did come, he was visited by a dream, old and familiar. He stood outside his cabin on the low bluff. An orange sun inched above the eastern horizon while the moon, pocked and full, still shone in the west. He looked out over his holdings, the wheat silver in the flanking light, stretching beyond the reach of his vision, filling the entire valley, fading into shadow. All of it, his.

He woke. Clammy, acutely aware of his heart, a furiously beating otherness; his heart, betraying his deepest fears, exposing him to his truth. A truth he denied.

WHEN THOMPSON FIRST BROACHED HIS request, Benito continued hoeing in the bean field as if he had not heard, but Thompson could see the impact, the muscles of Benito's jaw working. The bean plants were knee-high and the pods swollen.

"I do not covet your land," Thompson said.

"So you've said."

"You do not believe me?" Thompson asked.

"I believe that you believe yourself," Benito said. "But I see you afield, pacing off your domain. I see you staring off into the distance, laying out crops, pasturing animals in your mind."

"Your vision is more acute than mine," Thompson said. "My design is more modest. I want only to trade my share of the corn harvest this autumn for produce now. To sell. To buy a small parcel from Captain Upperdine."

"Then you will be without cornmeal for winter," Benito said.

"I made do largely without last winter."

"We have so little to spare," Benito said, talking to the hoe.

"Think of it as an investment." Thompson knew that every egg he begged, every pound of butter, of cheese, would deprive Benito's family until the full harvest began. But his plan depended upon it. Eggs, cheese, butter. A few half-ripe melons, this constituted his capital. Hungry miners his market, clamoring for fresh food and willing to pay dearly for any small morsel not looking or tasting like hardtack or rancid fatback.

"You won't have to sacrifice," Thompson continued. "One-tenth of the proceeds will be yours plus the additional corn. With your share, you can buy flour at the mercantile, coffee, a little sugar, perhaps. The boys would love sugar."

Without giving it voice, Thompson knew the leverage he exerted over Benito, counted on it. Without Thompson's help, only a fraction of the crops could have been planted last spring. A piddling harvest, another cold and hungry winter to dread. Thompson could see the weight of these obligations settle on Benito as he worried his hoe between the rows.

30

The wagon loaded, Thompson climbed aboard and slapped the haunches of the team Upperdine had chosen for the trip. The Captain insisted that he employ horses. "You carry perishables and you travel alone, both arguments for speed." Thompson was more accustomed to mules or oxen, but could not fault the Captain's logic. His destination: the near goldfields, the Fountain Creek stakes, and other rough camps pitched beside the rivulets and streams veining the foothills. He did not know what to expect, only that with luck he'd meet prospectors with a few flakes of gold and large appetites.

As he guided the wagon from the Upperdines' compound, Carlos approached, calling, leading the burro and, in the cart, Benito. Benito climbed down with Carlos's help and held out a cloth package. "More butter," he said. "Fresh-churned." Thompson halted the team. Benito passed the butter to Thompson and caught hold of the wagon siding and hitched onto the bench and fit his broad hat about his head, pulling it firm, and propped his walking staff against the front board. Carlos handed up a rucksack, which Benito stored beneath the bench.

"This is not a good idea," Thompson said. "Sitting for long stretches will stiffen your leg. The road will jostle."

"My leg will be fine."

"The mining territory is rough, and the tolerance for Mexicans is not high. Or so Captain Upperdine reports."

"I think tolerance increases with the value of the goods you carry," Benito said.

THEY TRAVELED EACH TO HIS thoughts, the clump of hooves on packed dirt stupefying, the creaking sway of the wagon over gentle swells and troughs. The breeze wandered across the tableland, occasionally raising dust devils that swirled up from the trail like snakes coiling to strike. Thompson studied the rising dust. An omen? He and Benito riding alone, his senses peaked. He noticed bends in the trail, rifts in the land, hiding what? A vast, open wildness. If Benito shared Thompson's heightened vigilance, he did not show it. He rested behind the cover of his hat, low over his eyes. Thompson followed the trail for as long as it paralleled the Arkansas River. When the passage dipped southeast, Thompson kept to the river with plans of locating Fountain Creek and turning north, hugging the low hills, all the way to the diggings at Cherry Creek if need be.

Along the route, almost immediately they encountered men eager to trade gold or currency for fresh food: eggs, a dime apiece, a goose quill packed with gold dust for a fist-sized lump of goat cheese. They arrived at a collection of rough, brush-roofed cabins along Fountain Creek, windowless, wagon canvas for doors. It seemed an entirely foreign place to Thompson. A reminder of ancient ancestors, scratching the earth, living one day to the next, each day brutal, life tenuous. The miners were gaunt, sunken-eyed, and hungry. A whore's tent sat off from the line of cabins, a sign painted in red on the canvas: Come, all who are weary. The stream banks were gouged into pits, and mounds of waste rock towered over the men. An ugly scar, an obscene monument. A latrine was dug beside a hillock but left unconcealed, and Thompson noted men squatting over the pit.

He and Benito set camp to graze the horses and to sell what they could before working north. The miners had found little gold, but several who had resisted the call of the whores still carried hard currency from the east, and were eager to trade for their produce. By evening of the second day, prospectors wandered in from nearby camps to buy fresh butter for their mush. Benito set up a stove and men stood in line to pay a dollar for a meal of eggs, cheese, and fresh tortillas that he made from the masa dough Teresa had wrapped in cloth and sent with him in his rucksack, the last of the family's corn stores until harvest. The prospectors, to a man, looked haggard and short-tempered. Not everyone paid without complaint.

"You asking a dollar?" one gangly man accused. His thrusting point of a chin reminded Thompson of a beak. "A dollar give up to that greaser for a few eggs?"

"I'm not asking a dollar from you," Thompson said, bristling. "I'll ask nothing from you except to be out of my sight before I take this fry pan to the side of your head." Benito remained bent over the stove, cooking.

Grumbling, the man sulked off. A companion held out his dollar, grinning. "He's just boiled over on account he had hisself a couple of layers this past spring. Making his own money from the eggs like you is, but he lost them."

"Foxes?" Thompson asked.

"Nah. Got drunked up one day and et 'em." The man took his plate of eggs and cheese and a stack of tortillas. "Didn't share a lick. Not one stringy wing. Them chickens had no more fat on 'em than a snake, but I sure would a loved to gnaw a bone."

A man with a seeping bandage on his forearm and a soft accent from the South bought the last melon for a dollar and a quarter. The man casually remarked to Thompson that he'd gotten into a knife fight with someone who had designs on that same melon.

An acre of land, Thompson thought as he took the money, for the price of an unripe melon.

After another day, the supplies ran out. The wagon sat empty except for provisions to fuel their return trip. Thompson's purse held twenty-seven dollars in hard currency, approximately twenty dollars in gold flake, and a few nuggets the size of a corn seed. After Benito's share, sufficient for his initial acres with perhaps enough left for a plow. Working alone with Upperdine's oxen, he might break eighteen, twenty acres that first season. He'd plant as much in wheat as the seed allowed and however many acres remaining in produce dear to the emigrants: watermelons, cantaloupe, and sweet potatoes. For whatever reason, they'd craved sweet potatoes and were disappointed he had none. He'd plant for market and live off of game and the yield from a small garden he'd sow in potatoes and onions. And he'd buy more land with the harvest proceeds, begin to hire tenants or wage labor from Bent's Post to put additional acreage into production. Glancing about, Thompson felt sure there would be no lack in the foreseeable future of men with empty pockets looking for work. This new land swarmed with opportunity.

THEY LEFT EARLY, BEFORE LIGHT, not wishing to call attention to their departure. Thompson eased the horses from camp and then pushed them hard, whistling encouragement and slapping at them with the reins until they panted and frothed, hides gleaming. Driven by vague uneasiness about separating prospectors from gold and their disposition upon the realization that their stomachs once again were empty and their pockets lighter, he wished to put miles between them and the miners. Earlier, Benito had irritated him with his deliberation at breaking camp, his careful stowing of supplies, the harnessing, and a pause off by himself for devotion while Thompson fumed.

Five miles out, the day just opening, two riders came up from the arroyo and blocked the trail. They rode mules, and later, much later, when Thompson relived the incident, he pieced together that they must have been waiting in ambush. The mules could not have outpaced his horses, even with the wagon in tow. The riders carried muskets and leveled them on Thompson and Benito from ten yards. Thompson reined his team. He considered trying to pull around, run for it, but the arroyo guttered one side of the trail and to the other, thick scrub confounded the route.

For a short time, no one spoke. Thompson noticed that the riders sat uncomfortably in the saddle and the mules seemed willing to test their control, shuffling and trying to dislodge the bit. Their guns looked ancient, both still fitted with flint and pan.

"Deliver and be on your way," the steadier of the two riders demanded, his voice high with nervousness. Only then did it register with Thompson that they were mere boys, within spitting distance of Joseph's age. Neither yet grew face whiskers.

"Young pups," Thompson whispered to Benito out of the side of his mouth. "Babies." And, to the boys, "What do you want of us?"

"You know. The gold."

"Armed boys," Benito said, under his breath. "Give them what they demand."

"My gold? My land?" Thompson said, more agitated now.

"Money only. We can recoup," Benito said, soothingly.

The boys waved their muskets excitedly. "No funning. Be quick."

"Yes, sir," Thompson said, and reached below the seat and came up with the money bag in his left hand, and as the boys' attention turned to the bag he brought up the Allen pistol with his right.

"Wait," Benito said, and reached for his staff, pushing himself erect, extending his hand. "Wait." Thompson raised the pistol and fired off rounds as quickly as the revolving barrels allowed. The mules bucked wildly, the two muskets discharged, knocking one of the boys backward off his saddle. Apparently uninjured either by Thompson's volley or the tumble, as soon as he hit the ground the boy rolled into the arroyo, continued head over heels until he reached the sandy bed of the dry gully, and took off running. The other mule had bolted into the brush with its rider clinging to the saddle pommel, having dropped both reins and weapon.

Thompson whipped the team into full gallop, throwing Benito back onto the bench. For ten minutes, Thompson slapped and shouted, driving the horses. His blood pulsed. For the second time in his life, he'd been fired upon, experienced adrenaline flush his body. The horses finally slowed of their own accord and Thompson's hands began shaking so violently he feared he could not control the team, so he pulled to a halt. He sat with his elbows on his knees, interlocking his fingers, attempting to steady himself.

"Too close," he said once his breathing regulated. Benito did not answer. Thompson turned to him. "Are you irked with me?"

Benito wanned, his face ashen, his lips a thin slash. He slumped back on the wagon bench, legs splayed. Thompson looked down and saw one leg of his trousers soaked in blood, hip to ankle. Blood dripped from his pant cuff and pooled in the boot box. Concentration creased Benito's face and his eyes strained for focus. Thompson set the hand brake and jumped from the wagon. He went around to Benito and lifted him from the bench and laid him in the wagon bed. When he stepped away, his own shirt was stained red and he noticed a red trail in the dust. He dipped water from the barrel and climbed into the wagon and lifted Benito's head and brought the tin to his lips. Benito drank a little and his eyes found Thompson.

"I should have let the Captain have the leg after all," Benito said, and forced a smile.

"It will be all right," Thompson said.

"It's not as bad as I'd thought," Benito said. "This business."

"No."

"It will be fine."

"Yes."

"See to them," Benito said. His voice sounded hoarse, his breathing rattled.

"Of course," Thompson said.

Benito reached out and grasped Thompson's forearm. "See to them," he repeated.

"Yes. Don't worry," Thompson said. He took his knife and slit Benito's trousers and saw at once the entry wound on the inside of his upper thigh. Blood pumped from the round hole with each beat of Benito's heart. Thompson grabbed an empty sack and tore it into wide bandages and fashioned a thick compress and tightly wrapped Benito's leg with the remaining strips, but the bleeding would not stanch and the bandage was soaked through even before Thompson had finished tying it off.

"Prop me up," Benito said. "I want to see what there is to see."

For hours, Thompson forced his mind blank, willed himself to concentrate only on the team, refusing to acknowledge the dark accusations fomenting somewhere deep within. He blocked out the moans from Benito when the wagon jostled over broken terrain. But eventually the demons surfaced, real and substantial as the young desperados he'd faced that morning. They stood before him, blocked his vision, and passed judgment. He halted the team, again unable to handle the reins, shuddering so. He searched the pitted, wind-scoured barrens for an answer. He craved dominion over *this?*

Overwhelmed, Thompson jumped from the wagon and descended an arroyo. He picked up a fistful of sand and threw it into the wind. *"This?"* he shouted. He followed the twisted course of the dry streambed aimlessly until an object caught his eye, and he bent and picked up the fragile bone of a desert animal, bleached white, small and neatly formed as the finger of a child. The animal long forgotten in this forgotten place. The bone only. He dropped to his knees and shut his eyes and held the bone in his hand like a talisman and attempted to summon the spirits of his wife and boys. He wanted to tell them they would not be forgotten. He sought forgiveness. But they did not answer his call, and after a time he dropped the bone and returned to the wagon. Benito had paled and seemed asleep. His chest rose and fell in barely perceptible rhythm.

Thompson climbed aboard and put the team in motion. The hours passed. The horses cast ever-lengthening shadows ahead of them until it appeared as if a second, phantom team was leading them. Wind sliced through the grass, a thin, high sound. The iron rims of the wagon clattered. The horses plodded on. Benito bled.

Long after nightfall the trail dipped from high ground to meet the river. Thompson allowed the team to water for a short time. Benito refused food. He had not spoken again since morning, but when Thompson steadied his head to offer drink, Benito held his gaze for a long moment. His eyes were not unkind; they expressed neither accusation nor condemnation, but seemed to offer a gentle reassurance that bore into Thompson's soul more than damnation ever could have. Trust. When Benito again closed his eyes, Thompson climbed onto the bench and urged the horses, but before they had advanced even a short distance Benito called to him in a strong, calm voice. "Here."

Thompson reined the team and jumped from the seat and went around to Benito.

"What do you require?"

"This place."

"Yes."

"It is a fine place?"

Thompson looked around. Dark, and in the shadows, rough scrub, low-growth willows along the trail and beyond the sound of the river, shallow, a murmurous suggestion. "Yes."

"I am weary. Stop a while."

"We should push on."

"Stop a while."

"For a short time," Thompson said. He walked around the wagon and slumped against the wheel hub, exhausted but impatient. He listened to the horses pulling at grass, to water caressing pebbles. Time passed. The wind gusted and then stilled completely, the horses quieted, even the river-flow seemed to hush, and Thompson knew that Benito had died. He sat against the wheel, unwilling to move. The moon hung in the sky lopsided, out of symmetry. Finally, he stood and went to the back of the wagon. Benito sat against the drop gate, eyes glazed and half-lidded, his face calm and still like the night, and in the moon glow Thompson saw how he must have looked as a young man. His creases smoothed and his expression innocent. Thompson eased him prone and closed his lids and crossed his arms at his chest and began to cover his face with the blanket, but could not, and instead folded it into a pillow and tucked it under his head. He continued toward the Purgatoire, toward the placita of Benito Ibarra. Somewhere along the trail, he wasn't sure where or when, the low rattling began far inside his skull, a constant, humming rattle of bone on bone, the army advancing. Let them, he thought. I don't care.

31

Teresa came for Benito to clean his body and prepare him for burial. Carlos had been working the field, seen Thompson approach, and after learning Benito's fate run ahead with the news. "Do not bring the wagon through the gates," she'd instructed. Dressed for mourning, she walked from the placita with dignity, dry-eyed, her bearing erect and proud. Paloma followed, her face distorted with grief. Teresa approached Benito, smoothed his hair. Remarkably, Benito's face retained the same peaceful expression, as if his body refused decay until taking leave of his family. Teresa leaned close, whispered into his ear, "Foolish man." She caressed his face. "Foolish old man." She straightened, looked at Thompson with level, intense eyes.

"He died well?" she asked.

"Yes," Thompson said.

"It concerned him," Teresa said. "When the time came. How he would face it."

"He died well," Thompson said. He fought for composure, the drumming in his head.

Teresa motioned to Thompson and Carlos. "Please, carry him inside, to our bed. Then leave us to attend to him."

When they lifted him, Thompson noted dried blood staining the wagon bed a deep rust. He sensed that time would never completely fade it, a reminder, constant, silent, persuasive.

THEY BURIED HIM OUTSIDE THE south wall where he'd begun to construct the family chapel. Three cottonwoods grew a short distance from the wall, drawing water from some deep tap. In the shade of the broad-spread canopy, Carlos and Thompson dug.

When time came to cover him over, Genoveva, Teresa, and Paloma took turns reciting the burial rites, what they could remember. They read from the Bible. The boys stood mute, dumb with fear and sorrow. Hanna kept to the side, moving away whenever Destiny chatted or fussed. Captain Upperdine stood at the head of grave, looking down into the pit, brooding. Paloma and Genoveva wept quietly, but not Teresa, and when they lowered Benito into the ground, she sang a hymn in Spanish that reminded Thompson of mist drifting over the river on autumn mornings.

Afterwards, Teresa sat in a chair under the cottonwoods while Thompson filled the grave. The others stood behind her, the boys close at her side, looking up into her eyes for any sign, any sign at all that things soon would be as before. Paloma clung to Carlos for support, and with each shovel of dirt a moan escaped her lips. Carlos turned to her and talked low, soothing. As Thompson finished tamping the earth, the sun turned red on the horizon and day ended. Teresa rose from the chair and accepted Carlos's free arm and he led them into the placita. Thompson returned to his cabin. He sat on the stump and faced west and watched the purpling sky. Skeletons continued to rattle and drum in his head. He looked over the valley and wondered if he might abandon this land, move on to some other shack on some other waste.

He awakened the following morning hardly able to stand, so deep was his exhaustion. He started toward the fields, but found no one at work, a day given to mourning. He halted, unsure what to do, where to go. In the distance, he saw Teresa, a shadow in black, sitting beside the mounded, fresh-turned earth. Thompson walked to Upperdine's paddock and watched the horses shuffle. He went to the wagon and retrieved his money pouch and pistol from beneath the bench and he tried, but failed, to avert his eyes from the bloodstain. He noticed for the first time the clear outline of Benito's leg on the floorboards where blood had pooled around him. His eyes began to tear, and he swiped with his shirtsleeve and shook clear his head. The drums sounded.

Returning to his cabin, he stopped first at the placita and placed the pouch of gold at Teresa's door. He'd mentioned the money to her yesterday but she had raised her hand to cut him short and studied him without accusation but with a perfect clarity that washed him with shame. Near his cabin, he cut a branch from a juniper and sharpened one end. Inside, he hammered the peg into the chinking on the far wall and hung the pistol from the trigger guard and stepped away from it.

THOMPSON EXPECTED THE TREMORS TO abate, but they did not, coming at unexpected times, growing worse. Chopping wood, the ax would fly from his grip. Eggs spilled from skillet into fire. The skeletons rattled in his head, and drumbeats, at times thunderous, at times distant. And weariness overcame him, a constant weight. Harvest was upon them, so he forced himself into the fields. At times he seemed confused about the work and unable to follow conversations, often not hearing at all. He picked beans, stored hay, shocked corn. In the evenings he retreated to his cabin and took to his bed, shaking, unable to rest. Up and into the fields. Back at day's end, sometimes eating, sometimes not. Uncomprehending cycles of light and darkness, until one morning he did not rise. He lacked strength and had no will. He lay in bed and thought that, yes, he would quit this place, a sin offering. He would quit it this instant.

But he did not move, did not rise. His sense of being in the world ebbed and flowed. At times, the universe collapsed into his thumbnail and he felt a part of everything that ever was, the purple bloom on a thistle, the evening star, a vole, a church bell tried in fire; at times, he floated above his bed and rose upward, higher, higher, feeling a part of no thing, no place, looking down upon his corporal self growing small, insignificant, a nit, a mote, invisible, and then nothing. Nothing at all. Where in this world a place for sin? For grace?

Sometime during the day he became vaguely aware of visitors, a soft buzz, his head tilted to accept porridge and a sip of water. And that night, in stupor, he felt a presence beside him, warmth, the press of a body. A whispering, let it go. Die in your grief. Pass through the veil. Emerge renewed.

He attempted to turn to the voice. Was it a voice? He could not move. He settled into the warmth, a deep and abiding comfort. Something was pulling him into himself, a sinking, to an unknown place.

THOMPSON WOKE TO EERIE SILENCE. Full morning, light slanted through the window. He lay still and listened. Five minutes, a full ten. Nothing, a glorious silence. In his head, the drumming had ceased, the bones departed. The song of a lark filtered into the cabin, a sibilant stream, and he rose, a modest strength returned, and left the cabin with its stale air and stench of illness. Outside, he built a fire and boiled coffee. He had no food to cook but nevertheless was grateful for the sensation of hunger. To feel anything at all. The coffee tasted pleasantly bitter in his mouth, and heat traveled down his throat to warm his empty stomach. In the distance, Paloma and Hanna approached from the placita. Paloma stopped short when she noticed Thompson sitting by the fire and veered off toward the fields. He watched as she approached Carlos, how Carlos set aside his gathering sack and removed his hat and stepped toward her. Paloma handed him a pouch, his midday meal, Thompson supposed, and when he took it, she placed a hand on his arm and Carlos drew her near for a moment, a tender interlude, before she turned for the placita and Carlos to his work.

Hanna continued to the bluff carrying a small pail, held it out to him.

"Teresa's atole, for your health," she said.

"The thought of food had crossed my mind," he said, accepting the pail.

"Your color looks good," she said. "You concerned us."

"I'm much improved," he said. "I will be back at harvest presently."

"What more do you require? How may I help?" Hanna asked.

"Nothing more, thank you. You've done much already," Thompson said.

"I've done nothing," Hanna said.

"Someone fed me yesterday," he said.

"Teresa," Hanna said.

"Teresa?" Thompson asked. He deserved Teresa's scorn, she offered kindness. He deserved condemnation, she offered compassion. What right had he to accept such freewill gifts?

"We all worried about you," Hanna said.

"Your words last night," Thompson continued. The voice had been familiar, and female. "A comfort."

Hanna, quizzically, "I don't understand."

Thompson recognized her confusion, understood his mistake. "Of course," he said. "I've been muddled."

"But you are well, now?" Hanna asked.

"Yes."

Hanna, after a pause, "I'd gladly offer comfort if you would accept it."

Thompson studied her face, questioning and hopeful, but he had no response. Still, he wished her to remain with him a while, wished for her company after struggling alone with his internal demons for such a stretch. But she must have interpreted his silence as withdrawal.

"I'll leave you to your nourishment," she said.

Thompson watched her go. Who then, last night? A dream? Of course. He slurped the thick corn drink straight from the pail, appreciating the surprising hint of cinnamon and sugar, and tried to piece together the past few days, a blur of reality and fancy. The incessant drumming in his head: fancy. Being given water: reality. His dream: fancy, he concluded after some indecision. And he clearly remembered his resolve to quit the Purgatoire Valley. But quit it for where? Another barrens? Or, dare he return east, to Indiana or Kentucky, to his past? Thompson remembered his father's estate as if he'd walked it yesterday: rolling green hills; dense woods; tobacco fields; the aromas wafting from the curing shed and the smokehouse during autumn. Some days working the brown, water-starved earth of the prairie, memories came, sweet, tangy stabs of yearning. Sunday meals following church services, girls in bonnets and gloves. The scent of lavender water. Perhaps it was time.

Yet, this place! Tainted as it was by his transgressions, its raw beauty, its harsh climate, its yawning presence like a touchstone for his soul. Stay, to what purpose? Leave, to what purpose?

Teresa's atole revived him, and he planned to work the fields that afternoon. But the longer he sat, the less willing his body to action.

When finally he stood, he found his legs wooden, his arms leaden at his side, the aftermath of his debilitation. A short rest, he decided, and went inside and stretched out on his bed, and his next awareness was of a room dim with the shadows of waning day.

Outside, he kicked up the fire. Above, light softened and the land lay quiet. Thompson watched Teresa emerge from the placita to sit with Benito during the vesper hour. As evening deepened, the others returned from the fields and joined Teresa for a few minutes before leading her inside. When the gates swung closed for the night, Thompson imagined himself alone in the world. Except for the faint glow from the windows of Upperdine's house in the distance and the dim outline of placita walls still visible, it was Thompson only in the vast, darkening expanse of land and sky. He considered sleeping in the open, but night carried a chill and finally he rose from the stump by the dying fire and entered the cabin.

During the darkest hour, he woke. Someone called to him. He sensed a near presence, not unlike the night before. A deep longing pricked his skin and quickened his pulse. He lay in darkness until a slight differentiation in shading defined the window. He rose and went to the door and opened it and in that moment before the dream world left him, before the owl called again to jar him awake, Rachel stood in the night light, young and radiant, their boys shyly peeking from the folds of her skirt. She looked at him and smiled, and in that instant he felt redeemed. He reached for her, but she receded. He strained to refocus, to hold her in his vision for one heartbeat longer, but she was no more.

Thompson remained outside, no inclination to move, to disrupt the moment. The owl continued to question from its perch in the cottonwood. A warm calm settled over him, and the deepest peace he'd ever experienced. Like a clock spring unwound, tension left his body, a tension that had twisted and tightened around and through him for the past year without his realizing it. In departure, just before she faded back into the ether, Rachel had swept her arm across the valley. A benediction over the land, or permission to take leave? Thompson did not know, but it mattered little. He'd been forgiven, and the rest would become clear. He would make his choice and whatever happened, happened.

A paling in the east, the faintest tint, and Thompson stepped into the cabin, gathered his bedroll into which he'd packed his traveling gear, took up his rifle, and started for the junction of the Arkansas. At Captain Upperdine's township, Arkansas City, he stood beside the foundation laid in notched logs for what would become Hanna's cabin. The others had begun construction while he and Benito were away with the prospectors. Their return had interrupted work, and now it waited on the harvest. Thompson stepped inside the foundation's perimeter and imagined a family here, Hanna and Destiny, a husband and more children, some day. Outside, the surveyor's stakes foretold other cabins, other families. They would come. They would encounter hardships beyond comprehension attempting to carve out a living, and in the end the land would best most of them. But not everyone.

He turned in the direction from which he'd just traveled. Go, or stay? The bedroll lay at his feet. He could continue to the ford and decide, west or east. He could return to the cabin and begin his chores. He vacillated. What course? He felt no anxiety, because if only he waited patiently, the answer would come. He waited.

Dawn slowly opened the valley to another day, washed it in new light, soft umbers and rusts, the colors of flesh and skin and bone and blood, and it came to him with the sun. He would never leave. So intimate was he a part of this place that only the thinnest of membranes separated him from the dust at his feet and the firmament above. A membrane so tenuous that at any moment it might split and he would dissolve back into the soil or disperse into the air with the lightest of breezes.

The town might thrive or decay, but the people would endure. Crops may yield or fail, but the land would endure. And he understood now with certainty that he too would endure, in this place. He would never seek to own a part of it; he would not put himself to the test again. But he would nurture it. He would become a part of this land, a part of its history, help cast its future, and one day his bones would rest in its folds. As he followed the gentle tilt of the land onto the floodplain, retracing his steps, he turned and looked back at the foundation of Hanna's cabin. It would command pleasant views of the river and of the great openness beyond. He would continue with her wheat patch, if she so desired. He hoped she would.

Thompson returned to his cabin on the bluff above the river, his home. Across the floodplain, crops showed golden in the heightening sun. He watched Carlos and the boys emerge from the gates and turn out the goats to forage. He ducked inside, hung his rifle on the rack above the door, tossed his bedroll onto the table, and collected his corn knife and a burlap sack. Outside, the sun bore down and the wind blew fresh and strong, a fine morning to begin tending Benito's fields.

ACKNOWLEDGMENTS

I owe a great debt to the novelist William Haywood Henderson for his close reading and insightful comments, and to my colleagues in the Lighthouse Writers Master Novel Workshop who gave an early draft much greater attention than it deserved.

Heartfelt gratitude to Jennifer Carlson for believing in this book; the original manuscript gained immeasurably from her thoughtful suggestions.

I deeply appreciate Maia Larson for her untiring and often thankless job of editing, and the entire production crew at Pegasus Books.

Thanks to the Ucross Foundation for the gift of solitude on the rolling plains east of Buffalo, Wyoming. Every writer should be so fortunate.

My thanks also to Don J. Unser, author of *Sabino's Map*, a fascinating oral and pictorial history of life in the plaza, for the generosity of his conversation.

To the Writers Block for providing a desk, a lamp, and the good vibes of other writers struggling to pull off the same impossibility with words, thanks.

Thanks for the artistry of Jay P. K. Kenney and Catherine Hope.

Finally, I'd like to freely acknowledge the liberties I've taken with history. By intent, the fictional characters and events portrayed in *Crossing Purgatory* are historically plausible rather than factual.